# A RING FOR A SECOND CHANCE

ANNE LOUISE BANNON

Healcroft House, Publishers

Healcroft House, Publishers, a subsidiary of Robin Goodfellow Enterprises, Altadena, California, United States of America


Copyright 2017 Anne Louise Bannon
ISBN 978-0-9980838-6-5
Library of Congress Control Number 2017910898

## *Praise for Anne Louise Bannon and Fascinating Rhythm*

*Fascinating Rhythm is reminiscent of Agatha Christie or Dorothy Sayers' novels of the time period. A very nice story to cozy up to a fire with and imbibe. Legally, of course.*

*Literary R&R*

## **Bring Into Bondage**

*Bannon's depiction of rural small town life is every bit as convincing and entertaining as the views of big city life we saw in "Fascinating Rhythm".*

*Carol Louise Wilde*

## **The Last Witnesses**

*This is the first I have read of Anne Bannon – was nicely written, a complicated mystery with a happy ending! Look forward to reading more of Kathy and Freddie and their cuckoo friends!*

*GoodReads Review*

## *Praise for Tyger, Tyger*

*I like Bannon's main character, Brenda, enough to follow her anywhere. Her boyfriend (no! wait! they're "just friends") trains animals for the movies, and between Brenda, the BF and his tiger, "Sweetness," they are a fun, crime-solving trio. I enjoyed this book.*

*Petrea Burchard*
*Author of Camelot and Vine*

# ACKNOWLEDGEMENTS

Many, many thanks to my beta reader Caitlyn Alexander, whose insight helped tremendously. My second, but most preferred, beta reader is my wonderful daughter, Corrie Ann Klarner, whose notes were not only spot on, but very witty, too.

A massive thank you to my friend Carol Louise Wilde. She did an amazing line edit on this novel and it wouldn't be nearly as good as it is without her deft observations and thorough work.

I need to offer a profound thank you to Gingko Lee, who did the gorgeous cover to this book. She said she just wanted to help out. Boy, did she!

Finally, and as always, massive thanks to Michael Holland, historical consultant and all around great human being, and best of all, my husband.

# DEDICATION

To my daughter, Corrie Ann Klarner – At last, a story in your preferred genre!

# ROYAL FAMILY

King Tristam V (offspring):

Adele (m. Desmond, Duke of Raultberg):
    Queen Lanicia
    Marcella (m. Chester duGrackel)
Maria
Genvieve (d. as infant)
Alora
King Bartholemew III (m. Adriana of Greenwalt):
    King Steffan IV (m. Ella of Gittlesmarkdt)

# PROLOGUE

When the story ends one says, "And they lived happily ever after."

For those of us among the Faer Folke whose task it is to watch and give aid, this is hardly a satisfactory ending. The lives of people are lived in many stories, especially among the Landed, or those who, in the mists of early time, gave up their magic. In that early time, all human beings had magic. But those who became what we call the Landed gave their magic up to own things, especially land. We, the Faer Folke, have all we need, but we cannot build up wealth and the power over others that comes with wealth. As a result, our lives are much longer, but much simpler and our stories are much shorter.

Not so among the Landed, especially those whose lives cross with ours. Time was, we crossed back and forth quite frequently. True, those of the Landed who had power were bent on making those under them fear us. And magic, once lost is very hard to regain. But as the Landed grew more Enlightened and began to serve reason and logic, as their numbers grew and ours diminished, we found fewer and fewer reasons to walk among them and kept more and more to the wild places where their clamor and their lust for wealth could not bother us.

That's why those of us who choose to watch and

give aid are honored among us. We do not forget those who have lost their magic, either by greed or by falling in love. It's difficult work. Our magic, when we're among the Landed, is very weak and we cannot always protect our loved ones from harm or hurt. That's why we are also the storytellers because we have the tales to tell.

Which is why I've taken up this tale. The first part has been told many, many times and in many ways. I had watched over young Ella for many years, protecting her as best I could from one who had left our number to pursue her love of gold. I had also watched over Steffan, whose grandmother was one of our own. She had left us to marry one of the Landed but eventually managed to return to us.

This tale actually begins long before Steffan and Ella were even born. It happened in Panomia, one of several tiny kingdoms on the edge of the wild lands where many of us Faer Folke had settled. Elsewhere in the world, there were revolutions and talk of setting up republics. Few in this region thought much about their kings unless provoked.

And the people of Panomia were provoked. Their king, Bartholemew, had ascended his throne as a twelve-year-old boy, so his much older sister, Princess Adele, reigned as regent in his stead. However, she was greedy and began taxing her people in order to build up the army and take over one or more of the neighboring kingdoms. Her people were very angry and they planned a revolt. Young Bartholemew, who had turned sixteen by then, wrested control of the government from Princess Adele and managed to peaceably put down the revolt. He encouraged Desmond, the Duke of Raultberg, to marry Princess Adele.

Adele was furious that she'd been put aside in favor of her brother, a mere slip of a boy, simply because he was male and she wasn't. She bided her time, eventually giving birth to four daughters. The first, Lanicia, was taught all the customs and the manners of an heir to the throne, what Adele felt was her true station in life. The two middle daughters died young. The youngest, Marcella, was spared her mother's bitterness and became a great favorite in the court of King Bartholemew.

King Bartholemew grew in wisdom, and upon achieving his majority, fell in love with and married the Lady Adriana, of Greenwaldt, not knowing that Adriana's mother was of the Faer Folke. Several years passed before Steffan was born to the young king and queen. There had been several failed pregnancies and two more infants who did not survive their first years.

When Steffan achieved his majority, there was great interest in who he would marry. But he found Ella, a young duchess kept in hiding by her stepmother. At the same time, Steffan's cousin Marcella, who was close to Steffan's age, fell in love with Steffan's best friend, Chester duGrackel, a commoner. It was hardly the usual sort of friendship for a young prince, but that is yet another tale. Duke Desmond did not approve of the prince's commoner friend, even after Steffan had given Chester the Barony of Fin Reache, thus elevating his status. The duke would not have allowed his daughter Marcella to marry Chester, except that the two had married in secret anyway shortly before

Steffan and Ella's wedding.

Five years after Steffan and Ella's wedding, the kingdom was waiting.

# CHAPTER ONE

Steffan's father, King Bartholemew, was ill and had been for many months. Few thought he would recover. On the day of Steffan's fifth wedding anniversary, the old king rallied. Steffan spent a couple pleasant hours with his father that afternoon, visiting and sharing with him the affairs of state that Steffan had been managing during Bartholemew's illness. The king was pleased and sent Steffan to spend some time alone with Ella, as was their custom on their anniversary.

Steffan took her to the private garden behind the palace. It was spring, and the rich, mossy scent of a renewed earth filled the air. It had rained most of the week before, part of the usual spring storms. But that day, there was sunshine. Finally able to relax after weeks of worry, Steffan and Ella ran about like children, chasing each other breathlessly, as the sun began its downward course to the horizon.

Laughing, Steffan captured her.

"It's not fair!" she gasped, laughing also. "You run me about until I'm exhausted, and then you grab me."

"It's correct strategy, according to all the books," Steffan replied. He held up a satin slipper. "Besides, you lost your shoe again."

"Oh dear, I have. I thought I felt rather wet."

"You're good at that, you know."

She shook her head smiling, as she leaned against

him and replaced the errant slipper.

"You'll never let me forget, will you?" she chuckled.

"Never." He gently held her face. "Not when that's how I finally caught up to you. Oh, Ella. I've been so happy since that night."

She gazed at him fondly. "And I have, too. You've been so good to me."

"It's the least I can do. Never again will you wear anything but the finest silks and satins."

"May I please have a bit of wool in the winter so I don't freeze?"

"Why certainly, Madam, but only the best lambs' wool. I don't want anything harsh touching your skin again."

"Steffan, you're being silly. I wouldn't be able to kiss one of little Barth's beloved monsters, and that would break our son's heart. Nor would I be able to change Alicia's bottom."

"You can let the nursemaid do that."

"Which I often do. But I'm not so grand a lady I can't take care of my own daughter."

"Well, Alicia doesn't need to be changed anymore, anyway."

"She still has accidents. She's only two. Even Barth still has them every now and then."

"I know." Steffan grimaced, thinking of his four-year-old son and his uncle, the Duke of Raultberg. "I was there for the last one. I can't fault Barth. Uncle Desmond has been terribly moody since Aunt Adele died, and he was always a very imposing fellow, to begin with." Steffan paused. "Why am I talking about him? Relatives are the last thing I want to talk about right now."

"We were talking about our children."

"They are dear, but I'd rather focus my attention on you."

Steffan wrapped his arms around her, and they kissed, warm and full of strong love.

At the same time, the hands of the cathedral tower clock ground into place, and the great chimes sang out over almost all of the city. Steffan pulled away and glared in the direction of the clock tower in mock irritation.

"Forever interrupting us," he sighed. "I'm afraid my dearest, we'd best head home."

"It would be nice to see the children before they're sent to bed."

By the time the clock tower rang out the next hour, Steffan and Ella's coach pulled up in front of the townhouse where they lived in the capital city. They could have lived at the palace. But Queen Adriana had said even before they were married that a bit of independence was the best thing for the young couple. So the two lived in the home in the city where Ella had grown up.

The next day, Steffan and Ella returned to the palace, this time with their children and the nursemaid. The children would spend their morning visiting their grandfather and grandmother. Steffan and Ella also got a chance to spend time with the ailing king. But then it came time to focus on affairs of state, in particular, the ambassador from Karperia, who had arrived late the night before. The visit had been arranged over the past week or so, and it was hardly the first such visit by an ambassador from a neighboring kingdom since the king had fallen ill.

By the middle of the afternoon, Steffan and Ella were standing in the council room greeting Lord Aldebont, Minister of State of the neighboring kingdom of Karperia, and his retinue.

After the initial introductions, the ladies retired to the salon, except Ella, who remained at her husband's side. Aldebont seemed slightly perturbed by this, and after one or two awkward glances, nodded.

"Dear princess, if you are concerned for my needs," he said, "I assure you, they have been fully met."

"Your Lordship is most kind to reassure me," replied Ella.

Steffan smiled. "I suspect it is not the usual custom in your country for the ladies of the court to join their husbands in conferences. It's a relatively new custom here. My mother always accompanies my father. He is fond of saying that she is his best counselor. My wife has been blessed with similar gifts of wisdom and discretion, so I do the same."

"As your father rules well, and is loved by his people, you are wise to follow his example." Aldebont shifted. He was not comfortable with the situation, and even more disquieted by his mission. "However, if Your Highness will forgive me, I have been asked by my sovereign to deliver my message to His Majesty's ears only."

"A fair request," said Steffan. "But, unfortunately, not a feasible one. As I'm sure you're aware, my father is ill."

"I trust it's not serious."

Steffan nodded, fully aware of what Aldebont was really asking.

"It has been quite serious, I'm afraid," Steffan said, trying to sound reassuring nonetheless. "Fortunately, he seems to be improving. Our physician is still insisting that he rest completely. Your Lordship may be assured that my ears are his."

"Were my mission not so urgent, I might wait, begging Your Highness's pardon."

"Granted. Your first allegiance is to your king, and his particular orders." Stephan smiled graciously but groaned inwardly.

"You are most kind, Your Highness." Aldebont sighed. "I do not wish to be the bearer of bad news, but my sovereign has been much concerned by the recent activities of Duke Desmond of Raultberg. He seems to be gathering an army together, and rules his duchy with an iron fist."

"We are aware of his actions." Steffan smiled. The last thing he wanted was for Aldebont to know the truth about what was going on in the Duchy of Raultberg. "Our current course is to discourage his militia. If he continues, revenues from his duchy will become forfeit. We are trying to avoid sending the guard out against him, but we will if necessary. As for his duchy, the people there are very proud, and will not accept an over strong hand. They are also very loyal to the crown first, and then their duke. I'm afraid my uncle is not very popular there. We keep a close watch on Uncle Desmond."

"That is somewhat consoling. We've been hearing

the most alarming rumors, especially regarding His Majesty's health."

Steffan nodded. "It hasn't been good. However, we are looking to his recovery. And even if we weren't, my father's succession is firmly established through me. These past few months I've been working in his stead. You may assure your sovereign that should the worst happen, the transfer of power will go smoothly. And I am quite prepared to deal firmly with the Duke of Raultberg."

Aldebont nodded. "You have given me more than I had hoped. With Your Highness's permission, I should like to leave tomorrow to make haste back to my kingdom, and report to my sovereign."

"You may go."

Steffan waited while Aldebont left, then turned to Ella

"He's still not satisfied," she observed.

Steffan rubbed his face with his hands. "And what more could I have said to him?"

"Nothing. Your father has been gravely ill, and a change of government makes everyone nervous."

"The vultures. They could at least wait until it's happened."

Ella smiled. "And be out-strategized by someone else?"

A dull thud and outcry outside the chamber caused Steffan's face to light up. "Chester's here."

The door opened, and a young man Steffan's age walked in, nursing his elbow. Lord Chester duGrackel, Baron of Fin Reache and friend since boyhood of Prince Steffan, was not happy.

"Even when there's nothing for me to fall over," he grumbled, then suddenly made a grand bow. "Your Royal Highnesses."

"Well, what brings your lordship here?" Steffan asked.

"The king. What else?" Chester shrugged and found a chair. Sitting without invitation in the crown prince's presence was a very special privilege that had been officially granted the Baron of Fin Reache. "My fair wife and I were told that your father was expected to expire at any moment. Marcella was devastated and insisted that we come so that we might see her dear uncle one last time. We've since found that he's likely to continue a while longer. The ghouls, ready to bury the poor man before he's drawn his last breath."

"Everyone is tense these days," sighed Steffan.

"A slight understatement, dear friend. Was that not Lord Aldebont of Karperia I saw in the corridor?"

"It was." Ella led her husband to a chair and gently pushed him down on it. "He came for much the same reason as you. They're also concerned about the Duke of Raultberg."

"Hah!" Chester snorted. "He is not the one you have to worry about. The duke, also known as my dear father-in-law, is just barely sane. Marcella's sister Lanicia, on the other hand, she's the dangerous one. I should warn you, Steffan, there is more than a little truth in the rumors that Lady Lanicia believes she should be the heir and not you."

"How could that be?" asked Ella. "Her mother only ruled as regent. Princess Adele couldn't possibly have hoped to ascend the throne, not while there was a son living."

"I'm not sure exactly," said Steffan. "That all happened years before any of us were born. I'm told that Aunt Adele was very bitter that my father should have primacy over her just because he was a boy, even though he was so much younger than she was. That was one of the reasons she raised taxes and built up the army to conquer Leiderkeit and Karperia. She hoped to get support and stay in power. Father took power while he was just sixteen and then the people revolted anyway. Aunt Adele supposedly tried to blame the revolt on my father and take the throne from him. Fortunately, Father was able to keep enough of the army on his side. And that's why she was married off to Uncle Desmond."

Chester shook his head. "They should have done the same to Lanicia and married her off to someone strong with a good solid holding, instead of the landless little flop she did marry. May he rest in peace."

"I agree," said Steffan. "But I couldn't say that to the Karperian ambassador."

"They've nothing to worry about, in any case," Chester replied. "Lanicia couldn't care less about them. Her eye is on Leiderkeit, which Raultberg also borders. Not only is it larger, she's still peeved because King John refused to marry her."

Steffan laughed. "And I told him not to. John is too good a friend to wish Lanicia on him. Luckily for him, he's got two good brothers, and doesn't need an heir as urgently."

"It's not entirely lucky since it's aroused Lanicia's wrath. And she thinks often how she's next in line for the throne, after you, little Barth and Alicia." Chester shuddered. "Lanicia's a devious one. I can't think of anything she wouldn't do to achieve her ends. She's got her father completely under her control. She doesn't like me particularly, but tolerates me because of being married to her sister."

"Speaking of Marcella," asked Ella. "Where is she?"

"On her way here, I would imagine," Chester answered. "She wanted to greet the queen first."

"I suggest we go find them then," said Steffan, getting up. "I was planning on spending some time with Mother before we send the children home for their dinner."

Queen Adriana's face lit up as her son and daughter-in-law entered the salon where she'd been playing with her grandchildren. Lady Marcella, Steffan's cousin and Chester's wife stood by.

"Hello, my darlings," Adriana crooned.

"Hello, Mother." Steffan went over and kissed his mother on the cheek. "How are you managing with our little ones?"

"Mama!" Barth yelped and rushed to his mother's arms as Alicia whined and ran for her mother also.

"Well enough, dearest," Adriana said. "As you can see, they're feeling the same worry we've all had these days."

"Indeed," said Ella as she cuddled her children. "Madam Mother, would you mind terribly if I sent them home with their nurse?

"I wouldn't mind a bit," Adriana said with a weary smile. "I suspect keeping them to their normal routine is the best thing for them right now."

"I fear so," Ella said and rang for the nursemaid. "Marcella, darling, it's so good to see you. Does this mean you'll be joining us for the dinner with the Karperian ambassador tonight?"

"Yes," said Marcella, smiling.

"Oh, thank heavens!" Ella gushed. "It's not very kind of me, but I'm afraid the ladies of his party are terribly dull. I'll need you to spark things up a bit."

As it turned out, the dinner with the party from Karperia was a quiet meal. No one dared speculate on the king's health, never mind that it was uppermost in everyone's mind.

Ella and Steffan took advantage of the mood and the dinner ended somewhat early, to everyone's relief. After saying good bye to everyone, and spending a couple minutes with the queen, Steffan and Ella retired to their townhouse.

It happened quietly. Even Adriana didn't notice when she checked her husband shortly before midnight. The tower clock tolled two as she checked again. She cried quietly for a few minutes, then summoned the physician, and sent Lord Cedric, the chancellor, to formally notify her son.

Ella woke first. Sleepily, she reached for her nightgown and pushed her husband off of her. Steffan stirred.

"What?" he grumbled, just barely awake.

"Someone's knocking." Ella yawned as she sat up and looked for her dressing gown. "Alicia's probably had another nightmare."

Steffan groaned and got out of bed.

"Why don't you go back to sleep?" asked Ella, who was trying to get her nightgown on.

"I won't sleep until you're back." Steffan struggled into his nightshirt and slid into his dressing gown. "I may as well go with you. Barth will be awake also, and wanting attention."

Ella fumbled with the catch on her dressing gown and followed Steffan.

"We're coming," Steffan answered crossly to the repeated knocks.

He opened the door, silently cursing foolish nursery maids, then stopped. Lord Cedric was the one who had knocked, but he would not come to fetch them for a child's nightmare. But what...

Cedric dropped onto one knee.

"Your Majesty," he began solemnly.

"Oh, no." Steffan swallowed.

"The king, your father, has died," Cedric continued, hiding behind the formality of his duty. "You, sir, are now king, and supreme ruler of this kingdom, as decreed by birth and the will of your father."

"I know the rest, Cedric," Steffan interrupted tiredly.

"As you wish, Your Majesty. Long may you live and reign."

"Thank you, Cedric. You're excused."

Steffan shut the door and turned to Ella.

"Cindy..." he began softly, using the old nickname he'd given her years before.

She was holding him before he could ask. Tears slid out of his eyes, as the bell from the tower clock began the death knell.

# CHAPTER TWO

King Steffan's first royal command was to declare an official period of mourning for the old king to last one week. Then, as was the custom, he would spend a week initiating the preparations for the coronation. At the end of that week, he would leave the capital city to stay with his mother and her half-brother, the Duke of Greenwalt, to return in triumph for the coronation at the end of one month.

Lady Lanicia Cormorant smiled to herself as the herald gave the official proclamation in the courtyard of the ancient castle of Raultberg. She had known of the king's death within a few short hours of the event and knew the traditions as well as Steffan. It had been the intention of her late mother, Princess Adele, all along that Lanicia should have what she, the princess, had been robbed of by the ancient, ill-used tradition that gave males primacy, and Lanicia had been educated as carefully as her cousin.

After issuing formal condolences, Lanicia hurried to her study. It was a dark, rainy day, forcing her to light a candle even though the study boasted a large window. Lanicia spread out a map of the kingdom on her table and pondered.

The road to the Duchy of Greenwalt passed through Raultberg. Though not as mountainous as Greenwalt, there were several lonely, rocky places where an accident might happen, if it could be arranged discreetly. She had the complete loyalty of the Duke of Raultberg's regiment. Several members were acting as spies in the Palace Guard at that very moment. Still, it would be safer to trust as few people as possible.

The rain blasted against the window with new force, distracting Lanicia. The spring storms had been severe that year. They had already caused several floods, in spite of the sluice gates in the hills, designed to control the problem.

The local peasants had complained several times to the duke, as if he could help. The poor man sank deeper and deeper into his illness every day. Only Lanicia knew how badly he fared. Her ability to control her father created the illusion of some sanity on his part, and the duke frequently proved useful to Lanicia's schemes. The window rattled again with fresh pellets of rain. Lanicia smiled. Suddenly, the flood problem became less tiresome.

The day after the funeral, Queen Adriana left the city to stay with her half-brother.

"I need some time for solitude," she told her son. "Besides, I have happy memories of my father's house. They'll help to ease the hurt. Oh, how I'll miss him."

"I understand, Mother," replied Steffan.

Adriana recovered herself and touched Steffan's cheek.

"I'm certain you do. You poor thing. It's bad enough to grieve for your father. Then to have all this responsibility."

"It's what I was raised for."

"And well raised, at that. Your father would be so proud of you. He always was. Nobody wants his time to come, but your father's was made so much easier knowing you were ready to take over for him, I'm sure of it." Adriana sighed. "I feel as if a great hole has opened up in my life, and yet I feel at peace. Your father is at rest now, and I take comfort in that. You should, too."

"I will, Mother." Steffan kissed each of her cheeks, then led her to the front of the palace where the coach waited to take her to Greenwalt.

Steffan's soul remained heavy for the next six days, as he began the complicated arrangements involved in the transfer of power. Many trusted councilors asked to retire from the king's service. Steffan agreed that they had earned their rest, but regretted their departure, especially since the ones who did not want to retire were the ones he least wanted to stay. Then there was the bother of appointing new councilors, and the tedious responses to the surrounding kingdoms, reassuring and placating them, as well as the casting of the royal seal ring, which had to be cast and fitted several times until it fit Steffan's hand perfectly.

"You've had no time to properly grieve," observed Ella the night before they were to leave for Greenwalt, themselves.

"Well, I hope to get some of it in the next couple of weeks," Steffan replied. He slid into bed next to her. "That's one advantage in leaving the city. I won't be able to bring a lot of this work with me. Perhaps that's what the forefathers had in mind, besides a triumphant re-entry."

Ella snuggled up close. "Whether or not they did, it is certainly fortunate. Although, I hope you don't spend your time brooding over the new responsibility."

"Why should I? I've already had it for three or four months, not to mention staring it in the eye all my life. I was raised to be king, and my father never let me forget it. I used to be frightened of it when I was all alone, but I'm not alone anymore." He squeezed her. "Like my mother, I merely miss him."

"I will, too. He was a second father to me."

"And after you lost yours at such a young age. Cindy, how long did it take you to get over it your father's death?"

She frowned. "It's hard to say. Things were so awful after he died. I suppose I shouldn't speak of her because of the magic, but if it hadn't been for Godmother, I don't know how I would have survived."

"You dear woman. I know we're supposed to pretend that it was all mere good fortune, that there was no magic. But I am so grateful for it." He pulled her even closer to him. "This is so terrible, Cindy. I've never known real grief or hardship before. Everything has always gone more or less as I wanted. I knew my father had to die, but I didn't really believe it. What confuses me is that, in some ways, I'm glad he's gone. Now, here's my chance to do what I've lived my life learning to do. What a horrible thought."

"That you're ready to do your life's work? I think not. I think that your father would be pleased that you're so eager to do it. You're certainly not happy about his passing, nor were you interested in hastening it. But now that it's come, you're ready to go to work with enthusiasm, and with the same love for it, and the people, that your father had. That was his greatest hope for his son. I know, because he told me, himself."

"He did?" Steffan mused. "That's comforting to know. Cindy, you are my greatest treasure. This would be the worst experience of my life if it weren't for you."

"You would have managed. But I'm glad I've been a help." Ella stifled a yawn and blew out the last candle.

The trip to Greenwalt was to take place without pageantry or much notice. It had been planned that the royal coach be accompanied by only six men. The transfer of a well-loved monarch and family in a time of peace did not require more. That the men all wore the colors of the Duke of Raultberg created no comment. After all, the men of Raultberg were loyal to the king, or so it was assumed.

It rained steadily for two days as the coach crossed the fertile plains, then skirted the rolling hills of Raultberg. As afternoon approached on the second day, the party slowed. The hills had become mountains, and the narrow road was littered with rocks left there by the bad weather. The road began to climb as it ran alongside a stream, swollen with the spring rains. Both the stream and the road followed through a small canyon, filled with trees and brush. Steffan looked out the coach's window and saw in the trees the small sparkling lights of the Faer Folke. At least, that's what his mother had called them.

It was here that the coach stopped. Steffan looked at Ella, who shrugged.

"Is there a problem?" he called to the driver, who was climbing down off of his box.

"No, Your Majesty," the driver answered. "We're just a little stuck. There's no reason for any of you to leave the coach."

Four-year-old Barth lifted a sleepy head from his father's lap.

"Are we there yet?" he sighed.

"No," said Steffan. "But we're getting out anyway."

"Your Majesty, it's not necessary!" someone called rather urgently.

"It'll be easier on the horses." Steffan picked up Alicia and opened the coach door. "Besides we could all do with a stretch."

"I certainly could," Ella said. "Barth, watch your step, now. And stay away from the stream. That water is moving terribly quickly."

They had, fortunately, all gotten out of the coach. Steffan noticed that the guards were scrambling up the hillside next to them, so he led his family in that direction. But he didn't have time to think about why the guards were behaving so oddly. A huge wave of water came crashing down from up the canyon, dragging the coach and the panicked horses down the road with it.

While the little family had escaped being swept away by the initial rush, the water rose so quickly that they were soon swamped.

Steffan felt the magic buoying him and the others up. He didn't know how long it would last, after all, he'd heard that the magic of the Faer Folke was fairly weak when among the Landed. He swam as hard as he could to reach Alicia as Ella managed to push Barth onto a small ledge above the now roaring river. Steffan got his daughter onto the ledge, but then Ella struggled as the weight of her skirts pulled her down. Exhausted, Steffan helped her out of the water. Then she pulled him out the rest of the way.

It all happened in a matter of moments. Faint with cold, and the battering waves, Steffan staggered onto the ledge. Pain leapt like fire through his right leg. He fell, trembling, and struck his head on a rock, then knew no more.

They found the coach at the bottom of the canyon, with the mangled horses still hitched, and the body of one of the guards. But they never found the bodies of the new king and his family. The Duke of Raultberg, being in a lucid phase, led the search with three of his most trusted men. It was the duke's decision to wrap the branches and rocks into four shrouds, then quickly close them into coffins. He claimed that the bodies had been so battered, it would be too horrible to gaze upon them. And so the funeral was held, and Lanicia, being the next in line for the throne, was crowned a month later.

Steffan was aware that he was ill, and that time was passing. Darkness and dreams faded into each other without much rhyme or reason. He was given strong broth to sip, and then the dreams would come again. Ella was there, off and on, and the children. He knew there was another, a man. It was hard to say if the man was a part of the dream or not.

The man was there when the fever finally broke and Steffan opened his eyes for the first time to clarity.

"Who... Who are you?" he whispered.

"I am a friend of the one your queen calls Godmother," said the man in a soft, reedy voice. He was thin with wild, gray hair. "You can call me Mr. Murdren."

"You're of the Faer Folke." Steffan swallowed. "Ella said we'd never see you."

"I was of the Faer Folke," the man said with a sad smile. "I lost my magic seeking after gold I never found. But I have kept my friends among the Faer. In fact, I'm even your cousin. On your grandmother's side, obviously."

Steffan frowned. "We must be in serious trouble."

"You are. But rest. Her Majesty will be here shortly. You've been very sick."

"How long?"

"Drink this broth."

Steffan sipped weakly. It tasted somewhat different than the other broth had.

"The children?" he asked.

"They're well enough. They've had some injuries, but yours was the worst. You broke your leg, and hit your head pretty hard, too. Then you had to go and take sick over it."

"I'm back, Mr. Murdren." Ella appeared behind me. "Oh, you're awake."

"I believe so," Steffan replied with a weak smile.

Sniffing, Ella sank to her knees next to him. "Oh, thanks be, you're really awake. You've been in that healing sleep for so long, I was beginning to wonder if you'd ever wake up."

Steffan gazed at her, completely puzzled. There was something odd about her appearance. The ragged gown and shawl she wore were unexpected enough, and she moved stiffly as if bending were impossible.

"You're with child," he gasped.

"Yes." Ella smiled and patted the greatly swollen belly.

"You look as if you're about ready to deliver. Have I been asleep that long?"

"Only six months," laughed Ella. "I've just grown a bit more than usual. Well, a lot more. It looks as though we're going to have a very large child."

"That's enough shock for now," Mr. Murdren cut in briskly. "Your Majesty, you sleep some more. I need to brew some herbs."

Steffan obeyed. He continued to rest on his own rather than by the magic of the healing sleep. He gained strength and learned that Mr. Murdren was a hermit and that Steffan and his family were hidden with him in a cave. But it was a week before he was able to sit up and hear the worst about his situation.

"Lanicia? Queen?" he growled. "I'll have to go right to the palace and clear this up."

"You can't," said Mr. Murdren. "She's very powerful now. And she knows that your bodies were not in those coffins. She firmly believes you're dead but more than one family with two small children has disappeared or met with an untimely accident."

"At the palace they'll know me."

"Not necessarily," Mr. Murdren said. "Lanicia has completely replaced the entire staff, and it's her Raultberg Regiment that controls the army. They like their positions. Your Majesty, without any support, you wouldn't last two hours."

Steffan looked away, thinking. "A sluice gate must have burst to cause that sudden flood. How fortunate for Lanicia. In fact, suspiciously so. I remember seeing the guard fleeing into the woods."

Murdren sighed. "The sluice gate was sabotaged. No one can really prove that it was timed to coincide with the coach's arrival in the canyon, and so, officially, it has been recorded as a tragic accident."

"So now what?" Steffan looked over at Ella, as he scratched at the beard that had grown during his illness.

Ella shrugged. "We must remain hidden until we can pull together the support we need to get you back on the throne."

"It will take some time," added Murdren. "But it's not hopeless by any means. The queen is not proving to be very popular. She's moving slowly. However, not many are fooled by her patience."

"As soon as I regain my strength, the first thing to do will be to go to Leiderkeit," Steffan said.

"And have King John present you?" Murdren shook his head.

"I already thought of that," said Ella. "If John championed you, it would be a virtual declaration of war, which is just what Lanicia needs to solidify her position. She would have the perfect excuse to invade, and the support of the people, since they would be only protecting the homes Leiderkeit is attacking."

"The key, Your Majesty, is to let the queen do the damage to herself, then appear with the solution," said Murdren. "Our people have a long history of revolting under rulers they do not like."

"It will still take years," Steffan sighed. "If I am supposedly dead, how will I get anyone to believe me when I reveal myself?"

"How you go about it, you will find in time. But our friend, the one you call Godmother, has used her power so that no one else can wear the ring that was cast as your royal seal. Lord Cedric guards it. Already, one man has claimed to be you. The ring proved to be far too small, and the man was not unlike you in stature."

"The best thing to do, for now, Steffan, is get well," said Ella. "Hermit Murdren is arranging for us to take a small farm he owns in the south of Raultberg."

"Lanicia's duchy."

"True, but not Lanicia's people. They support her only nominally and being right under her nose, so to speak, it might prove to be a better hiding place."

"I farmed it for many years," said Mr. Murdren. "But I gave it up a few seasons back in order to see if I can regain my magic."

Steffan nodded sullenly. Murdren left to play with the two children. Steffan squeezed Ella's hand.

"It's going to be terribly hard," he murmured.

He looked at the wooden ring his wife wore. It had been his betrothal present to her after she had told him how she wished at times that wood was all he had to offer her. Her gold wedding band had already been sold. Ella had been so ashamed when she'd told him. But even he'd agreed she'd had little choice. Afraid that Lanicia's men would be hunting them, Ella had taken the hermit's advice to be ready to flee at any time, which meant selling anything of value so they would have some money. The problem was there hadn't been much to sell. Unlike her peers, Ella seldom wore jewelry during the day and had only been wearing her wedding band at the time of the accident. All they had was the money from the sale of the wedding ring and the small pouch of silver coins that Steffan carried for alms giving. And the jeweled medallions that each of them wore that identified them as a member of the royal family. Ella had hidden those. Selling them was out of the question.

"We have nothing," Steffan said.

"We have some silver," said Ella. "It's not much, but it should help us through. We'll be poor, is all."

"All? Good heavens, Ella. I swore I would never let you see hard times again."

"You didn't let this happen. Who would have believed that Lanicia was this treacherous? It's almost as if I'm fated to be poor."

"What an unhappy fate."

"I'm not in the least unhappy. The worst thing in the world is to be unloved, and I've already survived that. I shall survive this. I can't say I like it, but I've got you, and two beautiful children with another on the way. Besides, I learned a long time ago that the only thing that can make you happy is yourself. If you depend on other people or your situation, you will be disappointed."

Steffan smiled. "And I've many very rich and very unhappy relatives to prove it. I just hope the good hermit can show me how to farm. I have only the slightest understanding of the process."

Murdren proved to be very helpful, and as Steffan

grew stronger, the hermit put him to work in the little garden outside of the cave. There wasn't much to be done. Winter was coming on fast. Frosts appeared as early as the first days of November.

One morning, in the middle of the month, Ella felt the first twinges of labor. It was too soon, but the child was so large, surely it would be all right. She didn't say anything at first. Steffan was resting. Murdren had taken the children with him to purchase winter supplies in a nearby village. By noon, Ella was well into the advanced stages. Steffan was awake and completely terrified.

He paced at the front of the cave, wondering what he should do when he saw a light from a nearby tree leap from the branches and quickly form a bent-over shape. The light seemed to jump away and there stood a wizened old crone of a woman.

Steffan stared for a moment.

"Are you the one Ella calls Godmother?"

The old woman shook her head and bustled into the cave. "No. But she sent me. I'm better at birthing babies than she is."

"Thank goodness you're here," he gasped. "Now I can get the doctor."

He winced as Ella cried out.

"I seriously doubt you'll get back in time," she replied. "Besides, you are still in hiding. We don't dare risk it. You'll have to help me deliver it."

Steffan went completely pale. Ella yelped again, then grabbed Steffan's hand.

"I'll be all right," she gasped. "It was worse with Barth. Oh no!"

As Ella grimaced with pain, the woman felt her belly.

"It may yet be worse," the old woman sighed. "I've a feeling I know why you got so big. You're carrying twins."

Ella laughed hysterically.

"Twins," Steffan whispered. Slowly, he gathered his wits together. He took a deep breath and let it out. "Well, we've a long day ahead of us. Madam, you'd best tell me what to do. I'm afraid helping to deliver babies is another thing no one ever thought I'd need to learn."

The old crone patted his hand reassuringly, then set him to work heating water and gathering a clean, sharp knife, and rags. Murdren reappeared as dusk fell, and kept the two other children busy. The first baby arrived well after sundown. It was a girl. The second, a boy, did not appear until almost midnight.

"Twins," Steffan whispered again, as he cleaned up. The old crone had disappeared the moment it was clear that Ella was well.

Steffan dried his hands on a battered rag and went over to the makeshift cradle where his new infant daughter slept. Ella dozed as she nursed the boy.

"My daughter," Steffan whispered over the infant. "Dearest child, what are we going to do? When your brother and sister were born, my greatest worry was whether or not I could keep them from becoming spoiled brats. Now I'll consider myself fortunate if I can just keep you fed and sheltered."

"Steffan?" Ella's voice asked softly.

"I'm here." Steffan slipped to her side.

"You'd best take this one. I can't stay awake any

longer, and I'm afraid I'll roll over on him. He's finished nursing already."

"I've got him."

Steffan sighed as he took the tiny infant. He was learning a great many things very quickly. He still worried that he wasn't learning enough fast enough to keep his family sheltered and well. Then there was the far deeper dread that he kept pushed to the back of his mind.

Near the first part of December, Mr. Murdren decided Steffan had better face his fears. The two stood at the entrance of the cave, looking out as the snow quietly fell, burying the landscape in white mounds.

Steffan's eyes settled on the nearby trees. Tiny lights danced among the branches. He looked over at Murdren, who seemed to be watching them, as well.

"Do you see the lights in the tree?" Steffan asked.

"Yes," Mr. Murdren said quietly.

"My mother is able to see them," Steffan said. "You're the first person I've met besides us who can see them, too."

"They are the Faer Folke," Murdren said, longing filling his face.

"That's what my mother said. I didn't see them often when I was a child. Only when something important was about to happen. I remember seeing the lights the day I first met Ella. And I saw them again just before the accident."

"Your godmother wanted help."

"But this was before the accident."

Murdren shrugged. "It's hard to say what she knew. She may have heard from one of the others that something was amiss. She may have simply sensed it. The Faer Folke can't predict the future, but the way of magic is mysterious, and we sometimes get hints and gleanings."

"That's right," Steffan said. "You told me that you'd lost your magic or something?"

Murdren sighed. "Yes. I was one of the Faer Folke when I was young. There are two ways we lose our magic. One is to fall in love with someone who is Landed, or without magic. It doesn't happen nearly as often as it used to, but it does happen every now and then."

"My mother's mother, Graciella," Steffan said. "She fell in love with my grandfather."

"They fell in love with each other, by what I heard. So as soon as he died and your mother was married, Graciella longed to come back and got her magic back very quickly."

"And the other way to lose your magic?" Steffan asked.

"To want to own things. The Faer Folke have everything they need. But if you want more than you need, if you want wealth or power, then you must give something up to get it, and in our case, that is magic. I gave mine up for gold and soon realized that I had made a terrible mistake. And while you can get your magic back, it can take a great many years. I farmed for many of them, then abandoned my farm when I realized that the only way I would get my magic back would be to give up the land. I left the deed to the farm hidden in the house in the hopes that someone would find it and claim the farm." Murdren sighed. "It never happened. Now, here you and your family are, needing a safe place to hide and work. Yes, it was a terrible thing to lose your throne to your greedy cousin, but it will turn out to be my salvation." Murdren smiled. "I can feel the magic coming back. And you have magic, too."

"How? Aren't I part of the... what do you call us?"

"The Landed. And, yes, you largely are. But most of our Landed children and grandchildren seem to have some magic about them. We're not sure why. But you, specifically, Your Majesty, have a gift."

Steffan's brow creased in thought. "Mother did say that my ability to get about without being seen or noticed was part of my heritage from her mother. I've never really thought about it before. It's just been something I can do."

"But what is your deepest, darkest fear right now?"

"Not being able to support..." He turned away. "No, that's not it. I can't help worrying about that, but we'll manage." He swallowed. "It's being seen, and recognized, and losing my family, my children."

"I know. Your magic is weak. There is more blue blood in your veins than that of our kind. But you can use it."

"How?"

"Don't think about it. Just do it."

"What about the children and Ella? Will it be enough to protect them?"

"It should be. And you will have help. Your godmother is still watching out for you. The best help she can give is that which is subtle and looks like mere good fortune."

"If only it will be enough."

"You'll manage. Poverty is no easy thing, yet there are worse fates, as I know full well. And I imagine precious few of your noble subjects would do as well, even with help."

Steffan nodded and looked back at the trees. "I would imagine not."

"You'll do well, Your Majesty. I have confidence in you."

Steffan looked back at the cave and sighed. The hermit's confidence was no small thing. He'd have to rely on it.

# THE FIRST YEAR

## CHAPTER THREE

Amild winter passed. As the last of the snow trickled away from the hermit's cave, Mr. Murdren acquired a good stout farm horse, a wagon filled with a few household goods and some food, and a milk cow.

"You should be able to make it through to the next harvest with this," the hermit told Steffan as they prepared to leave.

"I just hope there will be one," Steffan answered.

"If you do as I told you, there will be." Murdren chuckled. "A meager one, perhaps, but enough to get you through the next year. And the next one will be bigger. You're no fool, Steffan. You'll learn."

"I have already. I'm indebted to you."

"Not necessarily. As I said, my gift is bringing my magic back. Is everything ready?"

"I believe so."

Steffan gave the wagon a final look-over, then loaded his family. As he climbed onto the wagon's seat, he turned back to the cave and saw Mr. Murdren suddenly glowing with light and disappearing. Steffan smiled softly, knowing that he would never see the hermit again.

It took a good day's journey to reach the farm where

they were to live. The sun was setting when Steffan reined in the horse. The Murdren farmhouse stood near the road into a small village. Mr. Murdren had said that the farm was on the outskirts of the community, and Steffan could see at least three other farmhouses and barns along the road to the village proper. Directly across the road, was yet another farmhouse and barn, surrounded by fields, half with newly-turned earth and half with the brown straw leftover from the previous harvest. Mr. Murdren had said that the farm across the road was owned by a John Asgarth and his family, and had called them good neighbors.

Steffan turned to the farm he now owned. It was a disheartening sight. Even Ella sighed when she saw it. Grass grew over the fields. Weeds and tangled brush grew all over the yard. The door to the house hung open on crooked hinges. Broken shutters covered two windows.

Inside the house, things were even worse. Abandoned chickens roosted everywhere, adding feathers to the built up dust and cobwebs that cluttered the little two room cottage. Dilapidated stairs led to a forbidding loft over the second room. A dark hole next to the huge fireplace suggested a cold room. An oven could be seen in the fireplace brickwork, but there was not much hope for its usefulness. Utterly discouraged, Steffan shook his head. Ella noted it and held back her own misgivings.

"Well, it's a good thing Mr. Murdren included a mop and broom on the wagon," she said with false cheerfulness. "That's all that's needed to set this place to rights."

"Mama," sniffed Barth. "Aren't we ever going to live in the palace again?"

"Sh!" Ella hissed quickly. Steffan glanced around nervously. "Remember what we told you? You must never say a word about that. We have to pretend there never was a palace or anything like that."

Steffan reached over and held the boy. "I know it's hard, son, but you must remember."

Barth nodded.

"The first thing to do is to shoo these chickens out." Ella flapped her skirt. "Come, son, this is something you can do."

It was an awkward, exhausting night. New sheets couldn't hide the rotting straw that was left for the beds. Alicia went into sneezing fits with the dust, and the infants were fitful. The best Steffan could manage for the night was a fire in the ancient fireplace and rags over the broken windows.

"This will be a proper house in no time," Ella promised as they finally crawled into bed. "You just leave it to me."

"Ella, please. I know you're only trying to be cheerful for my sake."

"A little for my sake, too." Ella sighed. "It is depressing, isn't it?"

"Yes. But it's better than nothing. My first task tomorrow will be to set out the field markers. I can take Barth with me to do that."

"I'll get this place cleaned up, then see what I can do about a chicken coop. Fresh eggs will be a big help, and maybe I'll be able to sell the extras."

"That would be nice. But first, let's concentrate on

making this place livable."

The twins woke first the next morning, in the early hours just as the eastern sky was getting lighter. As Ella tended to their needs, Steffan roused himself. Comfortable cackling informed him that the chickens had returned, and as he fumbled for a candle, he stepped on and crunched a reminder of their presence.

"See if there are any other eggs about," whispered Ella. "I'll use them for breakfast."

"If I can find a candle."

"No. It'll be light soon, and we don't have the candles to waste."

Gloomily, Steffan pulled on his pants and carefully retrieved the small white eggs. Barth awoke as Ella finished with the twins. He was instructed to watch them while Ella headed out to the yard with a pair of buckets. Steffan followed her, feeling uncomfortably unwashed.

"What are you doing?" he asked his wife.

"I'm going to milk the cow." Ella smiled confidently. "I may have been raised in the city, but Mr. Murdren assured me I had the right touch. Thank heavens, Daffy seems to agree."

"Daffy. You mean the cow."

"Yes, and I already knew how to make cheese and butter and other good things. Stepmother didn't like paying the dairyman any more than she had to." She paused, then handed him one of the buckets. "Perhaps you might check and see if the well still has water in it. I know you must be aching to wash up."

Steffan scratched at his beard. "At least shaving won't be a problem."

He went back inside to check the children, then visited the well. The weeds were overgrown around the bricks, but the winch functioned and the rope was intact, which was surprising. Perhaps it was help masquerading as good fortune. Still not feeling reassured, Steffan lowered the bucket.

Everything seemed so bleak he couldn't understand how Ella managed to remain so optimistic. But then, she was no stranger to hopeless situations. Steffan's life hadn't always been easy, but he'd never had to worry about wasting candles or scrounging for food, or even hiding his face lest he be recognized and his family wiped out.

Even as he scratched the beard he'd maintained to avoid recognition, he pushed his worries aside. If Ella could remain positive, so could he. After all, he did have his family, and they were all well and healthy, and they had a roof over their heads, and they wouldn't exactly starve. The bucket had long since splashed into the water at the bottom of the well. Steffan remembered what he was doing, and pulled it up.

Ella choked back a nervous sob as she faced the cow. Milking was not as easy as she had led her husband to believe. Daffy was prone to fits of temperament. Ella always got the milk, and as often as not, a bruise or two. She wondered if she should have been completely honest with her husband, then dismissed the thought. Steffan was depressed enough already.

Fortunately, Daffy was in a placid mood in spite of her disordered surroundings and the previous day's march. Ella quickly went to work, pulling and squeezing the teats. Milk squirted into the pail in a comforting rhythm. Hopefully, it would keep Barth and Alicia happy. If only the twins could be made as content.

That was another worry Ella didn't want Steffan to know about. Nursing two little ones was quite a strain, and it seemed as though they were always hungry. Ella was fairly sure her own milk would hold out, but how could she clean the house up, and care for Alicia and Barth when she was feeding the twins almost every hour, and they were already four months old? It had to be done, and so it would be. Ella sighed. It was not going to be easy.

The twins were crying again when Ella came back with the milk. She hurried over to feed them. Steffan smiled as he watched.

"They certainly know how to get their breakfasts promptly," he chuckled.

"I'm sorry," Ella groaned. "But what else am I to do? We can't afford a wet nurse, even if there was one we could trust."

"We'll manage." Steffan shrugged. "And there are some things I can do."

"And me too!" Barth chirped in. "Look. I dressed all by myself, and I helped Papa get water and wash up Alicia."

"We're calling her Grace, now," Steffan warned.

Barth grimaced. "Right. And I'm Lucas."

"You did very well," Steffan said. "I'm very proud of you."

"And I am, too, darling," added Ella.

"You and Mama are so scared all the time." Barth plopped down next to his mother.

Steffan sighed. "Yes, we are. We told you why in

the cave."

"Our cousin took away the palace and made us have an accident, so now we're poor." Barth pouted. "Why does she want to hurt us?"

"Because if a lot of other people knew we were alive, they'd help us take the palace away from her," Steffan answered. "But right now it's too hard for me to let enough people know, so we have to stay in hiding until I can get enough of them to like me."

"And then we get the palace?"

"Hopefully. But we may not, for a lot of reasons, so we can't count on it. That's why we've come to live here. We must be very careful, and remember not to say the wrong things, all right?"

Barth nodded. Ella glanced at Steffan, and they both sighed secretly. Not yet five years old, Barth was too young to really understand the danger. But he was old enough to remember the good times and miss them. Fortunately, Alicia, who had just turned three, had been too little to remember and genuinely liked being called by her new name.

As soon as Ella had the twins fed, she prepared breakfast for the others, then began setting the fireplace and cooking area to rights. Steffan was about to suggest that she sit and eat but something stopped him. Reminded that his own work awaited him, he finished quickly. Barth was already done. Steffan gathered him along and left for the fields.

It was a long morning. The stone markers had been scattered. Steffan lifted and replaced the heavy stones, while Barth ran about finding them. Even though the day was cool, Steffan was soaked with sweat long before mid-day.

He had sat down to rest for a moment when he noticed he and Barth were not alone. A man approached from the road along the field markers. His face was lined with years out working in the sun, and flecks of gray shot through the wisps of hair that appeared underneath his hat.

"Hallo!" he said cheerfully.

"Good day, sir." Steffan remained aloof. Lanicia's spies were said to be everywhere, and he did not dare take any chances.

"So you've arrived," answered the man. "Mr. Murdren sent word that he'd given the farm over. We been waiting for the new owners for most the winter. I'm John Asgarth. Our house is right across the road from yours." He studied Steffan carefully. Steffan realized that the man was equally suspicious of him.

"My name is Alex Murdren," Steffan said slowly.

"That's right. You're the hermit's kin." Asgarth's eyebrows flickered up with interest.

"Yes. My father's cousin."

"And what brings you here? He's not gone to his reward, is he?"

"No. He's quite well." Steffan thought of the bright flash of light and Mr. Murdren's disappearance and decided he hadn't lied. But then he paused. He and Ella had rehearsed the story many times, but he still felt nervous telling it. "I, like my father, am a merchant, or was. As you've no doubt heard, merchanting is not particularly profitable anymore, especially for those who are no longer in the queen's favor. When my father died, he told me to go to his cousin should I ever be in need, and Mr. Murdren sent me here."

"Aye. We've heard that story before, and we've been hearing it a lot more. But not everyone has a cousin with a farm to hand over."

"We are truly fortunate."

Asgarth smiled and nodded at Barth, who was busy running through the field. "Your son?"

"Yes."

"Any others?"

"Four total."

Asgarth nodded, pleased. "That's a blessing for you. We've seen more than one young family with only two children disappear."

"So I've heard."

"Papa!" Barth came running up. "Another stone."

"Good, son. Let's go get it. Excuse me, Mr. Asgarth. I'm afraid I've a lot to do if I'm to get this field planted in season."

"You do, indeed." Asgarth ran an experienced eye over the grassy land. "You'll have to mow that grass before you plow, and you'd best be doing it quickly. If this weather keeps up warm like it has been, that grass'll go to seed, and there'll be trouble for you."

"I know." Steffan walked over to where Barth had found another stone.

Asgarth followed him. "You'll never get it mowed fast enough by yourself."

"I have no other option, therefore, I will," Steffan grunted as he lifted the rock.

"You've a fair bit marked out, and not that much more to go. You'll be done getting them stones back by this evening."

"I hope so. I've still got to clear out the barn and patch the roof of the house."

Asgarth laughed "'Tis a job, ain't it? Tell you what. My two sons are almost grown, so between us, we're well ahead at my place. We'll be here tomorrow and help you mow this field."

Steffan hesitated. The offer of help was generous, and he needed it. Still, he and his family were too new to this life not to make errors. Asgarth was already moving away.

"We'll be seeing you tomorrow morning," he called as he sauntered back down the road.

Steffan thoughtfully heaved the stone into place. It appeared he had help coming whether or not he wanted it. Perhaps it was just as well. Given Asgarth's own suspicions, it would be better not to remain too aloof.

At the house, Ella's work was not progressing as quickly. As soon as she had gotten enough water in to clean the table, fireplace, and oven, the twins started crying again. She fed them, then Alicia wanted something to eat. Ella gave her some leftover milk. She had just barely finished with the table and was sweeping the hearth when someone knocked at the door. In swept a middle-aged woman, comfortably plump. She beamed at the activity.

"Excuse me," Ella said, a little more severely than she'd wanted.

"I shouldn't be bursting in on you so quickly, I know," replied the woman. "But neighbors we are. I'm Mrs. Berencia Asgarth. We're right across the road, there."

"Mrs. Cindy Murdren," replied Ella carefully.

"The hermit's kinfolk. We'd heard."

"My late father-in-law's cousin."

"You poor thing. This place is in a state, it is." Mrs. Asgarth scuttled about the room. "What a beautiful little girl. And what do we have here? Twins? They're a sign of good fortune if ever there was one, but a burdensome one it can be. They're so tiny. How old?"

"Four months."

"The poor little mites. Don't they eat?"

"All the time," sighed Ella. "They're always hungry, it seems."

"You're nursing them, aren't you?"

"How else can I feed them?" Ella shifted. It was a little embarrassing to be discussing such a private matter with a complete stranger.

Mrs. Asgarth tittered. "You're city-bred, my dear, aren't you?"

Ella turned red. "I'm afraid so."

"Don't tell me. Your husband was a royal tradesman and the queen don't want his service no more?"

"He was a merchant."

"We've been seeing enough of them, too. Don't be looking so scared, child. I'm here to help. The hermit's a dear, dear man, but only a man would be leaving a woman in a house like this." Mrs. Asgarth bustled about cheerfully. "Oh, good, you've got milk and eggs. Perfect. We've had more than a few twins in the village before, and it's a good thing I learned this trick or we'd've lost some." She quickly rinsed out a bowl and dumped milk into it, then put her hands in her dress pockets. "You'll be needing a couple kid teats. Look at this, will you? I forgot I was carrying them." She carefully cracked three eggs into the bowl and mixed it heartily. "Asgarth is forever telling me to empty me pockets. 'Berencia,' he says, 'you needn't be carrying the whole household with you everywhere you go.' But I'm never wanting for anything I need."

Ella sat back in bemused wonder. Within seconds, Mrs. Asgarth found and rinsed two flasks, poured the foaming mixture into them and tied the leather nipples to the tops. Gently, she propped the two babies up and gave each a flask. After a minute's careful prodding, the two babies were sucking greedily.

"There." Mrs. Asgarth stepped back, thoroughly pleased. "That ought to give you some time and keep them better fed. Poor thing, you can't keep them fed all the time yourself, not with two. No woman can. But you keep them on your breast when you can. They need that, too."

Ella blushed again at such coarse talk. It had been a while since she'd heard it, and she was accustomed to the more discreet manners of royalty.

"I don't know how to thank you," she said.

"Oh, it's a pleasure for me." It was Mrs. Asgarth's turn to blush. "I just can't get enough of babies, and yours are so beautiful. What are their names?"

"My little girl is Grace, and this one is Nella, and the other, James. And I have another son, Lucas. He's with his father." Ella stood, suddenly worried that she might have said too much and encouraged the woman to stay longer. "I'm afraid I'd better get back to work. There's a lot to do."

"You'll be getting it done in no time, I'm sure."

"Well, thank you again, Mrs. Asgarth."

"Oh, it's no trouble at all, Mrs. Murdren. We'll be seeing each other again soon." Mrs. Asgarth swept out of the door as swiftly as she had come in.

Ella let out her breath in relief. Getting too close to anybody, no matter how kind, could end in disaster. Yet Mrs. Asgarth had solved quite a problem. Her spirits restored, Ella went back to work with vigor.

By the time lunchtime came around, Ella had soup and fresh bread ready.

"Are you sure this is the same house we came into last evening?" Steffan teased as he sat down to eat.

"I'm quite sure," replied Ella. "It's amazing what a difference no cobwebs make. And I'm going to tackle the loft this afternoon. Our good fortune seems to be helping me today. If it continues, we'll be able to move up there tonight, and let the children have their own room."

Ella's good fortune held, and she and Steffan spent their first night alone together in almost a year.

"I wonder if we should have brought the twins up," Ella sighed as they rested together in each other's arms.

"Probably. Knowing them, they should be waking up any minute now."

"They should have woken up an hour ago. Thank heavens for Mrs. Asgarth."

"Mrs. Asgarth? Was she here?"

"This morning. She showed me a special mixture for the twins and made up two special flasks so I don't have to be feeding them all the time. She's a terrible busybody, but I'm immensely grateful."

"Her husband is not much better. He and his sons will be here tomorrow morning to help me mow the field. I truly need the help, but I think they're watching us."

"Why? Could they have guessed?"

"No. I don't think so. He's too suspicious of me. He's probably wondering if we're spies."

Ella laughed. "I can't blame them, but it seems so ridiculous. The difficulty is, no matter how meddlesome Mrs. Asgarth seems, I find it hard not to like her."

"I was thinking the same thing myself about her husband."

"Mr. Murdren did say they were good neighbors and we are going to have to make friends with people if we are to get you back where you belong."

"True. But we'd better do it slowly. The wrong friends could be deadly."

# CHAPTER FOUR

In the house across the road, Berencia Asgarth set a bowl of steaming porridge next to a platter of sausages.

"Well, go on with you, Asgarth." She merrily prodded her pensive husband. "The boys want to be meeting with their friends, and you've a meeting yourself tonight."

"Another meeting, Father?" sighed the older boy, a young man of seventeen named Edward.

"Aye." Asgarth snapped out of his reverie. "Her Majesty is letting loose with more of her trouble, and I've got to listen to the men grumble about it. Sooner or later we'll be getting to doing something about it."

"What they ought to be doing is finding King Steffan," said fifteen-year-old Giles.

His three younger sisters giggled.

"The man and his family are dead," Asgarth replied.

"But there's families still disappearing," said Gen. She was the youngest of the five, and ten years old. "Mary Miller says there were three families what got taken, in the dead of night, they were. 'Twas in the duchy of Greenwalt, but that ain't all that far from here."

"I've been hearing the same, Father," Edward added. "And from young Mr. Cyril, too. If anybody knows, he does."

Asgarth shook his head. "Her Majesty isn't wanting anyone taking advantage of the rumors and putting up an impostor to get rid of her. She's no fool, that one, and not foolish enough to believe she's loved."

Meg, the middle sister, and twelve years old, smiled dreamily.

"What if the new family across the road was them?" she whispered.

The others laughed, except Berencia.

"It's not possible," Asgarth chuckled. "They've got four children. It's been almost a year, but nobody whelps them that fast."

"The youngest two are twins," said Berencia. "And they're only four months old."

Asgarth counted. "Well, it just might be possible, at that. But the odds are so long even Giles wouldn't bet on them."

Fourteen-year-old Arlette giggled. "And he would, too."

"I would not," said Giles indignantly.

"What do you think of him, Asgarth?" Berencia asked more seriously.

"A gentleman. The hermit's cousins married well. It don't surprise me none. The Murdrens have always done well for themselves. But he's scared, and well he should be if Her Majesty isn't wanting his services no more. He's not looking to be taken into any confidences, which I say is a good sign."

"Are we still mowing his field tomorrow?" asked Giles.

"Aye. I want to be sure of him. And what are you

thinking, Berencia?"

"Same as you. She's city-bred and said as much, but she seems to be getting on well enough. I pushed my way in, gave her a bit of help, and she thanked me quite prettily for it, too. But she's not about to trust me. I think a spy would be more friendly like."

"Aye," her husband replied.

His mind was full of these musings as he made his way to the village tavern that night. He paid his coin for a tankard of beer and went into the back room. Four men had already gathered. Asgarth took the last place at the table.

"Woodman, Kiffs." He nodded at Woodman, whose shirt bore the dark stain of his trade as a cobbler, and Kiffs, whose broad arms proclaimed him as a blacksmith. Asgarth grasped the hand of the man to his right. "Lyle."

"And me?" asked the last man, with just enough humor to not be offensive.

"Cyril." Asgarth smiled and clapped the man on the back with more warmth than he felt. "I heard you were back."

"This afternoon, I was. I tell you, with what I've been learning on this trip, we'll have the other provinces with us in no time."

"As usual, you're moving too quickly, Cyril," sighed Woodman, the oldest of the five. "We've not even got the rest of the village with us, let alone our own duchy."

"They keep hoping for a dead king to save them," snickered Lyle. Another farmer, he was younger than Asgarth and more prone to humor.

Kiffs shook his head. "Those rumors aren't dying, are they?"

"Of course they're not," said Cyril. "With no proof, how can the queen prevent them? Why just yesterday in the capital, another young man tried to prove he was King Steffan. And like you're thinking, the ring didn't fit. No one can understand why it doesn't. I hate to be thinking what became of the poor fellow that tried it."

"Aye, that's what we need to do." Lyle chortled, merry with the silliness of his plan. "Get an impostor of our own."

Woodman's eyebrow flickered up. "With the proper support, that could be just the diversion we'll be needing. Asgarth, you frown."

"Frown?" Asgarth shifted. "No. I was just thinking. It's a little soon to be planning a revolt, don't you think? Shouldn't we be just keeping the queen in control with the Commoner's Council?"

"You're dreaming, Asgarth." Cyril shook his head. "Consider the latest outrage. The queen has disbanded the Commoner's Council."

The others looked at him, aghast. Cyril grinned. He was of an age where he should have had a wife and a few young children. He had managed to remain unencumbered. As the local miller's son, he had numerous occasions to travel to the capital and other cities in the kingdom, selling flour from the local district. He was the best source of news in the village. While Asgarth didn't care for his impatience and slightly ambitious nature, he was honest and considered a good-natured fellow.

"You may yet be right, Cyril," said Kiffs. "But I

agree with Asgarth. A revolt should be our last resort. I don't doubt it could come to that. But, please, let us try everything else first."

"I'd like to be thinking that went without saying," sighed Woodman. "True, it'll be difficult with this newest outrage. But the letters I've been getting from the other provinces and villages tell me that a revolt is what they're most frightened of. We don't have a better replacement for Her Majesty. Besides, there's more than one kingdom that'd be happy enough to take advantage of such unrest. It's a backwards blessing for us that they don't like Her Majesty either, and don't want to solidify her position with an invasion. Our task is to plan resistance, nothing more, and by that resistance, keep the queen's greed under control so we can live in peace. And plan carefully we must, for whatever resistance there will be, the other provinces will follow us."

"That's only natural," said Cyril, with a smug grin. "Considering how it was you and your father who led the last revolt, Woodman."

Woodman shifted. "That's not important, nor will I be leading any others. I'm too old, and I don't care for the responsibility of a kingdom on my shoulders anyway. The only reason I called this group together is because I know how to reach my former comrades and because things are bad enough to need it. But remember, Cyril, just because my family left our village to come here and changed our names doesn't mean we're safe. The queen's eye is already on Raultberg. We don't want her attention drawn to this village and what we're doing. She's already arrested a couple of the old leaders, and I've heard she's looking for me. Now onto other business. Asgarth, you've got a report to give, I believe."

"The new family." Asgarth sat up straighter. "According to them, he was a merchant who fell out of favor with the queen. They're suspicious of us and aloof, which I'm thinking gives credit to their story. They have four children, all very young, and the youngest two are twins. He's definitely a gentleman, and Berencia says his wife has pretty manners. I don't think they're spies. The children are too young, and they're too suspicious of us."

"But a young family." Lyle nervously bit his lip. "Won't that be attracting the queen's attention?"

"Not with four children," said Kiffs.

"That's the bothersome part." Asgarth scratched at his beard thoughtfully. "The twins are four months old. That means they had to have been started at least a month before the old king died. It don't seem like the queen knew her cousin's family was having another baby. You'd think she would have known there was one coming. But if she did, why isn't she looking for a larger family?"

"Good point," said Cyril.

"I doubt they'll be drawing any attention to us," Woodman said. "There aren't any of the duke's guards here often enough to notice new families, and that rascal, Willert, will only note the four children. He's too stupid to consider counting months."

"I'll still be watching," said Asgarth. "We may yet be fooled. But when he does prove honest, I've a feeling this Mr. Murdren could be a great help to us."

"If there is nothing more..?" Woodman paused. There wasn't. "Then I propose we end this meeting. Next Monday, again, as usual, unless something comes up."

Kiffs left first, while the others chatted. Woodman left with Lyle. Asgarth waited a moment, then got up.

"Asgarth, a moment, please." Cyril touched Asgarth's arm.

"Yes, Cyril?"

"Why are you so against a revolt?"

"I think Woodman made it clear enough. You might add to that I don't care for bloodshed, and I can't see how we can have a revolt without it."

"But you could be king. You heard Woodman. It's us that'll be leading this thing. Our village. You're the most respected voice here, and Woodman don't want it."

"Nor do I." Asgarth suddenly smiled with paternal warmth. "Cyril, I wouldn't worry about getting your share of glory. Much as I don't like it, I've a feeling we'll, sure enough, have a revolt. But I will not do a thing to hasten it, and things will have to get a lot worse before anyone else will."

"And by that time we may not have the means."

"That is why we're having these meetings."

Asgarth left, trying not to be bothered by Cyril's attitude.

In the capital, in the palace, Lanicia sat in her sitting room, brooding. The message from Raultberg was disquieting at best. The old duke was getting restive, his fits of madness increasing. More and more often he'd go ranting through the castle, swearing that Steffan was alive and coming for him.

That was foolishness, of course. Everyone had seen the coffins. True, there were those who were concerned because they were never opened. It was a ridiculous and revolting custom, Lanicia thought. It was just as well it had been decided that the funeral should commence without the display.

The important question, however, was what to do about her father. She had put her youngest sister, Marcella, and her odious husband in charge of the old man. It was a convenient situation. The duke particularly loved Marcella, and it kept Chester out of the palace and away from Lanicia. But it was becoming obvious that even Marcella could not control their father anymore.

An accident would be perfect. But Lanicia balked. While she hadn't thought twice about arranging an accident to put herself on the throne, arranging an accident to dispose of a mad father made Lanicia uncomfortable. She sighed and brooded some more.

The next morning, Steffan and Ella were up again just before the dawn. Ella fed the twins while Steffan drew water and collected eggs from the hens that had again slipped into the house after dark. It seemed to Steffan that already a pattern was forming. He helped Barth and Alicia wash up and dress while Ella made breakfast.

Half an hour later, fed and washed, Steffan stood in the doorway, running a whetstone down the long blade of a scythe. It was in surprisingly good shape given its abandonment. Steffan suspected that it was more help in the form of good fortune. He watched with mixed feelings the signs of life in the house across the road. Ella tapped him on the shoulder from behind.

"I need to go milk the cow," she said.

"Oh, excuse me." Steffan stepped out of her way.

"You're watching our neighbors rather intently," Ella observed.

"I wonder if they'll come."

"I'm sure they will. They have chores they have to get done first, just as we do."

"And I wonder if I should be happy about their coming."

Ella smiled. "Let's be thankful for whatever help we can get, and remember that there's no law that says we have to answer any of their questions."

"And who should know that better than me?" Steffan chuckled and grabbed Ella by the waist. "As usual, my princess, you are right."

"Thank you, my prince. Now, will you unhand me so I can get the cow milked before she gets obstinate and decides not to give any."

Steffan released her, somewhat surprised by how easily the laughter had come. Although he only remembered six months of it, it had been a year since he had felt that relaxed. That he could made an otherwise grim future look bearable.

He was just about to start for the fields when the Asgarth family descended on them en masse. Asgarth and his sons came with two scythes. The women were loaded down with food and flour. Berencia quickly shooed the men to the fields, then turned to Ella, who was just returning with the milk.

"My goodness, what is all this for?" Ella gasped, completely surprised.

"To eat!" answered Berencia cheerfully as her daughters giggled. "Those men will be plenty hungry come mid-day, and I don't doubt we'll be working up a good hunger, too."

"But we have food."

"You save it, dear. You'll be needing all you can to get you through the harvest. Good heavens! Don't these chickens have a roost?"

"There are several roosting boxes in the barn," sighed Ella. "But they're probably such a mess the chickens can't use them."

"We'll set that to rights this afternoon, then. But for now, let's get the cooking going. I brought my soup bone, so we'll have that for tonight. Come along. We've got to set the bread to rising, and I'm sure those twins of yours are hungry again. Girls, you'll be minding the little ones while we cook. Arlette, you help me and Mrs. Murdren. She's my oldest girl, and fourteen. Time she started really cooking, don't you think?"

Ella merely nodded. By the time she was fourteen, she'd been the cook for several years already. Arlette went to work, flushed with pleasure at being considered old enough to do the "real" work. She fetched water and cut vegetables, singing old love ballads all the while. The tunes were infectious, and Ella found herself singing along.

"My dear," Berencia sighed just before lunch. "You sing in the loveliest way."

Ella felt her face growing hot. "Thank you."

"It sounds trained. Where did you learn?"

"Learn?" Ella paused, then glanced around. "Grace, where did you get that filthy rag? Give it here to Mother, and I'll get you a clean one."

Berencia chuckled softly to herself.

After lunch, the men returned to the field, taking Barth to help Giles tie the bundles. The women went to the barn.

"The roost is in the middle here," Ella explained as she led the way through the clutter of tools. "All Alex has had a chance to do is clean up the stalls for Daffy and Max, the horse. I've been trying to get the house settled."

"And a fine job you've done of it," replied Berencia. "I would never have believed it was your second day in that place without my own eyes to see it."

"Well, it's time those chickens had a place of their own. Wait. Did you hear that?" Ella softly padded over to the tall, terraced boxes along the wall. Balancing on one of the lower boxes, she peered over the edge of the top row. "Here's why the chickens are in the house. Kittens. Shhh, mama cat. I'm your friend. If you'll let me put your family in the house, you can lie by a nice warm fire, and have a saucer of milk. Mrs. Asgarth, I think we can move this entire box. Then we won't have to disturb mama and her kittens. Calm now, mama cat. I was wondering why I hadn't seen any rats."

With Berencia helping, Ella carefully lifted the wooden box. Together, they brought it into the kitchen, and set it near the fire. Alicia, Gen, and Meg were fascinated and had to be cautioned to keep their distance. Ella and Berencia went back to the barn where

Arlette had already started work. Dust and mildew were everywhere. Old, rotting straw had to be cleared out of the nesting boxes, and fresh straw packed into them. Berencia insisted on spreading the boxes out so they weren't so tall.

"That'll make it easier to collect the eggs," she explained.

It was about two hours before sunset when they finished.

"That looks wonderful," sighed Ella. "Now all we have to do is get the chickens to roost here."

"Spread your feed out," Berencia replied. "They'll roost where they're fed."

"Then we'd better get back to the house."

"I'll get supper started while you feed them."

Ella breathed a silent sigh of relief. The only feed she had for the chickens was stale crusts, and she didn't want Berencia to offer any. She owed the Asgarth family too much already.

While Berencia was fussing over the twins, Ella furtively collected the leftover bread from lunch. Slipping out of the house, she started for the barn. A ragged figure on the road caught her eye and stopped her. He hobbled over.

"Have pity," he said in a wavering voice. "I've been in the queen's prison for the past year. I've no home. Nothing left. It was all taken because I dared speak out against her evil."

"We're not much better ourselves," replied Ella. "But we have a roof and food. You're welcome to stay."

"No, madam, I couldn't stay. I've got shelter in the village. All I ask is a bit of food."

"Of course. Wait here." Ella hurried back into the house.

Muttering that she had forgotten something, she grabbed some cheese and a small fresh loaf and hurried out.

"There you are," she said. "It's not much, but take it with our blessings."

"And God bless you, madam." The beggar took the food in shaking hands, then shambled on his way.

In the fields, Steffan watched the interchange with confused feelings. Asgarth looked at him and chuckled.

"I know how you feel," the older man said. "My wife and I've seen more than a few bad years together. I remember when Edward was eight, crops failed. We almost ate our shoe leather. Berencia gave part of our last bit of bread to some children whose father had already starved to death. I was so angry, and yet, I couldn't tell her not to."

"I'm more worried about there being enough for us." Steffan hefted the sickle again. "Although, someone very wise said to me not too long ago that I'll manage better than a lot of other folk in my situation could."

"Well, you're a long ways from begging, even if you're not much closer to being a farmer. Swing wider. There you have it."

Steffan corrected his stroke, wondering if he would ever develop the easy swing born of years of practice.

# CHAPTER FIVE

Four days later, the Sabbath arrived.

"If we stay home, everyone will notice," said Ella. "And we will not be looked upon favorably."

"That should be the least of our worries," Steffan retorted.

"It would be far more dangerous to call attention to ourselves. Furthermore, you can't afford a bad name if you're going to regain what you lost." Ella paused. "I don't care if you wish to leave things as they are. I just thought you wanted..."

Steffan sighed. "Even if I were a decent farmer, I can't afford to let Lanicia rule. Asgarth told me she dissolved the Commoner's Council. She's only waiting until she's built up enough strength, and then our neighbors are in peril."

"Steffan, we should go to mass. The least we can do is honor God in His own house."

"We can worship here."

"We still should go. There is the rest of the village to think of as well."

"All right. Perhaps it is better." He sighed and shook his head dismally. "I wonder when we'll be able to live our lives without all this fear."

Ella only sighed.

Barth and Alicia were excited about going into the village, but not happy when they were told it was only to go to church. Before the family left, Steffan pulled Barth back and warned him yet again to speak to no one unless spoken to and then to be careful of what he said. Nonetheless, the children ran about as they walked with their parents along the road into the village, about an hour away.

They were the last to arrive at the church and stood in the back. As the mass ended, they left quickly but were stopped by the Asgarth family.

"You've come all this way, and you won't be seeing the rest of our fine village?" Asgarth asked. Before Steffan could reply, Asgarth turned him back towards the square. The others followed. "Come along. We visit on Sabbath, and I've got a man here you'll want to meet. Woodman! Here a moment!"

The older man wandered over.

"Mr. Ernst Woodman is our cobbler," continued Asgarth. "With such a growing family as you've got, Murdren, I'm sure you'll be well acquainted with Mr. Woodman."

"I fear I may," replied Steffan with a quiet smile.

"Shoes are not cheap." Woodman shrewdly gazed at Steffan. "But I do my best for the people here."

"Mr. Woodman, even if you didn't, you deserve your wages," said Steffan. "It is a craftsman's due."

Woodman smiled. "You are kind to remember that, Mr. Murdren. I wish some of my other customers did. Still, with growing families, and in these times, too, I can understand their complaints. It's not been easy to keep my family fed either."

Ella spoke up. "Perhaps, Mr. Woodman, we might be able to trade some of our food for your work. We seem to have plenty of eggs."

"That might be possible," Woodman replied, somewhat startled. "We'll talk it over when the time comes."

"Thank you, sir."

"I believe we'd best be off," said Steffan. "Thank you, Asgarth, for presenting us to Mr. Woodman."

Trumpets began blowing in the distance as several horsemen rode up the main street, all wearing the Duke of Raultberg's colors.

"You, peasants, prepare for the parade!" called the leader. "The duke's coach shall be passing through here in a minute. You will show your loyalty and love for him."

Two of the guards remained as the others rode off, preparing for the oncoming coach. Steffan swallowed his fear. He had always had a gift for remaining unnoticed if he so wanted. But would it hide his family, too? If they left the square for the road, they would be too easily spotted. There was some hope that they could be lost in the crowd of villagers gathering to pay their reluctant respects.

The trumpets blew louder and nearer. A wave of cheering, spurred on by the duke's Guard, rippled along the village road.

"But I want to see!" whined Barth to his mother.

"No, son. I already have the babies. I can't carry all three of you."

"Quiet, son." Steffan pressed the little boy next to his leg.

The coach appeared with a great deal of rattling and jingling.

"All bow to the Duke of Raultberg!" called the guards. "All bow to the Duke of Raultberg!"

Steffan glanced at Ella. Her face was hidden as she made a deep curtsy. The thought of bowing to his most disliked uncle galled Steffan to the point of nausea. But it did afford him the chance to hide his face. For the first time, he consciously willed that no searching eye would see him, or his family. He felt the good fortune wash over his family as the coach passed and knew they were hidden. He could not hide the anger he felt as he rose after the coach had passed. Nor did he notice that Woodman and Asgarth were looking at him speculatively.

"The fiend," grumbled a voice just behind Steffan. "If only he hadn't sired that she-devil."

"Enough, Cyril," warned Asgarth.

Steffan turned to face the younger man.

"Oh. The new farmer." Cyril started as if Steffan's appearance had caught him by surprise, then laughed heartily. "Murdren, isn't it? It's a pleasure meeting you. I hope we'll be able to do a good bit of business this fall."

"Excuse me?" asked Steffan.

"James Cyril, our miller's son," said Asgarth. "He and his father work together."

"The old man is a pretty sturdy fellow," Cyril explained. "It don't look like I'll get a chance to inherit it all for a good while yet. Fine by me. Just that much longer I can avoid burdening myself with a wife." He smiled at Ella. "Of course, if I'd been around to meet you, Mrs. Murdren, those could be my children."

"You're very kind, Mr. Cyril, but I doubt you could

have caught me." The twinkle in Ella's eyes caught Steffan by surprise and softened his irritation.

"I had a hard enough time, myself," Steffan added, with a smile. "I wish we could linger, but it's a long walk and the children are getting tired. Mr. Woodman, Mr. Cyril, it's good to make your acquaintances. Mr. Asgarth, thank you again for the introductions."

Steffan nodded and directed his family towards the farm. Cyril rocked on his heels until they were out of earshot.

"So that's them," he observed. "She's a fine looking woman, and I'll say he's discreet enough. You were right about those pretty manners. I'd say he's a gentleman. I'll eat your leather, Woodman, if he isn't."

"Hm." The older man mused, his eyes on the street where the Murdren family had gone.

"Shall we see you in two nights?" Asgarth asked Cyril.

"Well, of course." Cyril paused, wondering if Asgarth was trying to get rid of him and if he was, what was the best way to save face. "I do believe I see my mother calling me. In two nights, friends."

Asgarth shook his head as Cyril departed.

"Yes, he's young," said Woodman. "But he's good at heart, and he can bring us news and deliver messages better than anyone else in the village."

"He wants it all, Woodman."

"Of course, he does. At his age, didn't you?"

"At his age, I had two sons and a wife to support."

Berencia laughed. "And you imagined yourself king of your own little kingdom. If Cyril's over anxious, it's only because something might just be within his reach that none of us could ever have."

Woodman chuckled. "Mrs. Asgarth, you are so very right. The trick for us is to temper Cyril's ambitions with reality. I suspect we have another in this village who might be a better leader and champion, and who is young enough to still want it."

"Murdren?" asked Asgarth, almost gaping. "It's a bit soon to be saying that, don't you think?"

"You, yourself, said he could prove useful."

"But to lead us? He's not one of us. How do you expect the rest of the village to follow someone who is not their own?"

"They follow me. And that young man. He did not bow willingly to the duke."

"Did any of us?" asked Berencia.

"No. But in him, there was fire burning. He has no love for the duke, and yet, Mr. Murdren seems to be a man that can be reasoned with, whose passions are in control."

Asgarth nodded. "Woodman, you have wisdom. I'll see you two nights from now. Come, Berencia, children. It's time we went home."

The Asgarth family followed their father along the road Steffan and his family had taken earlier.

Steffan remained moody for the rest of the day. He managed to hide it as he helped Barth learn his letters before supper. But as soon as Barth and Alicia were in bed, he left the house for the last remnant of daylight. Ella found him behind the barn, sitting sullenly on a pile of discards.

"You seem disturbed," she said quietly.

"To my very core." Steffan shifted. "I have never

done anything as distasteful as what I had to do today."

"Meeting our neighbors?"

"No. When the coach came through."

"Oh, that. I didn't give it much thought. At least we had a good way to hide."

"Cindy, I have never bowed to anyone in my life!"

"Not even your parents? And what about all the other heads of state you visited before we were married?"

"Heads of state do not bow to each other, and that includes heirs apparent. Of course, I paid respect, a mere inclination of the head. But to get on my knee, and to Uncle Desmond, of all people. And you didn't give it much thought. Cindy, I wish I had your humility."

"It's easy when you have no sense of personal value. Steffan, I spent most of my life bowing and scraping to people equally as odious as your uncle. When you first brought me to the palace, it felt so uncomfortable to have people bowing to me. But thanks to your love, your mother's and your father's, I finally felt as if I was someone worthwhile, and though I still didn't like being bowed to, I got used to it, and I liked holding my head up. Bowing to Desmond might seem like a step backward but it wasn't. I know who I am. Even if I'm poor, I'm still the same woman who held her head up in the palace."

Steffan chuckled and dropped his arm across her shoulders.

"You are a treasure, my dearest. You are more than a helpmate. In many ways, you are my better."

"And in some ways, you are my better. So we pool our strengths, and together we're far stronger than either one of us could be alone. Oh, Steffan, I know how hard this has been for you. You were so proud of rescuing me."

"Only to drag you back into it."

"Don't say that. It's pure silliness." Ella pressed her lips together, trying to hold back the anger. "I can't help it. It's just too ridiculous. Why should a man's pride be so dependent on how he supports his family? Steffan, the greatest gift you gave me had nothing to do with your position, or how well you dressed me, or anything like that. You didn't earn it. You were born into it. What you gave me were yourself and your love, and that's the most important part, and that's the part nobody can take from us. Even now, when we have nothing but what we sweat over, you couldn't support me and the children without me doing my share, any more than I could survive without your work. So curse your stupid pride! You'll feel a lot better about yourself as soon as you realize that it's both of us who have to support this family, with or without rank, money, or anything else!"

"And that is the hardest part of all to accept. In the palace, Cindy, I valued your wisdom before anyone else's. You were my greatest strength. But now we are truly partners. This whole disaster may yet have a blessing or two tucked into it."

"I suspect there will be many of them." Ella looked into the sky. "Well, look at that. The stars are out in force tonight. I hope that means a fair day tomorrow. I've got washing to do."

"Washing?"

"The first day after the Sabbath every week."

Steffan sighed. "What a pleasure it will be to get into some clean clothes. That's the one thing I miss more than anything else, being clean. Oh, how I wish I could soak in a hot tub."

"I wish I could, too." Ella thought. "That is one luxury we might be able to manage. Of course, we'd only have lye soap, and it is a lot of work to fill a tub. Maybe you could use some of this spare wood to make one."

Steffan grimaced. "I wasn't too bad at the carpentry the good hermit taught me, but a bath tub? That sounds rather difficult."

"Well, if you had something you could build around." Ella stood and started picking through the pile they'd been sitting on. "There's something under here that seems kind of big. Maybe it's hollow."

"Ella, it's too dark to be looking now," said Steffan, even as he helped her. "You could be right, though. Wait a minute. Let me get this mess away. My darling, I do believe we have another bit of good fortune."

Ella chuckled. "In on other words, Godmother is still watching and caring for us."

"Exactly. Stand back. I'll turn it over."

"It's a tub! Dearest, this is wonderful."

"We'll have to look it over in the morning to see what shape it's in. It certainly doesn't smell too good. But with luck, we could be washing ourselves tomorrow evening."

Their good fortune held. Steffan cleaned the massive tub in between furrows as he plowed his fields. With Ella's help, they pushed it up into their loft, and set it next to the fireplace there. After supper, Steffan helped Barth bring in bucket after bucket of water for the huge kettle Ella had brought upstairs.

"I don't want a bath!" moaned Barth. "I hate baths."

"Well, you're getting one," Ella said, relieving her son of his last small bucket.

"I don't want it, and it's not fair that I have to bring in all these buckets of water to fill it."

"I wouldn't complain, son. I wasn't much older than you when I had to fill up twice as many baths every day."

"But you're a princess."

"I wasn't always."

"But you were a lady, weren't you?" Barth looked at her, puzzled.

"That I was. But I didn't live like one for a long time. It's like now. You're a prince, but you don't live like one."

"Was I a prince in the palace?"

"Of course, and that's how most princes live."

"Mean old queen. Made me stop being a prince."

"Barth, darling, nothing can make you stop being a prince." Ella knelt on the floor beside him. "That's why you must always act like one. That doesn't mean putting on airs, and thinking you're better than everyone else. It means being courteous, and using good manners, and not complaining sometimes when you want to. It's hard. Being a prince is a tremendous responsibility. People look up to you, and you must be a good example, or they will be sad."

Barth angrily flopped into her lap. "It's not fair, Mama. I didn't ask to be a prince, and I am, and I can't tell anybody, and I can't live in the palace. It's not fair."

"It isn't. I wish it were, Barth. The best we can do is be fair to our family, and to each other, and to all our neighbors. Then maybe things will work out. In the meantime, when it gets too hard to take, you come running to me, and I'll listen, and hold you, and love you."

"Mama, am I a good boy?"

"A very good boy."

"Do I still have to carry the water?"

"Yes. That will help make you a strong boy."

Barth heaved a sigh. "I don't know if I want to be a strong boy."

"It will make your father and me very happy."

"All right." Barth fumbled and crawled out of his mother's lap. "I guess I can."

Steffan rewarded his son for his industry by allowing Barth the first bath, and by staying with him and playing until the floor around the tub was soaked. Ella washed the twins and Alicia together. After the children were in bed, Steffan insisted that Ella bathe.

"No, my darling," she protested. "I know how badly you've wanted this."

"Actually, Ella, I'm being very selfish." Steffan smiled sheepishly. "I'm planning on a good long soak, and I'd feel terrible if you were waiting for me to get out so you could get in."

Ella laughed and made a point of washing quickly.

# CHAPTER SIX

In the middle of the week, as dawn slowly showed its face, Steffan lay in bed, thinking. He glanced at his wife. She stirred.

"Ella," he whispered.

"Hm?"

Steffan propped himself up on his elbow and leaned over her.

"Ella. Darling, are you awake?"

"Just barely. Is it dawn?"

"I'm afraid so. Do you know what tomorrow is?"

"Thursday?"

"Yes, but it's also our eldest son's fifth birthday."

Ella opened her eyes. "It is."

"We should do something special, don't you think?"

"Yes, but what? There really isn't much of anything to celebrate with."

"What about those little nut cakes he likes so much? There are walnuts in the cool room."

"We don't have any sugar."

"Oh." Steffan fell back on his pillow. "Things have just been so close. I was hoping a little something might lift our spirits some."

"Well, Alicia's coming out of the toes of her shoes again. Do we have a spare silver piece or two?"

"Yes, but what do you propose?"

"Going into the village, getting Alicia's shoes fixed, and buying a bit of sugar. The only problem is how am I going to carry the twins?"

"I don't like it, even aside from money being so dear." Steffan sighed. "But I suppose we'll have to go into the village periodically for shoes and the like. As for the twins, leave them here. Barth can watch them while I work on the plowing."

"Steffan, Barth's too young to be left like that."

"No. They can all come out to the field with me. I'll be right there."

"Are you sure you can manage? What if they need changing?"

"Ella, who changed them last winter when you had the influenza?"

"Well, they're mostly getting bottles during the day, and I don't think I'll be gone that long. It's only an hour's walk to the village."

"Then it's settled."

"I guess it is. We'll leave right after breakfast. I'll set out bread and cheese for your lunches, and the bottles." Ella sat up and got out of bed. "Steffan, are you sure it'll be all right? They're only five months old."

"They'll be fine. In fact, I hear them calling for their breakfast now."

Ella quickly dressed and hurried downstairs. Steffan continued to reassure her as she collected eggs and three silver pieces and a few farthings from their tiny collection. He felt somewhat relieved as he watched her stride off down the road, with Alicia toddling alongside. It was embarrassing to admit, but Steffan felt more capable taking care of the children than he did plowing.

With some leftover swaddling clothes, he strapped the slightly smaller James to Barth's back, and Nella to his own. Out in the fields, with the babies gurgling and cooing, Steffan felt somewhat self-conscious as he hitched Max, the horse, to the plow. But the work was getting done, the babies were happy, and Barth seemed content as he guided Max along the previous furrow. Besides, Steffan recalled another farmer he had observed in his youth who had done the same thing when his wife had died in childbirth.

Asgarth appeared shortly before noon. Steffan had unwrapped Nella to feed her, and Barth was holding James' bottle.

"I was thinking that was an odd bundle you had on your back," Asgarth said after the greetings had been exchanged.

"Cindy had to go into the village, and it would have been too hard to manage both Grace and these two."

"You're changing their bottoms, too?" Asgarth looked bemused.

Steffan blushed. "Last winter, Cindy was ill, and we had no help. I learned quickly. And Cindy's been out here leading Max, and hauling rocks."

"Good for you. Thanks be, Berencia was always healthy, at least while the children were small. I don't know how I could have kept them fed, let alone changed."

"You would have managed. When the need must be met, one does."

"Well said by one who knows. And speaking

of managing, your furrows are looking straighter." Asgarth held Steffan with another long speculative look. "You were a merchant, you say?"

"I did."

"Well, farming's not in your blood, but you don't do badly by it. You're learning fast."

"I haven't had much choice. It's kind of you to mention it."

"You're welcome. You know what you're planting, don't you?"

"Wheat." Steffan paused. "That's what I should be planting, isn't it?"

"Of course. That gets the best return around here. But what about that small field on the other side of your house? You already got your kitchen garden laid out behind the house, so that's not your plan."

"Wheat also, I suppose."

"That's an awful small field for the amount of work you'll be doing and the return you'll be getting on it. Maybe hops would be good there."

"Oh, no." Steffan smiled and shook his head. "It's not a bad suggestion for you, perhaps. But the only customers for hops are the duke's own henchmen. I'm better off keeping my distance from them."

"Aren't we all?"

"True. But I am not a farmer because I got on well with the duke's people."

"Hops would still be good, and the duke isn't the only buyer for them. We have a tavern in the village here that brews a very good beer, and Mr. Aleman needs hops to do it. And whatever hops Mr. Aleman won't take, the Cyrils can be selling for you."

"They get a good return?" Steffan thoughtfully scratched at his beard.

"Better than wheat."

"Well, I do have some seed for them. They're certainly no riskier than wheat. Thank you for suggesting it, Asgarth."

"What're neighbors for?"

"Lucas, has James finished?"

"He's asleep." Barth smiled proudly.

"Good. So is Nella. Why don't we get some plowing done while they nap, then we'll eat when they awake, and they can roll and stretch themselves while we do."

"Yes, Father."

Steffan stood. "If you'll excuse us, Asgarth. I don't want to keep you from your plowing."

"I've two strapping boys and only one plow. I've a bit of time to meddle, as Berencia puts it. Why don't you have to, and we'll see about getting you a better hand at it. You, lad, Lucas is it?"

"Yes, sir," answered Barth politely.

"You follow behind and pick out rocks. I started out that way for my father when I was just about your age, and my boys did the same for me. Ready, Murdren?"

"Yes."

Reluctantly, Steffan picked up the reins and went back to work.


Even allowing for Alicia's slower pace, Ella arrived in the village square in good time. Stalls crowded the square, tended by women from the local farms selling vegetables and fruits while village wives got their shopping done early in the day. Ella went first to the cobbler's shop.

It was on a small side street, not far from the square. The close built brick houses towered above, leaving the ancient alley in perpetual shadow. Alicia clung tightly to her mother. The door under the sign of the shoe was made of two pieces, and the top half was open. A voice floated out. Ella hesitated.

"...And another impostor was presented. Of course, the ring didn't fit. Why they can't be letting that poor prince lie in peace. They should've left those coffins open." The speaker was a middle-aged woman, short with a pinched face and a long, pointed nose. She spoke to an older woman who had the calm bearing of one who had seen hardship and refused to be conquered by it. The middle-aged woman balanced unsteadily, as Woodman, the cobbler, laced a shoe onto her foot. "I said so at the time, and I still say so. Oops! Steady, Mr. Woodman. And, Eudora, did you hear about that tramp that came through the other day? Stole Gertrude Aleman's laundry right off her line, he did. And Baker Simpfl lost three pies that very day. I don't care if the sheriff said the tramp wasn't anywhere near the Aleman's when the laundry was taken. That tramp should've been run out of the village first thing. It's bad enough the hermit just handed over his farm to total strangers. Cousins, they say. Hmph! Easy, Mr. Woodman. And they've uppity manners, I'm told. If they keep to themselves, that'll be fine by me. He's a handsome fellow by all accounts. He'll be coming to town to visit you know who soon, sure enough, although

I've heard she's pretty enough. Maybe they did fall out of favor, but that don't speak well of them to my mind. Aren't you done lacing that yet, Mr. Woodman? I tell you, Eudora, if they'd tried, they could've been right with Her Majesty. There's something about that pair. Mark my words, they'll bring trouble, they will. Finally done, Mr. Woodman? It still pinches. Well, you'll just have to try again some other time."

"I need the two farthings now," said Woodman with infinite patience.

"Not til this shoe is fixed properly."

"Two farthings, please, now."

"Oh, all right. Hmph!"

Ella quietly stepped into the shop as the woman doled out a copper farthing, and four of the smaller copper groats. The woman whirled around and stopped in front of Ella and Alicia.

"What?" The woman looked surprised, then a cold smile cracked her face and she suddenly dove at Alicia. "Why, what a sweet little girl. What's your name, child? Speak up!"

Alicia backed into Ella, terrified, as the woman pinched her cheek.

"Please, she's a little shy," Ella intervened firmly.

A small puddle appeared at Alicia's feet.

"Hmph! Look at that. You should be able to hold your water better than that, young lady. Mine were half your age and able to hold themselves through anything. Hmph!" The woman swept out.

"And now they can't go at all," said the woman who had patiently listened. "Oh, don't worry about the mess. Here's some rags. Isabelle Plainfield is just a silly old busybody. All wind and no substance, even if her wind isn't very pleasant."

"Well, thank you for your kindness." Ella finished mopping up, then pulled Alicia's wet bloomers off. "Here, Grace, I've another pair of bloomers. I was afraid with the long walk there might be an accident. I'm sorry it had to be here."

"It wasn't the child's fault, or yours. Besides, I've raised eight children. An accident or two is nothing new here." The woman smiled, then paused. "You must be Mrs. Murdren."

"I'm afraid so."

"I wouldn't worry about what Isabelle said. Nobody trusts strangers these days, but there are those who are speaking well of you. I'm Eudora Woodman. I'm told you've met my husband."

"Yes, Sunday."

"It's a pleasure seeing you again," said Woodman from his bench. "I had a feeling you'd be visiting soon."

"Grace's toes are coming out of her shoes. I hope you can patch them."

"New shoes would be easier on her feet."

"Probably. But we've only got a little silver to see us through the harvest. I did bring two dozen eggs."

"Fresh eggs?" Mrs. Woodman's eyes lit up. "Why, Ernst, look at these beauties. And just the other day Eric was longing for an omelet."

Woodman chuckled. "Come here, little lady. Let's see how much leather those little feet will need."

Alicia hesitated, then smiled shyly. A minute later, she was in Woodman's lap, happily showing him the shoes that were too small. Woodman carefully considered and nodded.

"Mrs. Murdren, I charge two silver pieces for shoes in the size she'll be needing. But two dozen good eggs are worth a fair bit. Can you spare a silver piece on top of them?"

"It depends. Is it that difficult a mend?"

"In some ways. But as I said before, a whole new set of shoes would be better for her. The eggs and the silver piece would just about cover a pair."

"Not quite, I suspect, but if that's your offer, I'm glad to take it. How long before they'll be ready?"

"I don't see why it should take me longer than a day or two. I've a couple other orders to fill first, you see."

"That'll be more than adequate. Thank you, Mr. Woodman."

Ella smiled as she watched Woodman break away from his usual reserve to play with Alicia as he traced the outline of her feet onto a piece of paper. As soon as he was done, she handed over the eggs and the silver piece.

"In advance?" asked Woodman, amazed.

"I'll not put you to the work of making a pair of shoes, and be worried about whether or not you'll get your money."

"And you trust me to get the shoes made?"

Ella laughed. "There's many a tradesman I wouldn't. But a man who can play so honestly with a child is not usually one who won't keep his end of a bargain. Did you say they'll be ready Saturday?"

"If that's two days from now, I did."

"We'll fetch them then. Thank you again, Mr.

Woodman." Ella gathered up Alicia and left.

Back in the square, she bought the sugar, then stopped as she passed the butcher shop. A bit of meat would be terribly extravagant, but also worth it. She went in.

The room was dark and smelled of aging meat. Two carcasses hung from hooks in a corner near a long table that separated the front of the shop from the back. On top of the table was a display of chops, steaks, organs, and assorted poultry. In the front part of the shop was a small round table with two chairs.

The first chair held a heavy woman, whose roundness belied the bitter downward turn to her face. She was gossiping with Isabelle Plainfield, sitting in the opposite chair, and another woman behind the counter. This second woman was pale and flighty, with curly hair that ran in all directions from the cover of her mobcap.

"And I saw him go to her house two times last week," the heavy woman was saying.

"His poor wife," said the second woman obsequiously. She noticed Ella in the doorway as the other two sighed their scorn. "Hello. Can I help you today?"

"Yes. I was thinking of buying a small roast," Ella replied quietly.

The heavy woman turned on her. "You might be introducing yourself to us."

"I beg your pardon. I didn't wish to intrude. I'm Mrs. Cindy Murdren."

"Mrs. Isolde Dirkman. This is Isabelle Plainfield and there's Penelope Drusse behind the counter."

"It's truly a pleasure. Mrs. Drusse, is there any roast today? A less tender cut would be perfectly adequate."

"I've a bit of rump."

"Are you sure you can afford it?" Isolde queried. "Meat is so dear these days."

"So I've been told. How much, Mrs. Drusse?"

Penelope flashed a weak smile. "Five groats."

"That is dear." Ella frowned as she fought to hide her shock at the price. "I think I might be able to manage four groats."

"That's all right," gasped Mrs. Drusse in high pitched relief.

"We never bargain here," said Isolde. "I suppose it's normal for city people, but here we consider it uncivilized."

"Indeed." Ella took the wrapped meat and put it in her basket. "Here's your farthing, Mrs. Drusse. Thank you very much."

"Mrs. Murdren, don't be in such a hurry to rush off." Isolde fixed her eyes on Ella. "Join us for a bit of chat."

"That's very kind of you, Mrs. Dirkman, but I really can't now. Perhaps some other time. Come along, darling." Ella took Alicia firmly by the hand and left the shop before Isolde could answer.

Isabelle's voice floated out. "Didn't I tell you? And I'm told they have four children. I wonder where the other three are?"

Ella shook her head and hurried into the square to find the road back to the farm. Berencia Asgarth hailed her from a fruit stall, then hurried up.

"Shopping, too?" she asked. "I've always preferred

mid-week, myself."

"I wasn't sure which was the best day," confessed Ella. "There were just some things I needed."

"It's all week long, here, except on the Sabbath, of course. There's a lot who come Saturdays. But it's too crowded for me, and I'm certain I get better choices. What do you have? Been to the butcher shop, I see."

"I'm afraid so."

"Isolde Dirkman and Isabelle Plainfield holding court with Penelope again. That's why anyone who can butcher their own does. It's really Isolde that's the problem. Isabelle is all wind, however unpleasant it is, it's merely wind at that. But Isolde, she's vicious. Not as I like to gossip, but there are those who say Isolde nagged her poor husband to his grave. It's Penelope who I pity. She thinks the world of those two biddies, and they run roughshod over her, and the poor thing doesn't even realize it. Her husband brags about how he beats her, so I guess she's grateful for any friends she can get."

"That's so terribly sad."

Berencia shrugged. "It is, but what's to be done about it? She could take it to the magistrate, but he's in the pay of the duke, and it's said he beats his wife even worse. Of course, that's only rumor. She doesn't say anything. They could be as happy as piglets at the teat for all I know, and I hope she is. Well, look at that. Selling your piglets, Mrs. Kapman?"

The large jovial woman looked up from the small wooden pen she'd erected next to a fruit stall. Her grin was mostly black space punctuated with a few brown and yellow teeth. In the pen, six piglets scurried about under the watchful eye of a monstrously huge sow.

"I'm selling them, I am," said Mrs. Kapman. "These will be some mighty fine bacon this fall. Look at them. Only four weeks old, and look how big they are."

"They're huge. Ours were only half as big. Just sold the last of them 'bout a week ago. But, Mrs. Murdren, maybe you'll be wanting some meat for the winter. Mrs. Kapman's pigs always give the tenderest chops."

"It does sound interesting," said Ella. "But I don't know. It must cost something to feed them."

Mrs. Kapman laughed merrily and without malice. "I heard you was city bred. Pigs don't cost nothing to feed. Just give him your scraps, and let him loose every so often to dig up what else he wants, excepting your garden."

"You've got those two orchards behind you, you know," pointed out Berencia. "Apples and cherries. Pigs love fruit, and you won't have to put up with all the flies from all the rotten fruit that falls. Just let the pig through."

"Well, if they're not too hard to care for, it might be good for Lucas to have some responsibility." Ella paused. "How much are you asking?"

"Two and a half silver pieces."

"Two and a half!" screeched Berencia. "That's robbery, that is. Ours only went for one and a quarter, and there's nobody in this duchy who'll pay more than one and a half for a piglet."

"I've been getting two and a quarter. Just look at the size of these beauties. There aren't bigger in the entire kingdom."

"That may be, but you can't be getting better than two pieces for one."

"Two and a quarter."

"Really now?" Berencia's shrewd eyes narrowed.

Mrs. Kapman squirmed, then giggled. "Well, I got it for one. But, seriously, Mrs. Asgarth, you wouldn't begrudge me a good price on exceptionally fine piglets as these."

"Of course not."

"Neither would I," said Ella. "But, Mrs. Kapman, being new and all, we haven't much, and I've already bought more than I should have today." She sighed. "Of course, the same amount of meat and sausages would cost much more than that, and it is my son's birthday tomorrow. Would you take two silver pieces for one?"

"Gladly." Mrs. Kapman bobbed her head, hitched her skirts, and hopped into the pen. "Come here, my little darlings. One of you's getting a new home. Aha! You, my fine little fellow." She swooped down and snatched up a handsome dark brown piglet with a bright pink nose. "What do you think, Mrs. Asgarth? He's the finest of the litter, and a smart little fellow, he is. Kind of hate to think about him ending up bacon, but that's what he was born for."

A strong doubt pushed its way into Ella's mind. But it was too late. Berencia was lending her wholehearted approval to the purchase, and Ella found herself parting with her remaining two silver pieces, and wondering what she was going to tell Steffan.

When she got home, she hid the piglet in the

loft and firmly instructed Alicia not to say a word. Fortunately, the piglet went to sleep and stayed quiet. Ella didn't tell Steffan about her purchases until the children were in bed, and they were preparing to go up to the loft themselves.

"Mr. Woodman said he'd leave plenty of growing room in Alicia's shoes," she told Steffan as she mounted the ladder ahead of him. "And I was thinking I could sell eggs at the marketplace, and the fruit when it comes in, and that should help some."

"I hope so. A farthing for that bit of meat. Is that a lot?"

"I thought so at the time, but it's been a while since I've had to buy anything. Mrs. Asgarth said I was overcharged, but not by much. She told me all the current prices as we walked home."

"Ella, what is this?"

The piglet stared at Steffan from his pillow.

"How did he get up there? Here, pig." Ella quickly removed the piglet and placed him on the floor. "You're only staying here tonight, then it's to the barn with you."

"Why do we have a pig in the first place?" Steffan asked, somewhat irritated.

"It's for Barth, for his birthday. He's old enough to take care of a pig."

"How much did it cost?"

"Well, you've got to consider, Steffan, that this pig will give us all the meat we'll need for the whole winter, and maybe even to next summer. He's going to be huge. You should see his mother. And all we have to feed him is scraps. Food for him won't cost anything."

"How much, Ella?"

"Two silver pieces."

"Two silver pieces."

"You're angry."

"Yes, I'm angry. But it's been done, and I can see why you bought him. It's not a bad idea. We just have so little right now."

"He'll pay off, Steffan. I'm sure he will."

"We'll leave it at that, then. Just get that blasted thing off our bed!"

Ella rushed to remove the piglet again.

Barth named the pig Roscoe. Steffan went to great lengths to explain to Barth that the pig would be butchered in the fall and that it would have to sleep in the barn. That night, Roscoe broke out of his pen in the barn, got into the house and slept on Barth's bed.

# CHAPTER SEVEN

"It's too dangerous, and we haven't the money," said Steffan angrily. "I'm sorry, Ella. I can't allow it."

"But, Steffan, the children want to go so badly. They've been working so hard, even Alicia."

"Blast those Asgarth boys."

"They did nothing wrong when they told Barth and Alicia about the spring festival. Everyone goes and they assumed we would, too. And we should."

"What if the duke comes through, or any of the guards that used to be at the palace?"

"We bow to the duke, just as before, and avoid anyone in a uniform. Steffan, people are going think of us as odd, or worse yet."

"Then they'll just have to. It's too risky."

"Don't you want to regain what you lost?"

Steffan glared at her. "Of course, I do."

"Then how do you expect to do it? Are you going to run up and present yourself for the ring? Lanicia would have you murdered before it could be brought out. Or even when it fits, she would still deny you. She's got all her own people in the palace. Not all of them know you, and those that do are going to deny you for fear of losing their positions, or are too few and too frightened of Lanicia to do any good. You need support, Steffan, and you're not going to get it by alienating our neighbors."

Steffan moodily gazed at the fire on the kitchen hearth.

"Ella, I'm not ready to risk it."

"Oh, dear. I was afraid of that."

"What?"

"That for some irrational reason, you're blaming yourself for what happened to us, and that you're afraid of failing again when you try to restore yourself."

"No. It's true I feel as if somehow it was my mistake that got us here, and I know it's irrational, and that there was nothing I could have done, except possibly foreseen the future. But my greatest fear is losing you, or the children. If I'm lost, there's always Barth to carry on, and Alicia, and James and Nella. And you'll be there to help them. But if I lose the children and you, what will it benefit me? I'll be dreadfully lonely without you, and since I will die eventually, without the children, it will all go back to Lanicia, or worse yet, her son. Then what have we gained? Absolutely nothing."

"I'm afraid I can't argue with that. My only thought leans toward over-caution. Steffan, please don't think of yourself as expendable. Losing you might not be a catastrophe for posterity, but it would be for me. I don't want to think what life would be like without you. If I'm at all able to bear up through this, it's because your love is carrying me."

Steffan pulled her next to him. "Ella, we must find a way to minimize the risks. You're right. We must build friendships if I'm to have any chance to regain my throne before Lanicia wipes us all out. But how to do it without exposing ourselves? We've been to spring festivals, and yet we were only observers. I've seen the drinking that goes on."

"Steffan, you've got a stronger head for liquor than anyone I know. Why remember the dinner that was held for the Karperian ambassador? You had two steins of strong Fin Reache ale before dinner, drank two glasses of wine through each of seven different courses, then nursed along three brandies before the man finally went to his chambers, and you stayed clear headed through all of it."

"I was bred to it. My father made sure I could handle strong drink simply because of state dinners."

"And I'm sure you could nurse along a Raultberg beer or two without noticing the difference."

"You win on that one. But what if we're asked to dance?"

"That." Ella frowned. The one courtly skill that Steffan had never been able to manage was dancing. "Everyone does the slip step."

"And the Raultberg dance."

"You know both of them."

"Yes. But do I do them well?"

Ella paused. "Well, I'm certain that there must one or two people who aren't terribly adept. Keep in mind, all the people we've seen were usually the best the village had to offer. Oh, dear, Steffan, I just thought. The nice genteel slip step we did at the palace might be rather different when the people do it, and if we want people to believe that you're not gentle born, then you'll have to do a more active version."

"Which I have supposedly known all my life. We have a problem, my princess. We don't know how to be commoners. We've never done it. Even you, my love. Everyone knows you're city bred. And I know if I ever get anywhere near a merchant, I am going to be found out as never having done it. I don't bargain well enough."

Ella laughed. "I remember a treaty you negotiated between our kingdom and Iggenstein. I kept thinking that my poor late father would have been so pleased to see that his daughter had married a man that took after him so much."

"Trade treaties are something completely different."

"How? What is bargaining but trying to get a better position for yourself? And prices have gone completely askew because of Lanicia's taxation and everything else she's doing, so if you don't know them, it's to be expected. Steffan, we never thought we could make people believe we come from their level, and we were right. They all know we come from a higher station in life. They just don't know how high, and it is up to us to make sure they don't find out."

"True."

"Then can we go to the spring festival?"

"I suppose we should."

"Oh, thank you, darling!" Ella kissed him happily.

Steffan chuckled. "Are the children asleep?"

"I don't hear anything."

"Is that pig locked up?"

"As well as can be. Part of it is that he keeps digging out. Barth and I put stones all along the pen and put his straw right next to Daffy, so he'll be warmer. Although, I don't think Daffy likes him much."

"Interesting that we have so much in common."

"Oh, Roscoe's sweet."

"Thinking like that is going to be a problem come butchering time."

"I know. But we'll overcome it. That is why we have Roscoe."

"Hmm. You have taken your bath, and I have taken mine."

"Mm-hmm." Ella laid her head on his chest.

"Then I recommend we bank the fire and make our way upstairs."

"I suppose I am getting sleepy."

"That wasn't what I had in mind."

Ella chuckled, then kissed her husband once more.

It was the first Sunday of May. The planting was done, and the people of the village were ready to celebrate. Dressed in their best, they proceeded out of the village church, following the old priest as he blessed the fields of the surrounding farms. There were a lot of farms to bless, and it was nightfall before the villagers returned to the town square.

That was when the merrymaking began. Lanterns were lit, large casks were broached, charcoal was set afire, and the smells of cooking sausages, fried dough and beer filled the air. On a platform at the end of the square closest to the church, musicians gathered and tuned their instruments. Game booths lined the square, along with booths offering treats of all kinds. Hawkers cried out, selling their wares and offering fine prizes for their games of skill and chance. Near the tavern booth, tables were set up, and several men gathered and began playing drinking games. At other tables, men gathered with their coins and took turns shaking five dice out of a cup.

Caught in the press of people, even Ella began to get nervous.

"Maybe this wasn't such a good idea," she whispered. "The children are sure to get lost."

"There you two are," cried out John Asgarth's voice. Acting like a battering ram, he led his family through the crowd.

"You're worried about the babies, aren't you?" said Berencia the moment the two families met. "Well, Edward and Giles are taking our young ones home. Might as well take yours, too. Arlette will be happy to mind the babies. Come along. Hand them over. It's too late for the little ones to be out, and there's no point in you two missing the fun. There'll be plenty of festival tomorrow, too, young Lucas. Giles said he'd take you around personally."

"I don't know if it would be wise..." began Steffan as Berencia lifted James from his arms and handed him to Arlette.

"For heaven's sakes, man, do you see any children here?" Asgarth asked, laughing. "It's time you two spent a night like adults anyway. Come on, Murdren, the dice are calling."

"Hurry along, children. The little ones need to be in before they catch a chill." Berencia sent her brood off.

"Grace was practically asleep, anyway," said Ella. She looked at Steffan, who shrugged.

Asgarth steered Steffan towards the dice tables. Steffan went along, but with a few misgivings. He had always liked gambling, but before losses had only meant that the dice were impartial, and the money he spent went unnoticed. He didn't have the money to waste on a bad throw anymore.

"I don't hold with gambling usually," Asgarth explained as they approached the tables. "But at a festival it's fun."

"I think I shall have to content myself with watching," replied Steffan.

"What? You don't have a few farthings to throw away?"

"I wish I did."

"Well, it looks like all the seats are taken, anyway. I've an idea. I'll loan you some farthings, and you can pay me back out of your winnings."

"What if I lose?"

"Send over a couple dozen eggs and some milk tomorrow. Berencia's been talking about making up some custards for the children. She'll need the extra, and I'd as soon buy it from you as go into the village and pay the higher prices."

"I don't like taking loans, however, it might be interesting to see if I can pay you back this evening."

They watched for almost a half an hour when two seats finally became vacant. Asgarth started for them, but Steffan held him back.

"We don't want to play at that table," Steffan whispered.

"That one gent is very lucky, but his luck's sure to turn."

"Not until he gets caught. You watch. He's about to get the dice. Notice. He scoops them in, and then he wins. He's switching dice. Catch him in the middle of a throw and you'll find he's shaved a few edges."

"Good heavens! I just saw him do it. You've got a good eye, man."

"I've lost my share of money to shaved dice. Fortunately, I had a friend who showed me how to spot dice switchers, although not before he'd won a small fortune from me. There are two seats open over there, and the table looks honest."

"And I'll spot you a farthing for saving my money for me."

At the table, Steffan decided that the small stack of coins he had could be considered spent in eggs and milk, and having so decided, bet with some caution until he had won back Asgarth's money. After that, he abandoned all concern about winning, and judiciously increased his bets, losing large amounts, but winning even more.

"Did I say I'd spot you a farthing for saving my money for me?" grumbled Asgarth good-naturedly an hour later.

The others at the table were not as amused by Steffan's winning streak.

"I suppose it's time to find our wives, wouldn't you say, neighbor?" Steffan clapped Asgarth on the back.

"Before you ruin me, that is."

"What? You're leaving?" One of the men growled.

"It'd be rude to leave without giving us a chance to win our money back," snarled another.

"I gave you your chance a while back," replied Steffan with a smile. "Unfortunately for you, the dice seem to be rolling in my favor tonight. I thought I'd leave before I took any more of your money."

"I'd roll again." The first man rose menacingly.

"As I'm sure you know," said Steffan with quiet firmness. "The first rule of gambling is to leave the table while you are still winning. If you had done so earlier, I would not be leaving with your money."

"Easy, Friederich," said Asgarth. "You know how to lose better than that."

"I say we check his sleeves," said the second man.

Exasperated, Steffan opened his sleeves and shook them. Nothing fell.

"That man is two tables down," he said. "Mr. Asgarth, do you care to remain?"

"No. I'll go with you." Asgarth rose with Steffan.

Friederich knocked the table over as he grabbed for Steffan. Steffan whirled, ducked a punch, then sent his fists flying with deadly accuracy. Friederich fell back onto the table, blood streaming from his nose. Steffan glanced around at the small crowd that had gathered.

"My apologies for the disruption," he said quietly, then turned into the square.

Asgarth followed.

"You handled that nicely," he said. "Friederich's been drinking, you know. Gets a few too many steins in him, and he's looking for a good brawl. You certainly hold up well in a fight. I haven't seen anybody put down so soundly in such a short time since I was a small lad."

Steffan shrugged. Boxing was considered a manly sport, excellent for the training of young gentlemen, and also a young prince.

"I prefer to avoid such incidents," he said. "I wonder where our wives went to."

"Well, if I know Berencia, she's been to all of the

wine booths, and is now busy throwing her groats away on a greased plate in the hopes of winning some fancy ornament that would be cheaper and prettier for her to make."

Steffan chuckled. "But it's more fun to say you won it."

"That may be. What did I tell you? There they are."

Berencia was still pitching her groat. Ella watched her with great amusement and a feathered ribbon in her hair.

"Lost it again," groaned Berencia. "Oh! Asgarth! Caught up to me, you did. I was hoping I'd have something more to show for myself than an empty purse and a crick in my back."

"I believe the Murdrens are the lucky ones tonight," Asgarth sighed.

Ella looked at Steffan. "Dice? I should have known."

"I wouldn't complain. My purse is a great deal heavier than when I started this evening. How many groats did that cost you?"

"Would you believe only two?"

Berencia snorted. "I couldn't believe it. And she says she's never had the nerve to pitch to a plate before. I tell you, it's a lesson to me. She kept her head clear tonight." Berencia giggled. "I tried a few too many different wines. Oh my! They're calling for the slip step. I think I'll be slipping more than stepping."

"That makes two of us," Steffan muttered. He turned to Ella and made a gentlemanly bow. "Mrs. Murdren, shall we?"

"With pleasure." Ella curtsied elegantly.

"Mrs. Asgarth?" Asgarth made a bow as graceful as Steffan's.

"Ooh, Mr. Asgarth, of course!" Berencia giggled, curtsied and stumbled getting up.

"Did you taste all the wines?" Steffan whispered as they went to their places.

"Tasted, unlike Mrs. Asgarth. Some of them were pretty bad. I've been spoiled, I'm afraid."

"No good ones?"

"A couple very good ones. The rest were adequate."

In position, the drummer began the beat. The dance was livelier than at court. But incompetence was not much of an issue, as half the dancers were rather inebriated. As Steffan anticipated, as long as he danced with Ella, the steps didn't confuse him, and he matched her grace and ease. But partners were soon switched, and Steffan stumbled rather badly, just barely keeping up. The dance almost broke down completely when he and Berencia were matched up. The result was more hilarious laughter than scorn. More than one couple was having trouble.

Steffan and Ella laughed about it later as they carried their sleeping children to their beds.

"Everyone must have thought I was falling down drunk," Steffan said.

"I doubt it. How much did you drink?"

"I believe I had two or three beers. I wanted to keep my head clear at the dice tables."

Ella paused as she put Barth's blanket over him.

"That worries me," she said.

"Why?" Steffan was surprised.

Ella nodded at the loft. Steffan waited until they were upstairs.

"Steffan, I know you're not obsessed with gambling, but I also know you enjoy it. I'm afraid that with tonight's success and things being so dear, you might try to keep winning to make things more comfortable."

"That is a very good way to lose everything we have. Ella, darling, I'm well aware of the danger. I always expect to lose when I sit down at a gambling table." He opened up his purse and poured out the coins. "Look at this. Fourteen silver pieces, that is two pieces beyond a half gold crown, you know, and that is all pure winnings. I always pull out my stake right away. We'll save one apiece for Barth and Alicia's treats at the festival. You shall have four because you are the loveliest woman there, and I shall have three for my own gambling. That leaves us five pieces ahead, with plenty of pleasure to be had. A nice treat, don't you think?"

"Our good fortune helping us again?"

Steffan mused. "I usually get a feeling when it happens. And tonight I didn't. I suspect actual chance and some skill at betting won us this extra money."

"Good. I would be mortified to think we were winning over our neighbors unfairly." Cindy smiled. "Oh, Steffan, I think we've gotten ourselves something far better than silver pieces."

"What? Feathered ribbons?"

"No, silly. Good friends. We've not done anything to court the Asgarths, and yet they've been so kind to us. Better yet, Mr. Asgarth's voice is one the villagers listen to. I do like Berencia. She's such a dear."

"They are good people, even if the only reason they befriended us was because they didn't trust us."

"There's a lesson in that, Steffan. We won't know who we can trust until we get to know them."

"Even that... What was her name? Mrs. Dirkman?"

"Oh, her." Ella snorted in disgust. "While we were trying wines, she had the nerve to suggest that I was already drunk, just because poor Berencia stumbled into me."

"And so you know, I may have made an enemy or two, myself. A certain man by the name of Friederich was not very happy that my luck was better than his. He wanted to settle the matter physically, and I bloodied his nose."

"With as much to drink as there was, that sort of thing is bound to happen. We can't please everybody, Steffan. The Asgarths know we're good people, and I'd rather have their approval over a good many of the nobility."

"And as usual, you are right, my dearest."

The next morning, Berencia awoke with a slightly queasy stomach, but a clear head. Asgarth was sitting up in bed, waiting for her.

"You want to know about Cindy Murdren, don't you?" she said.

"Well?"

"A finer, sweeter young woman never walked the earth. You don't know what a time I had convincing her it would be all right to shed a few groats on some wine and that silly game. She was worried for her husband. John, they lost everything when the queen dismissed him. They're not even sure they'll make it through the summer with the money they have. And they won't take charity easily. They've got their pride."

"And we don't?" chuckled Asgarth. "She told you all that?"

"No. I've had to guess. She's a close one. They still fear the queen."

"I know. He's very cautious. I suspect that's why they didn't want us to take the children. Giles said last night that the boy is as close as one person can get. Not that he pressed, mind you. Whatever secrets the Murdrens have, I've a feeling they're better off kept, and I told Giles so."

"What did he say back?"

"He said what if they were spies? And I said I was sure they weren't, and besides, I knew of ways to test them without trying to weasel out their secrets."

"I agree, John. We don't want to be harming them if they're innocent, and I believe they are."

"Good. It looks like we'll have to buy their eggs after all. Murdren's also very lucky at dice."

"Then I'd best be up and fetching them. Ooph! John, why did I agree to make custards today?"

"You should remember that the next time you go tasting wines."

Berencia playfully shoved her husband, then slowly made her way out of bed.

# CHAPTER EIGHT

It was three weeks after the spring festival. Steffan, with much satisfaction, noted that his family's spirits remained high. Perhaps it was because Steffan's luck had held at the festival, and he won another half crown's worth of silver and farthings. Perhaps it was because it was a fine late spring morning, with summer just about ready to hurry in.

Ella sang as she made breakfast. Barth and Alicia were still doing the slip step as well as they could and, Steffan had to admit, better than he. The twins were cooing and gurgling and beginning to crawl.

Outside, the air was crisp and clear. The chickens had reconciled themselves to their roosts and were contentedly cackling. Daffy chewed her cud amiably. Max, the farm horse. nickered and stamped with satisfaction. The cats prowled about and napped. Roscoe was showing signs of some exceptional hams.

Admittedly, the pig would not stay penned at night. He had decided that he wanted to sleep with Barth, and Barth was not discouraging the pig. There wasn't much Steffan could do that he hadn't already done. An amiable enmity existed between Steffan and Roscoe, and for the moment, Steffan was content to leave it at that.

Having tended to the livestock, Steffan returned to the house for breakfast.

"So, what will you be doing today?" Ella asked as she dished out the porridge.

"If you don't mind, I was going to spend the morning looking over the cherry orchard," replied Steffan.

"Why don't you make a day of it, and go into the woods and gather some kindling? We're almost out."

"That's an idea. Maybe I'll set a trap or two, and see if I can bring home some rabbit meat."

"That would be good."

Having been raised with the understanding that his dignity was to be maintained at all times, Steffan was not given to behavior that attracted attention. Nonetheless, he found himself whistling a merry folk song as he walked out to the cherry orchard on the other side of the field behind the house.

The trees were bursting with fruit, and would soon be ready for harvesting. Ella had promised preserves, and Steffan had indulged her by purchasing several jars, wax, and sugar. Steffan noted which trees would be ready the soonest, cleared out tendrils of ivy that were starting to grow, and made things neater. Shortly before noon, he made his way into the small forest at the far end of the orchard.

He set a couple traps, then started gathering large twigs and small branches, binding them together with twine. He was on his third bundle when he heard someone crashing through the brush and a soft female voice cursing. A second later, a young woman fell at his feet.

"It got away," she groaned.

"Are you all right?" asked Steffan. "Here, let me

help you up."

She was of average height, and thin. Her pinched cheeks and drawn eyes marred an otherwise pretty face. Brown hair tumbled about her face and shoulders. Her bodice was cut low, and Steffan couldn't help noticing the generous breasts heaving as she gasped for air.

"Are you all right?" he asked again.

"As well as I'm going to get. Damn, I'm hungry." She flopped down onto a fallen tree trunk.

Steffan's ears turned pink at the sound of the curse.

"Business has been terrible lately," she continued. "So I'm out here risking my neck trying to hunt. With my luck, the duke's guard will catch me at it, and I'll get my neck stretched without having caught a decent meal."

"You're not hunting deer, are you?" Steffan sat down next to her.

"Anything I can catch. At the moment, I'm aiming at rabbits."

"Those aren't illegal to hunt."

"Haven't you heard? The queen declared all game royal property, even squirrels and field mice. Heavens, that was over a year ago."

"A year ago I had other concerns. The nerve of that woman. That was purely self-indulgent."

"Tell that to the duke's guard if they catch you."

Steffan pulled his lunch sack from his belt. "You have a point. In the meantime, would you care to share my lunch? There isn't much, but it will be something."

"Oh, why not? I've done it for less." The girl watched greedily as Steffan split the hunk of bread, and then divided the piece of cheese. "The worst of this hunting is that I set the trap, then when I open it to get the beastie out, it escapes on me. I wish I could find a trap that kills the silly things. I can't bear looking them in the eyes while I breaks their necks."

"It's not my favorite part, either. But food is food."

"Now that be truth. I still can't do it. If business were better, I wouldn't have to. It's that damned Isolde Dirkman, you know."

"I've heard of her."

"She's been sitting across the way, watching my door. She's scared off all my clients. What's a girl to do, I ask you? I can't change quarters. I haven't the money, even if I could find new ones."

"That's a difficult one. Have you tried taking the matter to the magistrate?"

"Me?" The girl burst into laughter. "Ah, you're fooling me, you are. That's a rich one, me going to the magistrate. What's your name? I've not seen you before."

"Alex Murdren."

"I'm Dora. I know now. You're the new one. That took the old hermit's farm, you did. I've heard about you. The gentleman's manners you do have, and glad I am of it."

"Thank you. It's my pleasure to be of service."

"I could get used to this kind of talk. Well, there, I've finished. Oh, Alex, I know I'm beholding to you, but could you help me once more? I've got one more trap to check, and it's my last chance at putting something on my supper table."

"I'd be more than happy to." Steffan smiled. For

all her coarse manners, there was something intriguing about Dora, and endearing.

A good-sized rabbit waited in Dora's trap. Steffan loathed the feeling of an animal going limp in his hands, but as he had said, food was food, and Dora was watching. He got a good grip on the rabbit's neck as he pulled it from the trap. Taking a deep breath, he covered the rabbit's eyes, looked elsewhere, and wrung. The rabbit jerked once and was still.

"There's your dinner," he said, nonchalantly handing the carcass over.

"Thank you."

To his surprise, Dora laid the rabbit down next to a tree and approached Steffan.

"Miss?" he asked, completely bewildered.

Dora's arms went around his neck, and she kissed him with the kind of passion he had only known from his wife. He struggled loose.

"What in heaven's name were you doing?" he gasped.

"I thought you'd want payment."

"That's payment? Good heavens, woman, what kind of a person do you think I am?"

"A man."

"I can't imagine what kind of man would take payment that way. Good Lord. You had need, so I supplied it. If any payment were necessary, I'd take it in copper, not in flesh."

"You would?" Dora was bemused. "You're a curious one, all right." She started. "What was that?"

"Someone's coming."

"The duke's guard." She grabbed the trap and

rabbit. "I can't let them catch you with this, especially since it's mine."

She ran off. Steffan wiped his mouth, utterly confused.

The someone turned out to be another farmer looking for a lost calf. Steffan had no help for him and returned to gathering wood. He didn't tell Ella about Dora until they were in bed that night. Ella laughed.

"Steffan, you were too sheltered."

"Because I don't care to have another woman kiss me, let alone in payment for lunch?"

"The payment wasn't just the kiss."

"Ella, are you saying she would have... That's disgusting."

"I agree."

"She wouldn't have. No one would do such a thing."

"That is what I meant when I said you were too sheltered. Steffan, haven't you figured it out? The woman is a prostitute."

"A what?"

"Steffan, you do know what a prostitute is, don't you?"

"Of course. There's a law against it, and I've known every law in this kingdom since I was twelve."

"I'm surprised your father let you learn that one."

"He didn't tell me what it was until after we were married. I still don't believe people would do such a thing."

"It happens quite frequently, and not just among the lower classes. That's why Mrs. Blythe was never admitted to the palace. Your father wouldn't allow her in. He could never prove it, of course, but he knew what she was."

"Oh. I never knew her. But Dora. She seemed so nice. Coarse, but nice."

"I wouldn't doubt it. From what Berencia has told me, and I've heard, she hasn't had much of a chance in life. Her mother died in childbirth, and her father used her as a wife until he sold her into her trade to her predecessor, who has since died."

"That is utterly disgusting. What kind of a man would do that to a woman? Or go to a woman that way?"

Ella shrugged. "Most are hard men, who never learned to be gentle, and as a consequence have wives who are cold and frightened. Or their wives have refused them for any number of reasons, or they just like something different."

"You grew up with this knowledge, didn't you?"

"I learned it as I grew. Being forced among the coarser lower class, I was exposed to that kind of talk. Fortunately, I had a friend who was brutally honest, but very reassuring."

"So that's why you were so calm on our wedding night."

"Calm?" Ella laughed. "I was terrified. But at least I'd known what was coming a lot sooner than you did. What a terrible thing, springing it on you the night before your wedding."

Steffan laughed also. "Poor father. He was so embarrassed and so anxious that I understand this was nothing terrible. It was just necessary."

"Oh, surely we could have waited a night or two,

and no one would have been the wiser."

"No, we couldn't have."

"Steffan, you would have rather eased into it. You can't tell me you wouldn't have."

"I'm not saying I wouldn't have. Oh, that's right. I never told you."

"Told me what?"

"The marriage had to be consummated that night because it had to be witnessed."

"You mean..." Ella's face grew hot.

"Poor Lord Cedric got stuck with the job."

"But why?" Ella was aghast.

"Royalty, my dear. It's partly to ensure the legitimacy of the issue, which is profoundly important, and partly to prevent annulments, especially in the case of strategic marriages. Why do you think I was so nervous?"

"I was nervous, and you were so naive, it made perfect sense."

"And I'm still naive."

"Not about marriage, fortunately. Just about the way the rest of the world functions." Ella stopped. "Steffan, did you like it?"

"That first night? Of course, I did."

"No. When she kissed you."

"Well, it wasn't you. Actually, I was so shocked, I really didn't feel much of anything."

"And you're not curious?"

"About other women? No. The funny thing is, when she kissed me, I thought that it was like you, but not. And the part that wasn't was the unpleasant part."

"I guess I just find it hard to believe that you've

never been tempted."

"Oh, Cindy, you are so good to me, and I love you so much, I don't think there is anyone out there who could tempt me."

In answer, Ella pulled herself close to him.

A week later, the cherries were ready for harvesting. Steffan and Ella and the children worked continuously for three days. The cherries were fat and sweet, and after three days, no one in the household wanted to eat another cherry. Ella set aside enough to fill all of her jars with preserves, then went with Steffan to the town square to sell the abundant supply left over.

Towards the end of the second day of selling, Steffan went to the tavern to get some hard-earned beer for himself and Ella. Arlette Asgarth had the children at her father's farm, and Steffan had promised Ella that they could purchase dinner at the local inn. It was a tremendous extravagance, but the cherries had sold extremely well, and Steffan knew Ella tired of doing all the cooking.

As he returned with the steins, he saw a crowd gathering around the small booth where Ella was.

"I know he's here," cried a vaguely familiar voice.

"My apologies, miss," replied Ella, sounding a little flustered. "He's left for the moment."

"What's going on here?" Steffan set the two steins down on the table next to the few remaining cherries and turned to face Dora.

Tears streaked her cheeks. Her hair was even more disheveled, and her dress was torn.

"You've got to help me!" she sobbed when she saw Steffan. "You're the only one that can."

"Where are you, you cheating wench!" another voice roared. Its owner burst through the crowd. He was a large man, a cart driver, and he carried a whip. He was balding, and his fury had turned the top of his scalp scarlet.

"Whatever trade this woman may have, there is no reason to call her such names," said Steffan with quiet authority.

The carter stepped back. "I've a right. I've paid her money. I've come to get what she owes me, and she won't give it."

Nervous tittering rippled through the crowd. Steffan looked at Dora.

"Is this true?" he asked.

"I'm giving up my trade. I can't live this way no more."

"That's an honorable ambition. Can you return his money?"

"I've already eaten it. I told you business hasn't been so good, and we all know why. He gave me the money a month ago. I couldn't change a half-crown, so we put it on account."

"How much do you owe him?"

"She owes me her flesh, and that's what I'm taking!" shouted the carter.

"What is your name?" Steffan asked.

"Wright."

"Mr. Wright, a contract made for illegal services is not binding by the laws of this kingdom."

"If I was worried about laws do you think I'd have given my money to her?"

"I was merely pointing out that you have no

legitimate claim on this woman. Technically, she owes you nothing."

"She owes me her flesh!" the carter roared.

"So you have said. But there is no way morally, or legally that I can help you achieve it. The best I can do is recommend that she return your money as she is able."

"I'm not taking that. I'm taking her."

Dora shrank back.

"Miss Dora, how much do you owe Mr. Wright?" Steffan asked kindly.

"Ten silver pieces."

Steffan swallowed, then opened his purse. "Mr. Wright, here are five silver pieces. You'll have to get the rest from me after the harvest. You can consider your contract with Miss Dora fulfilled."

Wright grabbed the money. "I'll take the rest of it out of her hide."

John Asgarth stepped forward. "No, you won't. The woman tries to turn from her wrongdoing, the least you could do is respect that. Here's the rest of your money, and this village will be a lot happier if you never show your face here again."

Wright snatched the coins from Asgarth and counted them. Angrily, he strode off.

Oh, no," groaned Dora. "Now I'm beholding to two of you."

Berencia appeared and giggled. "To my husband you are, but since you're giving up your trade, you won't be paying him back your usual way. I hear you do stitchery. With my boys, I've always got mending to do and no time. You can work your debt out sewing for me."

"And I can use some help in my house," said Ella. "I'd be happy to have you work out what you owe. Then maybe someone else can pay you some real money."

"In this village?" An older woman stepped forward, chuckling. "Mrs. Murdren, we haven't had a chance to meet yet. I'm Mrs. Dorothea Kinsell, or informally known as Widow Kinsell. I do stitchery for the village. I haven't any children, and I could use a good apprentice, providing she's willing to work hard, cheerfully, and virtuously."

"I'll do my best, ma'am," said Dora with a sniff.

"And it'll be a very good best at that. Well, ladies, I'm afraid you won't be getting your help. Mr. Murdren, Mr. Asgarth, I'll see to it that you get your silver back. It may take a while. I'm not a rich woman, and I can't afford much in wages."

"The important thing is that Miss Dora has a new trade," replied Steffan.

"She'll have that, and a roof, and food, and some decent clothes."

"Then thank you, Mrs. Kinsell," said Steffan. "Your kindness has made the difference."

"Only because yours did first, Mr. Murdren, and your just decision. But I'll be warning you. The tongues will be wagging in this village."

"Only because some people are so narrow-minded that they can't see beyond their own strict interpretations of the law to true justice. If I'm to be censured, I'd rather it were because I chose compassion instead of the letter of the law."

Mrs. Kinsell nodded in approval. She put her arm

around Dora's thin shoulders and helped the girl to her house. Steffan picked up a stein and turned to his wife. She held up her stein.

"To justice," she said with a smile.

Steffan touched her stein with his and began breathing again.

# CHAPTER NINE

The tongues in the village were wagging. In the butcher shop, Isolde Dirkman was in her glory.

"She said he didn't know what her trade was," she said triumphantly, almost two weeks later.

"Was that when he met her in the woods?" asked Penelope.

"Of course, you goose."

"I can't believe he didn't take her favors," said Isabelle. "She's only swearing to it because she likes him."

"Well, it don't surprise me that she went to him for help," said Isolde. "He's a close one, and that kind can be up to no good. He shaved the dice at the festival. Won three gold crowns, he did. And he certainly knew what her trade was when he defended her. Imagine, defending the likes of her, and his wife, too, wanting to take her in like that."

"She probably wanted to keep Miss Dora where she could keep an eye on her," said Isabelle. "If my Clarence were foolish enough to visit one like Miss Dora, I wouldn't mind keeping an eye on her myself."

"Well, I did. I was keeping her honest enough, and she blamed me for starving her." Isolde snorted. "It's no better than the likes of her deserves. I tell you, I'll not be taking my sewing to Widow Kinsell no more. Imagine a Christian woman taking a creature like that into her house. There'll be trouble over it, mark me well."

"Did you see she went to mass yesterday?" Isabelle lifted her eyebrows. "The priest must have shriven her, and to think he did so with no proof that she really has mended her ways. You'd think she should still be doing penance before she darkened the church doors."

"The poor man is as daft as the rest of them. She'll return to her trade. Those kind are not honest women. A little hard work, and she'll be back to her old quarters. You can trust me on that one."

In the tavern, the men were also still discussing the incident.

"What I don't understand is why she thought he was the only one who could help her," sighed Sigmund Lyle. "After all the years I spent with her. All of us did, and I was kind to her, never used her roughly."

Georg Kiffs laughed. "Lyle, my friend, haven't you heard? He was the first man she'd met who didn't want her to favor him."

"I don't understand," said Cyril, who had been away from the village when the incident occurred.

"They'd met in the woods, or so she tells it," said Lyle. "He gave her some food, and wouldn't take her usual payment for it, which is an odd reason to like a man if you ask me."

Cyril's eyebrows lifted. "It is indeed. And she's turned to a new trade, I hear."

"Widow Kinsell took her in as an apprentice," replied Kiffs. "There'll be little comfort to be had around here for a while."

"There was little enough before," grumbled Lyle.

"What with that old biddy, Dirkman, watching that girl like a cat at a mousehole."

"Which is probably why she went to Murdren," pointed out Kiffs. "If the rest of us wouldn't even been seen darkening her doorstep, who else would have the nerve to defend her?"

"Odd that he'd take such a risk being new here, and all," said Cyril.

Kiffs shrugged. "Well, you can't fault his decision. You'd have to do a lot of walking in this village before you'd find another who could be so fair. There's many a man here who would have thrown them both to the law, and not given the poor girl a chance to mend herself, and many of them her best customers. Heaven knows I would have."

"Watch, now," hissed Lyle. "Here he comes."

Steffan entered the tavern carrying a large pitcher. Aleman laughed when he saw it.

"Drinking a bit, Mr. Murdren?" he asked.

"Just a bit," replied Steffan. "It's for my wife and me to share. We've had some eggs to sell, and it's thirsty work."

"That it is. And they're fine eggs, too. My wife bought some this morning."

"Then ask him!" Friederich burst out in loud anger. "But I know my coin."

A small, quiet man approached Steffan.

"Mr. Murdren, what do you know of weights?" he asked.

"Enough. Why?"

"My name is Elgar Richitts. I'm the village apothecary and chemist. Our friend, Mr. Friederich, presented me with a gold coin for some powders this afternoon, a half-crown, but my weights show it false. He says my weights are false, and it's not true."

"His weights are false," said Friederich. "I've checked the coin myself."

"I'm sure you were very careful, Mr. Friederich," Steffan replied. "Mr. Richitts, do you have your weights with you?"

"Yes, here." Richitts handed over the small weight.

Steffan examined it carefully. "Well, I can see no sign of falsehood. Mr. Aleman, you have cause to weigh coins. Might I check this against your weights?"

"Certainly, Mr. Murdren." Aleman placed the scale and measure on the bar.

Steffan carefully placed the weight on the scale. It balanced with the matching scale.

"I'd say that's a true weight, wouldn't you, Mr. Aleman?"

"As I value my gold, I would."

"Mr. Friederich, may I see the coin in question?"

Friederich reluctantly handed it over. "I don't see how it could be false. You can see right there where I bit it."

"I agree. It does look sound." Steffan ran his nail along the edge. "There it is. The lead is just starting to crack through. That's why your bite didn't catch it. Lead is even softer than gold. These are hard ones to catch. They're just coated with gold. It's a lot of work, but you can get ten halves from just one gold crown. I'm afraid, Mr. Friederich-"

"You'll not accuse me of making false coins!" Friederich sputtered.

"I was making no such accusation." Steffan remained calm. "I was merely saying that someone else cheated you, quite probably as innocently as you presented this coin to Mr. Richitts."

Friederich blushed, then glared at Steffan. "I've not finished with you, Murdren. You'll pay for this embarrassment, and you'll pay for your dishonest dice game."

"Dishonest?" Steffan stepped back in shock.

"I've heard about how you shave your dice. Won five crowns, you did."

Steffan laughed. "I only wish I had. I could use the money. My apologies, Mr. Friederich. You've heard a silly rumor. The dice I played with were untouched, as far as I know."

With a final glare, Friederich retreated, murmuring apologies to the apothecary.

"You've made no friend there," chuckled Aleman. "And for all you tried, too."

Steffan shrugged. "We've crossed each other before, I'm afraid. Here are your three groats for the pitcher."

"Aren't you going to weigh them?" Kiffs approached, teasing, but without malice. "A man who knows so much about false coins must have learned about them some way."

"True." Steffan laughed. "But I learned about them in a completely honest undertaking, which is why I am now a farmer. Good day, neighbors."

Aleman gazed after him. "He's a good man. There are few husbands who will bring their wives a sip of water after a hard day selling, let alone a stein of beer."

"What was he before?" asked Kiffs.

"A merchant he says."

"Quite a rich one he must have been, for all his fine manners. He's got a head for settling disputes."

"Since he defended Miss Dora, he's been asked to settle a few. If he keeps this up, our magistrate is going to find his court looking rather empty."

Kiffs thoughtfully sipped from his stein. "Sir Leonard isn't going to like that. His pay may come from the queen's treasury, but he adds to it with bribes from the duke's people, and takes his share of the settlements."

"And an informal court will not feather his nest as generously. The question is, do we want to defend Mr. Murdren, or leave him to his own peril?"

"You're asking me what I think?" Kiffs laughed. "Any way I have of cheating that rogue of a magistrate I'll gladly protect, and if it's better for our neighbors, I'm that much happier."

Back in the square, while Ella waited for Steffan's return, she noted with some dismay the approach of Isolde Dirkman.

"Eggs you have," the older woman noted.

"Very fine ones. How many would you like today?"

"Not so fast." Isolde picked through the basket and sniffed. "They're not as fine as all that. Hmph! Look at that one, misshaped, bad color. You ought to be ashamed for even offering something like this."

Ella took the egg. "You needn't purchase it if you don't like it. Would this one be better?"

"It would." Isolde slipped it into her basket. "I suppose I can do with a dozen. Here, I want these."

She put the twelve eggs down on the table.

"You'd best take two more, then, to go with the one in your basket," Ella said. "They're a farthing for a dozen, and I'll have to charge a groat for just the one if you don't."

She charged a farthing a dozen because, with four groats to a farthing, it made it easier to buy more or less than a dozen eggs.

"A farthing! For twelve ugly eggs as these? I've paid less for larger ones."

"I'm sorry, but that's the price. Do you want the extra two?"

"I'm not paying a farthing for a dozen eggs. I'll give you two groats and nothing more."

"Mrs. Dirkman, I thought it was considered uncivilized to bargain in this village."

Isolde's face went red, and her mouth opened, for once speechless.

"This is an outrage," she finally sputtered. "I won't stand for it. I won't, I tell you."

"Then you needn't purchase any eggs. I would appreciate it if you would return the one in your basket to me."

"Are you accusing me of stealing?"

"Were you? I thought you had intended to purchase the egg when you put it there."

Isolde removed the egg and slammed it onto the table, breaking three others in addition.

"There's your egg."

Ella held her breath. "Then I need two groats since you damaged four."

"Why, it was a sad accident. I can't be held

responsible for that."

"Yes, you can, by the laws of this kingdom."

"And what do you know of laws? Do you shave your husband's dice for him?"

"Shall we discuss this with the magistrate?" Ella snapped.

Isolde swallowed, then dug into her purse. "There's your groats. See if I ever buy anything from you again!"

"That could only make me happier. And I don't want to hear any more stories about my husband shaving dice, or I will be so pleased to make a claim against you."

Isolde went pale and hurried off.

Steffan came up. "What was that all about?"

"Please. It's been dealt with. I'm too angry right now."

"Fair enough. Here's some beer to cool you down."

"Thank you, my darling. A cool drink is just what I need."

"Where are the children?"

"Arlette and Meg took the twins again. They're both so fond of babies. And Edward and Giles have taken their sister Gen, and our older two two to look at the fish pond. They'll meet us back here or at the farm."

"Good. Why don't we pack it up for the day? I've some weeding to do in the garden before dark."

"I'll be quite happy to do so."

They packed and returned home, collecting their children along the way.

Towards the end of that week, the family returned to the village, this time to make some purchases. As they approached the square, Barth pulled at his mother's skirts.

"Mama, see those boys playing?" He pointed to a group of boys wrestling alongside a stretch of crumbling wall. "I played with them last time. May I play again?"

"I don't know, son." Ella watched as one, a sturdy boy of about eight, climbed to the top of the wall and walked its length. "We won't be here that long, and that wall looks dangerous."

As she spoke, a section of the wall came loose, and the boy tumbled with a shriek. The others watched dumbfounded as their friend lay still. Ella ran over, followed by Steffan, Barth, and Alicia. The stricken boy groaned loudly, his leg twisted into a sickening shape.

"It's broken," said Ella. Gently, she stroked the boy's forehead. "I know it hurts. But we'll get you home, and fetch the doctor." She looked up at the boys. "Which of you knows where the doctor lives? You? Good. Fetch him quickly and bring him to the boy's home."

"I'm his brother," said one, a little younger.

"What's your name?"

"Dirk. Dirk Friederich. My brother is Arnold."

"Will you help us get Arnold home? No, don't lift him. My husband will do that. Be careful, dearest. We have to lift the leg all of a piece, or we can make it worse."

Still carrying Nella, Ella gently slid her arm under the injured limb. Steffan handed James to Barth and positioned himself as well. Together, they lifted the boy, then followed Dirk to his house.

Mrs. Friederich was horrified when she saw what had happened. She ran ahead and prepared a bed for her son. Carefully, Ella and Steffan laid the boy down.

"Mrs. Friederich!" The boy who had gone for the doctor came running in. "The doctor's at the duke's palace, tending to his people. They say he won't be back for another three days."

"We can't leave Arnold's leg like this," sobbed Mrs. Friederich.

Ella took a deep breath. "I'll just have to set it myself."

"But, Cindy, have you..?" Steffan looked at her, surprised.

"I set yours. Now. Is there any brandy about?"

"I don't keep such things in my house," replied Mrs. Friederich indignantly.

"I don't hold with strong spirits either, Mrs. Friederich, but they're good for pain, and your poor son is going to be hurting worse before he's better." Ella turned to Steffan. "Hurry and go to the tavern."

Steffan nodded and left after instructing Barth to watch his brother and sisters.

The tavern was only half full when he arrived. There were several knowing grins as Steffan requested the brandy.

"So early in the day?" chuckled Aleman.

"It's for an emergency."

Something about the grim look on Steffan's face made the tavern keeper hurry.

"I'm not surprised to see the likes of you drinking

heavily," sniggered Friederich.

"Mr. Friederich, you'd best come with me." Steffan quickly paid Aleman and walked out of the tavern with Friederich close behind him. "I'm afraid your son has had an accident. He fell off a wall and broke his leg."

Friederich swore. "The doctor is at the duke's palace."

"And heaven forbid that the duke's people should not be taken care of. But it's not hopeless. My wife has had some training. She'll set it and with luck, it will heal. And if it's left for the doctor to set, it won't heal at all."

"She can?"

"She set my leg, and I'm no cripple. That's why I've got the brandy. It will help ease the boy's pain."

"It's eased mine more than once."

In the house, all was subdued. Arnold groaned, again and again, adding an eerie pall over the gloom and worry. Ella coaxed the boy into drinking several sips of brandy, then had his mother keep it ready to give him as the pain got worse. With Steffan holding the boy down, she firmly pulled the bones into place. Arnold screamed. It was over quickly, and Mrs. Friederich quickly gave him some more brandy.

"Well, there's no outward bleeding," said Ella, breathing heavily. "We'll need some sticks for a splint to hold the leg still, and some rags to tie them with."

Friederich nodded and fetched the materials. They tied the leg down and left the boy to rest with his mother.

As Steffan lifted Nella from the floor, Friederich spoke.

"I owe you an apology. I was drunk at the festival, but I wasn't earlier this week. You were more than fair to me. And today I've a feeling if it had been my leg, you still would have helped. There are not many who would do that."

"And there aren't many in your shoes who would have the grace to apologize. This wasn't easy for you to say. I appreciate that." Steffan smiled. "We'd best be going. Let us know how he does."

They shook hands, then Friederich held the door for them as they left.

Three days later, the doctor returned and looked at the young patient.

"Will you have to amputate it?" asked Mrs. Friederich fearfully.

"No. Whoever set it did a fine job. I'd like to meet the man."

"She was a woman. Mrs. Murdren. You know, the new family what took the hermit's farm."

"Yes. Well, she has quite a gift. I wonder when I'll get a chance to meet her. I'll come back in a few days to check on him. But he seems to be healing well, and with luck won't even have a limp."

The doctor left, cursing the call that had kept him away from his village and blessing the fact that there was someone else to help. On the road, he looked out in the direction of the Murdren farm. He decided not to go. By all accounts, the Murdrens were close people. He'd seen them at church, and they'd seemed nice enough. The man's face seemed vaguely familiar. The doctor pursued the thought, but all it led to was the duke's palace. The duke's daughters, perhaps? The doctor chuckled. If there was a relation, it was surely not of the sort one mentioned.

# CHAPTER TEN

The months moved along. The spring faded into a mild summer, which gave way to a chilly fall. A nagging anxiety filled Steffan as time for the wheat harvest approached. Not only was there his own inexperience, but he couldn't help noticing that the fields of many another farm had much taller wheat than his. Asgarth continually assured him that there would be a fair return. Steffan hoped it would be enough.

"We'll be all right, Steffan," Ella said the night before the harvest was to start. "We've got all those vegetables from the kitchen garden, and the hops look good. Besides, the apples will be ready soon. We got five silver pieces from the cherries. We're sure to get at least that from the apples."

"James and Nella need winter wraps. Both Alicia and Barth need new shoes, and you need more jars to preserve the apples."

"We'll make it."

"I suppose. We'll have meat enough, at least. I have to admit, Barth has done a good job with that pig. The beast is a monster."

"And so smart, too. Barth taught him to sit and lie down on command. He comes when we call, and Barth has him digging up roots. He helped harvest the carrots, and he was certainly a help when you had to pull out that stump in the kitchen garden."

"We bought it to butcher."

"I know." Ella sighed. "I've been trying to remind Barth. But he's so sweet, Steffan. The children love him. You should see him stand guard over the twins."

"Ella, I do not find that reassuring. If we do not butcher that pig, we have spent two silver pieces on essentially nothing. We do not have the money to spend on pets."

"I know. I'm sorry, Steffan. I had no idea a silly pig would become such a part of our family when I bought him. I was just thinking of the meat, and how proud Barth would be to have some responsibility of his own."

"I knew that pig was going to be trouble the moment I laid eyes on it. Ella, you're just going to have to harden yourself to it. Butchering animals is a fact of life on a farm, and the sooner we all face up to it, the better off we will be. Now, let's get some sleep."

Steffan rolled over, but sleep did not come.

They were all up before dawn, ready to go over to the Asgarth farm to help with their harvest. Other farmers from the village gathered also. Everyone helped when it was time to bring the wheat in. For a week, the men mowed, the children gathered, and the women cooked and threshed. Steffan's farm was one of the last to be harvested, and there were not nearly as many bags of grain in his barn at the end of it than he'd hoped. He had more than several other farms, and the other farmers expressed their surprise that he had as much as he did. Still, the return was discouraging.

"Two and a half gold crowns," he complained upon returning from the miller. "That's it."

"That's not bad, Steffan. It's more than we had when we arrived here last spring." Ella handed a saucer of milk to Alicia. "Now be careful, darling. The kitten will need only little sips."

"What's that all about?" Steffan asked as Alicia went to the hearth and picked up a small bundle.

"One of the cats had kittens, and then a weasel got her. By the time Alicia found the nest, the other kittens were dead. But this one was still fighting. Alicia's been doing a beautiful job nursing it."

Steffan smiled at his oldest daughter. "It doesn't surprise me. Alicia's always been very affectionate, and you, my dear, have a definite talent for nursing. You've no doubt passed it on."

Moved, and happy to forget his own troubles, Steffan went over to the hearth and sat down next to Alicia.

"It's eating," she said happily.

"Yes. You do very well at that."

They remained there for a long time, even after the kitten was fed and asleep.

Two days later, after the Sabbath, the whole family attacked the field of hops, except for the twins, who were happy to walk along the fence, holding onto it as they went. They couldn't walk by themselves yet and found the glory of being upright too intoxicating to do anything else. The next day, Steffan hitched the horse to the wagon and drove the sacks into the village. He was much happier with that return.

"Another crown and a half," he announced when he got home. "We're not rich by any means, but things aren't quite so dear."

"That's a blessing," said Ella, happier that Steffan wasn't depressed than at the money. "Perhaps you should just plant hops."

Steffan shook his head. "I don't think I could sell that many, at least not directly. Cyril could sell them for me, but my price would have to allow for him to earn some money."

The apples also brought a good return. Steffan counted out the money contentedly. Other farmers had done better that year, largely on the strength of their wheat crops, but Steffan had enough to keep his family fed and clothed for another year, and he was happy.

His biggest problem was the pig. Roscoe had endeared himself so completely to everyone in the family, except Steffan, that he was beginning to feel uncomfortable. The night before All Hallow's Eve, an intruder ventured into the farm's front yard. The family could only guess that the intruder had less than honorable intentions. With a great deal of grunting and squealing, Roscoe rushed out of the house faster than could be imagined of anything so huge and short-legged. The intruder ran off howling about ghosts and other strange beasts. Afterward, Steffan found that any mention of butchering resulted in baleful looks from everyone except the twins, who were too young to understand.

"This is ridiculous," he announced the next day at lunch. "Bartholemew, you and I are going for a long walk."

As soon as they had eaten, Steffan took his son by the hand and headed for the woods. Roscoe followed.

"Shoo! Go back!" Steffan gestured in vain.

Roscoe gave him the same baleful look everyone else had.

Steffan looked at Barth. "Can't you send him back?"

"He won't always listen, Papa."

Steffan decided against pressing the issue. In the woods, Steffan checked his traps, wrung the necks of a couple rabbits, and tried to explain to his son how death was a part of life, and that animals were not the same as people, and it was a very noble thing for a pig to give its life so a family could eat.

"We had enough to eat without him," Barth replied stubbornly. "And Mama said last month we had more money than we did last spring."

Steffan sighed. "You are your mother's son."

Barth stared at him without comprehension.

"Never mind, son. I guess you're just going to have to accept the fact that your pig has got to supply meat for yourself, your sisters, your brother, and your mother and me. I've put this off too long. Tomorrow is All Hallows. The day after, we will butcher the pig."

Barth did not sob and carry on. He knew how his father felt about such things. But the tears slid out of his eyes. Steffan was too compassionate not to allow the boy his grief. He held his son next to him, unable to do the one thing that would bring joy to his child.

Roscoe, blissfully unaware of his impending demise, rooted about.

"He likes to dig," said Barth, without enthusiasm.

"I know." Steffan thought of all the holes underneath the pigpen fence.

"There he goes!" Barth dashed off, following the mound of dirt that Roscoe was making with his strong snout. "Papa, you should see the things he finds, and he gives everything to me. Uh oh, these are icky."

Against his will, Steffan was drawn to the dark things Barth was holding out in front of him.

"Don't drop those," Steffan commanded. He pulled out a small sack from his pocket, then sniffed at Barth's hands. "Yes. These will be delicious."

"These?"

"These are truffles, and they are not icky."

"You eat them?" Barth was horrified.

"Whenever I can." Steffan carefully slid the fragile roots into the sack.

Back at the house, he presented the sack triumphantly to Ella. She grabbed it, enthusiastically.

"This is wonderful!" she exclaimed. "We can sell them for an enormous amount of money."

Steffan grabbed the sack back. "We are not selling them. We are eating them."

"Then we'll send Roscoe out for some more. I told you he would pay off."

"Ella, we can't sell truffles. Nobody in that village knows what they are, and the people who do are the very people from whom we're hiding."

"Then he can satisfy your appetite."

"He'll satisfy it better as chops!"

In the pause that followed, Steffan felt himself growing warm. Ella, Barth, Alicia and even the pig were looking at him as though he were a criminal. Steffan dropped the bag of truffles next to the hearth.

"Well, it looks as though it's time for dinner," he

said finally. "Shall we eat?"

Dinner was a silent, uncomfortable meal. The children didn't eat much, and even Steffan pushed his plate away before it was empty.

The next day was a church feast day. There was a procession after mass and a special dinner in the town square. Nothing was said about the pig by anyone. The next morning, Steffan was very aware of his criminal status among his family.

"I expect the best thing to do is get it over with," he said when the breakfast dishes were cleared.

Both Barth and Alicia broke down and ran for their mother's lap.

"I understand, children. But your father's right." Ella swallowed to keep back her own tears. "We bought the pig to be butchered, and we need the meat."

Steffan picked up the long knife and left the house feeling like a murderer.

He returned five minutes later.

"That was quick," said Ella with a trace of bitterness.

"I changed my mind," Steffan replied neutrally. "I suppose if the pig means that much to you, and he doesn't cost anything to keep, I guess we can find some other use for him."

Barth and Alicia yelped with joy and hugged their father. They ran off, only Alicia ran back and placed a sloppy kiss on her father's cheek. Steffan turned to Ella. She was smiling.

"Don't you dare," Steffan warned her. "Not one laugh, chuckle or chortle out of you."

"You couldn't do it."

"It looked at me." Steffan sank onto the wooden bench at the table. "It stood in the pen and just looked at me. Ella, I don't like killing things. But there are times when it simply must be done. So I do it." Steffan paused. "Two silver pieces. Gone. And all for a pig that will not be butchered."

"It's not a complete loss. You have your truffles, and he is as good as a watch dog. Besides, the thought of ham was making me nauseous."

Steffan's head snapped up. "You're not..."

"Oh no." Ella laughed. "It was just the thought of eating him. I couldn't bear it. It's all right to go to a butcher shop. There, what things do have eyes, there isn't any light in them, and so it doesn't matter."

"Butcher shops are expensive. I suppose we'll find our meat some other way. At least the children are happy."

Steffan got up and went to the barn to sulk. Asgarth appeared in the door.

"I thought today was butchering day," he said, coming in. "And yet I just saw the children playing with the pig."

"He's not getting butchered."

Asgarth laughed. "You couldn't do it."

"I am not amused."

"We knew you wouldn't. Berencia knew it as soon as Mrs. Kapman snatched up her favorite. That's why you got that one, you know. Same reason we have old Trudi. Mrs. Kapman knew we'd fall in love with her, and wouldn't have the heart to eat her. She has a favorite almost every year. She won't sell it until she finds the softest heart she can. This region is full of hog farmers, thanks to her. We do a steady trade in ham and sausages."

"Raultberg is famous for its pork."

"Mrs. Kapman is why. We take turns raising piglets, and sell them off to the pig butcher every year at the harvest festival. You've got a really big one there. I'd bring it along to the festival. It should win a prize for size alone."

"That would be nice, especially since I won't be eating him."

Asgarth gazed thoughtfully out the window. "He's a big one, all right. Should get some good-sized piglets out of him."

"You mean breed him?"

"Why not?" Asgarth laughed. "Why didn't I think of it before? My Trudi's due to come into season. I'll be glad to give you some meat in exchange for some piglets. How about two good hams?"

"I..."

"I'll throw in a side of beef. Trudi's always been a good sow. Throws good-sized piglets. Just think what she'll do with a sire like that. Still not sure? I'll throw in some sausage, say twenty pounds."

"But..."

Asgarth bounced with excitement. "All right, two large hams, a side of beef, and fifty pounds of sausage. It'll be worth it to take a prize at next year's festival, not to mention all the silver from piglet sales."

"But there's no guarantee you'll get large piglets or even any good ones."

"We'll keep them at it the whole time Trudi's in season. You and I should be able to take that kind of comfort." Asgarth chuckled as Steffan blushed. "That'll be one happy pig, Murdren. Is it a deal?"

"Of course," replied Steffan. "We were wondering how we'd get our meat."

The meat arrived the day it became obvious that Trudi was about to become a mother again. Berencia clucked and confessed she'd made considerably more sausage than she'd need, and they wouldn't feel the pinch of fifty pounds. At the harvest festival, Roscoe won a prize, and Steffan got three more hams, several chops, and some ducks in exchange for mating privileges.

"I told you he'd pay off," said Ella happily as she sorted through the meat. "And better yet, Roscoe is a continuing source of income."

"Until a bigger pig comes along. Then we can butcher him."

"Steffan!"

He laughed and pulled his wife into his lap for some lazy affection.

The days grew shorter. Christmas came and went. It was a meager holiday with few presents, but Steffan was content with having his family well and alive. The bitter cold of January wore everyone's tempers thin, and February seemed to last forever.

On the first day of March, Asgarth made his way through the lingering snow.

"Have I got news!" he announced. "Old Trudi delivered this morning. Sixteen piglets I've got! And little monsters, too. I've never seen such big newborns. They're all sucking away at the teats. Not a runt in the lot. Can you believe it? Sixteen."

Ella looked over at Steffan with a smug grin.

"Yes! You were right," Steffan replied. "He is paying off."

# THE SECOND YEAR

## CHAPTER ELEVEN

Ella stepped into the front yard and took a deep breath in spite of the moisture-filled air. The heat was almost oppressive, but not unusual for the height of the summer. There was no one abroad. Anyone with any sense at all was under some shade. The only sound was the humming of insects.

It had been a quiet, pleasant spring. Alicia had turned four and Barth was now six years old. The one-year-old twins were growing fast and running everywhere. The early summer weather had started fair, but over the past week, a series of storms had left the air wet and heavy.

Ella looked around. Steffan was in the barn, probably resting more than he was cleaning. He'd save that for the evening when it was cooler. The Asgarth girls had taken the children to a nearby stream to bathe. Ella toyed with the idea of finding a private bend and dabbling her toes. She sighed. Berencia was waiting, and she had said it was important.

Ella had long since given up the ritual of knocking at the Asgarth door. Berencia was at her table shelling early peas.

"Afternoon, Cindy," she said with a smile. "It's

certainly hot today."

"It is. But last summer was worse."

"The air's heavier this year, and have we had the storms."

Ella pulled pods from her own basket and began shelling also.

"They've been terrible," she replied. "The last one seemed as if it were going to blow the barn down. I'm surprised I've still got peas to shell."

Berencia coughed.

"Is that cough still bothering you?"

"Off and on."

"You've had it since winter."

"Well, it's not the consumption, if that's what you're worried about. The doctor was very sure of that."

Ella stopped shelling. "You've been to the doctor."

"Stop getting so worried. He came for Mrs. Aleman's last baby. We had a bit of trouble with that one. Anyway, while he was there, he asked me about my cough. So we talked about it, and we agreed there was nothing to be done."

"Berencia, please don't lie to me. You didn't just casually talk with the doctor in the middle of the night about a simple cough. You wouldn't have said a word to him if you hadn't thought it was serious."

"All right, it's serious. So's living. Cindy, it's just part of getting older."

"You're not that old."

"That's sweet of you. But that's what I wanted to talk to you about, anyway. No matter what you say, I'm not as young as I used to be. It's getting harder to get up in the middle of the night for the birthings. Ever since Lucy Schmidt died, there's only been two midwives for our whole village. Now, Gittel Markmardt is training another, and it's time I trained one, too. I know you've got the healing knack, and a clearer head than most I know, man or woman. So. What do you say?"

"Berencia, it's a tremendous honor." Ella sighed. "You must be terribly worried."

"About you? No. Why do you think I asked you? But I understand. You'll have to talk to your Alex. It's only fair. It's his rest that gets disturbed also, as often as not."

"I mean you're worried about yourself. Something is terribly wrong, isn't there?"

Berencia sighed. "I've had it for a good many years. It started in my teats. Little lumps. The doctor calls them tumors. I've got them all over me now. This winter, they started in my lungs. That's what my cough is. I could linger on for a good while yet. There's nothing the doctor can do. Some days it hurts. Others it don't."

"You're dying."

"We've been dying since the day we were born. It's where we're all headed, and I just pray it's the Good Lord's face I'll be seeing when I go. I'm only worried about my family. I did so want to see my girls married. But John will see to it that they get good husbands." Berencia chuckled. "I made him promise that, and good wives for my boys, too. I don't know if I'll be around for even Edward's wedding, for all he's sweet on Mistress Willman."

"At least this week he is."

Berencia laughed out loud. "That's my boy. Breaking a new heart every day. He's so serious, too. 'But, Mama,' he tells me, 'I've got to know them all if I'm to find just the right girl for me. Women like you aren't easy to find.' And then, there's my Giles breaking hearts, too, and for the opposite reason. He doesn't want to get married. Not him. He just enjoys the attention. Oh, you're right, Cindy. There's no point in burying me yet. I've still a ways to go. A short ways, perhaps, but I might as well enjoy it."

"You might as well." Ella returned to her shelling.

After dinner, she followed Steffan out to the fields.

"We've got to keep checking and destroy any stalk that has them. Put them in this bag, and we'll burn them." Steffan pulled at a stalk. "Here's one, and here's another. These blasted weevils are all over the place."

Ella looked over the sea of tall rich wheat. "It's like Berencia. She looks healthy, and inside the very life is being choked out of her."

"The very life will be starved out of us if we don't stop these weevils from spreading," replied Steffan. He stopped. "Ella, darling, I know you're upset about Berencia. But there isn't a thing we can do about it. Even if I were on my throne, I couldn't order it away. I learned very early in life that human power can only go so far. Right now, we can do something about these weevils. Hopefully, it will be enough."

They finished with the field just as the sun set. While walking back to the house, they met Asgarth coming from the village.

"Twice as many today," Steffan grumbled, holding up his sack.

"They're all through my field," sighed Asgarth. "There's nobody who'll get much of a harvest this year. There's nothing you can do about them."

"Well, I can keep trying."

"You're wasting your time." Asgarth looked over at his fields. Already his wheat was looking brown and wilted. "Then again, maybe your foolishness will leave you with some wheat."

"If only it's enough," Steffan sighed.

"If it isn't, you'll be no worse off than anyone else here. I've survived a couple blights like this. Your belly rumbles a bit more, but you live."

"I don't know if that's reassuring or not. Well, good night, Asgarth."

"'Night, Murdren, Mrs. Murdren."

Wearily, Steffan followed Ella into the house. He threw the sack onto the fire and moodily watched it burn. The worst of the blight was that the wheat had been coming in so beautifully before it had hit. Steffan felt as if he had finally gotten the knack of farming. Then the weevils began appearing, burrowing their way into the tender ears of wheat. They spread faster than Steffan could pull the bad ears. It seemed hopeless.

The next day, the air was even heavier, and a sense of expectant anxiety rippled along with the gentle breeze. Huge clouds piled up along the horizon like runners at the start of a race, waiting for the starting gun.

"It's another storm coming in," said Ella as she and Steffan went through the wheat, still searching for weevils. Barth and Alicia played with the twins nearby. The weather had left them subdued and cranky.

"It looks like a bad one, too," Steffan added. "Let's see how fast we can work. With any luck, we'll save some of the crop."

The weevils had multiplied again overnight. By mid- afternoon, Steffan and Ella had only covered three-quarters of the field, which was looking considerably thinned out.

The wind sprang up. Steffan looked up as saw that the clouds had covered the sky in a matter of minutes.

"We'd better get in!" he called.

"I'm getting the children together!" Ella called back.

A gust of wind brought a splattering of raindrops.

"Here, I'll help you." Steffan fought against the rising wind to the rest of his family. He picked up Nella and got a firm grip on Alicia's hand. Barth helped his mother carry the bag of weevils that she had collected.

The rain became a downpour when they were halfway to the house. Steffan left Nella on the floor and hurried out to the barn to secure it. The gale increased in fury as he fought his way back to the house, slipping and stumbling in the mud. The door burst open at his touch, and he struggled to close it.

Inside, the room was quiet. A fire crackled merrily on the hearth over the roar of the storm outside.

"You're a filthy, sodden mess," Ella teased. "Go upstairs, get out of those wet things, put your blanket on, and come sit by the fire. And don't give me any of your it's not proper nonsense. A little impropriety is better than you catching your death."

She was already cloaked, in a rather fetching manner, Steffan thought. If only the children weren't awake.

An hour later, Ella's petticoats and other underthings were dry and clean, so she dispensed with her blanket and just wore those, even though her oldest son was right there. Steffan mused over the lack of modesty. It didn't bother him. They were too poor for Ella to have an extra work dress. The only other dresses she had was one to wear on wash days and one for Sundays and festivals. Steffan thought it interesting that she preferred immodesty to the risk of ruining her only good dress. Perhaps it was because they were so poor.

And likely to get poorer, if the weevils continued. Lightning flashed and thunder rumbled. The two older children huddled together for courage. The twins napped. Ella hummed as she cleaned Steffan's pants and coat. She checked the steaming clothes on the hearth.

"Barth, you can get dressed now," she announced as she handed him his shirt and pants.

Thunder growled again, and Barth shivered and clung to his sister.

"I'll go with you, son," said Steffan, getting up. "Come along."

A leak opened up in the roof near Barth's bed. Steffan gave his son a reassuring pat, then grabbed some of the straw he'd been keeping in the house for such occasions, and stuffed it in the thatch where the water was coming through. The first thing he'd have to do when the weevils either let up or completely decimated his crops would be to completely rework the roof.

The storm continued for the rest of the afternoon, lessening every so often only to renew its strength and roar even more fiercely. Ella made soup for dinner, and the children went to bed soon after. Both Ella and Steffan had long since dressed. As Ella finished with the dishes, she noticed Steffan watching her.

"What are you looking at?" she asked.

"You. I was thinking how pretty you looked in your blanket this afternoon, and later in your petticoats."

"You've seen me in my petticoats before."

"I know, and you were enchanting then, and you are enchanting now."

"Really? I was thinking I was looking rather spindly again."

"Not in the important places." Steffan pulled her to him and buried his face in her breast.

The door burst open. Ella yelped and Steffan blushed.

"Oh, sorry, Mrs. Murdren, Mr. Murdren," Edward Asgarth gasped. "Mother sent me. It's Mrs. Friederich's time, and Mother says you should go with her."

"At all the worst times, and on all the worst nights," Steffan grumbled. "Asgarth warned me about this."

"Perhaps I shouldn't then."

"No. I may as well get used to it. I'm thinking I should go with you."

"You'd better stay with the children." Ella picked up her cloak and put in on.

"Father's coming with us, Mr. Murdren, and me, too."

"Then I'll leave my wife in your hands." Steffan stopped Ella long enough for a quick kiss.

Shortly after she left, the wind shook the house harder yet. Steffan stuffed more straw in more leaks and placed pans under the leaks he'd already stuffed. He opened the shutter on the side window by just a crack and saw that the barn was still standing, and it seemed to have everything attached. He paced for hours in front of the kitchen hearth, as the storm went on roaring. Close to midnight, he noticed a draft that came and went. He traced it to the front corner of the house. It was wet, as was the floor under it. Ella had laid out plenty of straw on the dirt floors, but now mud squelched up through the straw. Steffan examined the corner more closely. The wind whistled, the roof lifted, and Steffan got a blast of rain in his face.

"Damn!" he cursed. There was some pitch next to the oven that Ella had been collecting for roof repairs. But it wouldn't hold in all that water. There had to be a way to nail down the thatch, at least for the moment so that the rest of the roof wouldn't blow away. Steffan remembered the twine that held the bundles together. He took the ball next to the stove, got his hammer and some nails, and went outside.

The water hit his back like pellets. He fought his way against the wind to the corner of the house. Fortunately, the roof dipped low there, and he didn't need his ladder.

A burst of wind ripped the thatch up at the corner. Steffan grabbed on to the slippery straw and hung on. The wind slowed for a moment, and Steffan forced the roof down onto the wall, then leaned on it. As the wind picked up again, he fumbled with his hammer and a nail. He put the first nail through and it bit solid wood. The second nail didn't catch, but the third and fourth ones did. Relaxing for a moment, he stood up straight.

The wind grabbed the roof again and pulled it up even further. Steffan leapt at the corner and just barely caught it. Gasping, he tried pulling it down. The straw slipped from his fingers. He gripped harder, catching a finger on one of the twine bindings. The wind pulled. Steffan's arms ached as he fought to hold on.

He struggled, and got a better grip with one hand, then dug the fingers of his other hand through the binding. The wind jerked and Steffan yelped as the twine bit into his fingers. He took a breath, ignored the pain, and slowly pulled the roof lower. While holding the binding, he got his other arm on top of the thatch to steady it, then ran a length of twine through the binding, and released his hand. It was stiff and bloodied, but still working. Steffan wrapped the ends of the twine around it. The wind pulled, but the roof did not come loose.

The nails that had hit wood still stood straight in the beam. Steffan added a row of four others on the inside part of the wood. He wrapped the twine around the first three nails, pulled the roof down, slid the twine to the inside, and slowly released it. Another gust tore at the roof. It held. Steffan thanked the good fortune, then ran inside, grabbed the twine and wrapped it around the inside nails.

The nails bent with the pull on them but held. Steffan decided there was no point in hoping they would be able to withstand the rest of the storm. He put in a row of nails all along the top of the wall at that corner, fed twine through the thatch bindings and wrapped it around the nails.

Gasping, he stepped back to view his work. The wind continued to howl, but the roof held. He began to feel the chill.

He staggered over to the kitchen fireplace, and put some more wood on the fire. Then he stripped and laid his once clean clothes out to dry. After a few minutes warming himself, he went upstairs and put on his nightshirt. His fingers throbbed where the binding had cut them. He flexed them, and the blood began freshly oozing. With exhaustion weighing every part of his body down, he made his way back to the kitchen and pulled a strip of clean cloth from Ella's rag bag to use as a bandage. He pulled the table bench up to the fire, wrapped his blanket around him, and waited.


The walk to the Friederich house was uneventful, merely long and exhausting. Ella's limbs were heavy, cold, and complaining by the time the village came into view. Berencia coughed harder and harder.

As they approached the first houses, the men went ahead a bit. A sudden gust caught Ella and Berencia and slammed them against a wall. Berencia coughed for a long minute.

"Are you all right?" gasped Ella.

"Oh, sure. I've made it farther with worse." Berencia wiped her lips, but not before Ella saw the dark stain on her fingers.

"You shouldn't have come."

"Someone has to train you," Berencia said. "And don't try sending me back. It'll be three times as hard going against the wind."

"Berencia?" Asgarth called anxiously.

"Mother!" Edward ran up.

Berencia pushed herself from the wall. "I'm fine. Let me alone. I'm perfectly all right. Cindy, you're ready?"

"If you are."

The streets offered some protection from the wind's buffets. Ella felt wet and miserable and wondered why she had left her fire. Berencia slogged along without complaint. Ella resolved to imitate her, and comforted herself with memories of a hot fire in a warm, solid palace, with soft down comforters, and hot mulled wine.

At the Friederich house, Mr. Friederich was calm. It was his sixth child, and it was nothing new to him. The children were asleep. Asgarth and Edward chatted amiably with Mr. Friederich, while Ella and Berencia went to the back room. Mrs. Friederich was in the middle of a contraction and cried out.

"Go ahead and yell, Mrs. Friederich," said Berencia. "We're here, and everything's going to be just fine. Good. Mr. Friederich already put out the water and towels. And here's a good knife. Wonderful. Cindy, always check to see that warm water and towels are out, and the knife for cutting the cord. Someone with as many as the Friederichs you don't have to worry as much. They know what to do. It's these first and second-time fathers. They panic, and scare the mother, and they forget things. So check first. There won't be time later. Then get rid of the father. This is no place for a man to be unless it's the baby being born. What are you smiling for?"

"We were alone when the twins came. We had no help. Alex had to catch both of them."

"Then you know from experience what good men are." Berencia went over to Mrs. Friederich. "How are you, dear?"

"I've been laboring since last night. The water didn't break until after the storm came, so that's why we waited- Oh!"

Berencia waited until the pain subsided. "They're coming pretty fast, are they?"

"Not that fast."

"Well, not to worry. We'll see how you're doing in a minute. I've got a helper with me tonight. Cindy Murdren. You know her. She used to help at births before she came here, and now she's learning to midwive."

"She's a good nurse."

"She's got the healing knack, all right. Let's get your legs up, and your bloomers off, and we'll see how far down the little dickens is. Cindy, wash your hands."

Ella did so as another pain hit. "I'm washed."

"Good. Mrs. Friederich's ready. Put your hand up the passage."

"What?" Ella's mouth fell open. "We never did that."

"This is no time to be modest. Put your hand up the passage and tell me what you feel."

Nervously, Ella did as she was told. "It's smooth, and there's a small hole in the middle, about the size of a groat."

"You should be further than that for pains this

fast." Berencia's hands explored the swollen belly.

"Should we call the doctor?" Ella asked.

"If you were by yourself, I would. But I've done enough of these. Ah, there's a kick. The baby's all right. It's just a breach. Come here, Cindy. Feel this."

"It's a breach?" gasped Mrs. Friederich in fear.

"It's passing all right, or I'd have already called the doctor," replied Berencia, patting her hand. "There, Cindy, can you feel the head?"

"Yes. And here's the torso. Both feet are together."

"So, it'll pass all right. Breaches can be a real problem, but this one won't be. It'll just be a long night."

The hours passed slowly. Mrs. Friederich's labor was hard, and the pains kept coming faster, but the womb took forever to open. At last, the two tiny feet entered the passage. The rest of the baby came quickly after that.

"Mrs. Friederich, one more good push!" Berencia called as she stood over Ella's shoulder. "Careful, now, she's tearing. Well, I've my catgut. That's a trick I learned from the doctor. And here's our baby! A fine little boy. Here, I'll wrap it. Do some of your needlework, Cindy. She won't feel a thing. She won't even notice the afterbirth coming. Start sewing before she wakes up."

Ella swallowed back the bile and went to work.

The sun was up and shining with that brightness that only comes after a storm when Ella left the house with the others. The walk home was a blur. Ella stumbled into the house to find the children still asleep, and Steffan curled up on the bench in front of the fire.

She went over and gently shook him.

"Hm! What?" He bolted upright.

"It's just me."

"Oh. I must've fallen asleep." He blinked and looked at her. "Did you sleep any?"

"No. Arlette is coming over with breakfast for you and the children. I'm going upstairs."

"Was it a rough delivery?"

"Sort of. It was a breach. Mostly it just took its time."

"Breach?"

"Feet first." Ella yawned. "I expect you'll be learning a bit about child birthing, too."

"I already know more than I want. You can do all the midwiving you care to. I've done my share, and I don't care to do any more."

Ella laughed sleepily and went upstairs. Steffan followed her a few minutes later to get dressed, and found her face down on the bed with her shoes and cloak still on. Chuckling, he removed her top garments and put a blanket over her.

# CHAPTER TWELVE

The storm left behind all manner of devastation. Roofs were torn off, trees uprooted. Many a kitchen garden had to be replanted with quick growing carrots and turnips. The only good thing the storm had done was kill the weevils that had been blighting the wheat crop. Unfortunately, when it came time for harvesting, there was very little wheat left.

Steffan had only a third of the grain sacks he'd had the year before. Half of the apples had been lost to the storm. The hops had remained unharmed, but since Mr. Aleman's customers had less money to spend on beer, he needed fewer hops and had less money to spend on them.

"There's going to be a lot of babies this summer," Asgarth observed as he and Steffan sullenly rode back from the miller's.

"Why's that?" Steffan asked. He was driving Max and had let the reins loose in his hands.

Asgarth looked at him, then laughed. "And what do you do when your heart is down, and you've no money for beer?"

"I don't drown my problems in beer, Asgarth."

"But you drown them in your wife, don't you? If you don't, I'd like to know where else you turn."

Steffan shifted. "Ah. Now I've caught your meaning."

"It's the only comfort a poor man has, and a costly one it can be, too."

"Well, there's a great deal of contentment to be had from your children. Even that blight doesn't seem to matter as much when I see them gathered at the supper table. If I can just keep food on it."

"There won't be much this year, but we'll make it. I've kept my family through a worse one. We didn't have fruit, eggs or pigs to sell, and we lost the entire crop of wheat."

"You lost all your wheat this year."

"But I've still got my fruit and those two pigs, and I've got some coin saved."

"I've only got a little, myself. I had more, but I had to spend quite a bit when I repitched the roof."

"Then you'll be warm this winter. That's more than many families can say around here."

"True. Well, here we are." Steffan reined in the horse before turning into his yard. "Asgarth, you're right. I don't have that much to complain about, and feeling sorry for myself isn't going to help, anyway."

"Now, don't be so hard on yourself, Murdren. We all need to complain a little every now and then. And I suspect you never had to worry about feeding your family before."

"No, that's one thing I was spared. I'm still not used to it even after all this time."

"This is your first really bad harvest, too. We all go through it. After you've made it through one or two, you find out just how tight you can make your belt. Once you know that, another comes, and it don't seem so bad. You know you can make it because you've done it before. That's what makes you strong, providing you let it."

"And that is wisdom. I know you're not one for sentiment, John, and neither am I, but we couldn't have survived without you and your family's kindness. I just want to say thank you."

"You're a good man, Alex. You make it easy. And you're welcome." Asgarth let himself down from the wagon. "Well, I'd best be seeing what trouble my boys have gotten into. Thanks for the ride, Murdren."

"You're welcome." Steffan chucked the reins and started Max into the yard.

Soon after, the weather turned cold. There was snow on the ground for All Hallow's Eve, which ruined many of the late squashes and other roots. The harvest festival that year was subdued and frozen. A week later, there was a thaw, but it didn't last long. By Christmas, the snow was piled high around the houses.

Two days before the holiday, Edward Asgarth was starting for the village when he saw Ella leave the house and head for the barn.

"Hullo!" he called and trotted over. "It's too late for milking. Is something wrong?"

"No. Be careful on that ice, Edward. I've just got to check the animals."

Edward followed her into the barn. "Doesn't Mr. Murdren usually do that?"

"Yes, but he's been sick these past few days. He's better now, thank the Lord." Ella took a spade and shoveled dung and dirty straw from Daffy's stall.

"You should have asked us. We could have helped."

"Edward, out of the stall. Daffy hates strangers,

and I don't want you kicked. It's no trouble to do, anyway."

"It's a job for a man."

Ella laughed. "Well, the man is sick, and the job still needs doing, so I'm doing it. Mr. Murdren has had to bake the bread a few mornings. If he can do that, I can shovel dung."

"That's a queer way of doing things, but I expect we'd best get used to doing it that way at our house."

"How is your mother?"

"She's not taken to her bed completely, but Arlette's doing all her work. It's awful hard on her, trying to be the mother without really being one, and it's just as hard for Mother to watch. Poor Arlette's so young, too. She should be worrying about which boy she can catch, and not about whether we'll have enough flour to get through the winter, and if we'll have enough herbs to keep mother comfortable."

"Your other sisters help, don't they?"

"Yes. But they don't feel the responsibility as bad, and they shouldn't. They're only girls. They shouldn't have to."

"No. No child ever should, but it happens sometimes that they must, and frequently they're that much stronger for it. I'm sure it's a comfort to your mother to know that her daughters are so well prepared to care for their own families." Ella pitched some hay into Daffy's trough. "And speaking of that, aren't you off to visit with some sweetheart?"

Edward blushed. "Eleanor Keinfeld. The prettiest face in the village, don't you think?"

"She's one of them. But isn't there some

competition for her hand?" Smiling, Ella took up the shovel again and went to work on Max's stall.

"A bit. I admit I'm not the only who's sweet on her. But I've got a good farm coming to me, and Father will help me let a room in the village until there's space for us in the house."

"Steady, Max. Does she like you?"

"That's hard to say. You know how these girls tease a man."

"Not really. I must confess, I was openly willing to accept Mr. Murdren very soon after we met."

"Not to hear him tell it. He says he had a time catching you."

"Catching up to me would be more accurate. There were some complications, though they were resolved in a couple days. But you're right. I've heard other girls are more coy."

"That they are. Eleanor would be quite a catch. Her father's promised ten crowns for her dowry, and since he's a weaver, clothes wouldn't be so dear."

"The question is, Edward, do you love her?"

Edward frowned. "I don't know. I expect I could learn to love her. The trouble is, I could love her a great deal after knowing her a while, and that's the only way to love someone, you know. But if I don't start courting her now, she'll be married off to someone else, and we could have been the right ones all along."

"Sounds like you've got quite a bit of competition."

"Not real competition. True, most every boy around is after her, but she invites me to call more than anyone except Mr. Silbeck. He's looking for a second wife, you know, and him being a goldsmith, he's pretty wealthy."

"And he's not very old, either. Well, if you lose her to him, I hope it's for love and not his money."

"If it's to his money, I haven't lost a thing."

"Well spoken. You'd best go quickly to courting if you expect to have a chance."

"I guess I'd better." Edward started out, then paused. "Uh, thanks, Mrs. Murdren."

"You're welcome, Edward."

Ella finished with the livestock, then went back to the house.

Steffan's fever had finally broken, and he was resting. Barth's cough had been going for several days, and he was looking flushed. The twins were warm, also, but still active. Alicia was the last well one, and her eyes were starting to get red.

Christmas morning, a baby needed delivering. Ella returned home after dark, utterly drained and sniffling. The next morning she woke up with a fever. Steffan, at least, was up and took care of both her and the twins, who were throwing up. Alicia put Barth to bed in the afternoon and tended to him as best she could.

Ella was almost well three days later when Alicia took sick. Barth still had a small fever and remained in bed. While the twins no longer had fevers, they still had coughs and sniffles. Alicia refused to admit she was sick. But when she came to the table for lunch, Ella sent the little girl right to bed.

By evening, Steffan was worried. Alicia's skin was burning hot to the touch, and she tossed fitfully. Her cough was deep and persistent. Ella put cloth after cloth on her forehead and found enough mustard for a small plaster for her chest.

"Perhaps we should call the doctor," Steffan said late that evening.

Ella shook her head. "There isn't anything he can do that I haven't already done."

"He might have some medicine that would help."

"Not for fever." Ella wrung out another cloth. "We'll see what happens in the next hour or two. She doesn't have a rash, so I doubt it's scarlet fever. It's probably the same influenza we've all had."

"None of us has had that high a fever." Steffan sighed. "I'm sorry, Ella. You know what you're doing."

"I understand, dearest. She should be coming to the crisis point soon. Until then, it's just waiting to see how it comes out."

Steffan paced. An hour passed, as did another. Ella continued changing cloths on the hot little forehead. Steffan went to the well twice for more water. Finally, he touched his daughter's cheek.

"It seems cooler," he said.

"I was thinking it might be. Her cough has settled down. I'm going to wait a few minutes more, just to be sure."

Steffan returned to the kitchen, and moodily gazed at the fire. Fifteen minutes later, Ella joined him.

"We might as well try for some sleep now," she said. "She's still pretty sick, but the fever's lessened, and she's sleeping soundly."

"Ella, I know you're exhausted. But I feel so lonely right now, and so powerless. My baby could be dying, and there's nothing I can do."

"It came pretty close for a while there, but I'm

confident she's going to live. And you have done a lot. It was so much easier for me to rest and get well knowing that you were able to take care of the children for me. Now, come along to bed before you get sick again."

Upstairs, Steffan slid his nightshirt over the long woolens he'd been wearing steadily since the first snow. Ella remained in her woolen petticoats and stockings. Steffan's hand found its way to a bare spot on her shoulder after he'd slid under the blanket next to her.

"I shouldn't be bothering you," he whispered. "You're so tired."

"And you're not?"

"I am, but you've been working so hard, and I like being with you when I'm tired more than you like being with me when you're tired."

"That's true, and you're very nice about not bothering me when I am. But I get the feeling you need some comforting."

Steffan tiredly chuckled. "If you could possibly manage it."

"I think I might actually be able to."

"Thank you." Steffan reached over and tenderly kissed her mouth.

Alicia remained feverish for the next two days, but it diminished over that time. Barth remained in bed also, until Steffan angrily demanded that Barth stop playing weakling and made the boy get dressed.

By the time the children were well again, Steffan and Ella faced a new worry. Food supplies were getting low, and there were still two months of winter to get through.

"We'll be eating a lot of eggs," said Ella one afternoon, about a week after the new year began.

Another winter storm had passed the night before, and the snow had drifted up over the windows, leaving the house in eerie darkness.

"I just hope the grain holds out," grumbled Steffan.

"Well, we could kill a couple of the hens. That will give us some meat and some soup for a while."

"We could also butcher the pig."

"Steffan, quit teasing."

"I am now. But if things get bad enough, I won't be."

"If things get bad enough, we'll have to. But they'll be a lot worse before we do. I don't suppose we can all eat a little less, starting now. It would help."

"Then that's what we'll do." Steffan sighed silently. He'd already been eating less and was getting tired of the empty feeling in his belly.

A week and a half later, Steffan returned from the barn to find Ella screaming at the children. Barth and Alicia had been directing the twins to sneak portions of food from the cold room when Ella's back had been turned. Steffan sent Ella to the loft, then lectured the children, and made each of them sit on their beds without moving.

He left the children's' room and went to the loft. It was filled with a sour, nauseating smell. Ella sat on the bed, staring into space.

"The children are being punished," Steffan said. "I'd like to know why you were so upset. You've never screamed at anyone like that, Ella."

"I'm sorry."

"You've been so irritable the past few days. Is it being closed up in this house with so little?"

"I'm sick again, Steffan."

Steffan swallowed. "That's what I smell. Have you got a fever?"

"Not that kind of sick!" Ella snapped. She sniffed suddenly. "Oh, no. I've done it again. I can't seem to hold onto my temper. Steffan, I'm so worried."

"There'll be enough food. Somehow, someway, we'll make it be enough."

"Haven't you been listening? I'm sick again! Like I was with Barth, with Alicia, with the twins."

"You're with child." Steffan happily rushed to her side. "Ella, that's wonderful. Another little blessing."

"Another mouth to feed!" Ella began sobbing. "Another child to clothe. We can't even feed the ones we have."

"We are feeding them. It's not as much as we're used to, but they're eating. And, no, we don't have a lot of food right now. But by the time this new one's here, things will surely be better."

"What if they aren't?"

"We can't think like that. If they aren't any better, then we'll find ways to manage. It's not as if we can change the situation. We'll do what we've been doing, which is just doing the best we can. It will be all right, darling."

"I'm so scared, Steffan."

"Sh. It's all right. We'll manage."

"If you hadn't been so blasted depressed."

Steffan paused, counting. "That may be. As

Asgarth says, it's a poor man's only comfort, and sometimes a costly one. But, Ella, I can't help thinking it's still a blessing. We have such beautiful children, the thought of another one simply fills me with joy. I know you're worried, my dearest, and we should be. But if we're to have another child, then we have to trust that good fortune will provide us with the means to keep it."

"You're right, darling. Things have just been so close."

"I know. And you're feeling awful, and we have been snowed in for a very long time. You've been bearing up well, Ella. You deserve a good blow up. I just wish I could have been the one to take it."

"I should apologize to the children."

"After they have been soundly punished. It was Alicia's idea, you know, and Barth who decided they should do it. The little beasts."

Ella chuckled. "You just said a minute ago that we had such beautiful children."

"Well, they can be beasts. That just makes them children. Are you up to coming downstairs?"

"I don't know."

"That's one good thing about you being sick. You won't be eating as much."

"Steffan, don't mention food."

"Sorry. Oops! Here's the pail."


Berencia Asgarth passed from earthly life to the next in the later part of that winter. In the week preceding, Ella spent much of her time at Berencia's side, coaxing soothing herbs and a little opium into the dying woman. Whenever Ella was there, Asgarth spent his time with Steffan, talking about everything but the fact that Asgarth was losing the woman he had loved for twenty-one years.

When Berencia at last passed, there was almost a sense of relief, for she had been in great pain. Getting the body to the church for the funeral was difficult, for the snow still reached the rooftops. Paths had been cleared to the barns and across the road, but there was no path cleared to the village. Steffan helped prepare a sledge, and joined in the grim task of getting the body out of the house and to the top of the snow.

Asgarth had already purchased a grave, although it could not be dug because of the weather. The old priest put the body in the church's crypt and assured Asgarth that at the first thaw, Berencia would be properly put to rest. Hers was not the only body down there waiting, sadly enough.

# THE THIRD YEAR

## CHAPTER THIRTEEN

The first thaw started in the middle of March. Within days, most of the snow was gone, and the rivers were swollen. Then another storm arrived and covered the village and surrounding farms with almost a foot of snow. That stayed for another two weeks, and then, at last, winter left for that year.

The farmers of the village worked frantically to plow and seed their fields, praying that the snow would not surprise them with another visit. Instead, spring storms swelled the rivers in the neighboring villages, and many families were flooded out of their homes.

Steffan and Asgarth sat in the front room of the Asgarth house, watching the Asgarth's youngest, Gen, play with Steffan's children. Now two, James and Nella were talking and still very active. Alicia, who had just turned five, had trouble keeping up with them. But Barth, who was soon to turn seven, had little patience with the smaller children and hung on thirteen-year-old Gen.

Thunder shook the house.

"I hope it doesn't flood here," sighed Steffan, wondering when Ella would return from delivering another baby.

"It won't," replied Asgarth. "We're on much higher ground."

Steffan shook his head and looked out the window at the rain as it poured down on his muddy field.

"It's still worrisome. After that terrible winter, and the blight, we can't take any more losses."

"Well, worrying about it isn't going to change a thing. The worst that can happen is that we die, and we're all going to anyway. Does it really make that much difference if we go sooner than later?"

Steffan looked at Asgarth, puzzled. "You seem a little bitter."

"Perhaps I am. Gen was saying just the other day that I've been mean lately. I thought I'd accepted it."

"It takes time. Asgarth, there's no fault in grieving. My mother used to say a year for mourning, then it's time to get on with your life. But for an uncle of mine, it took three years, and my mother never once faulted him."

"You're right. I've never been alone like this before. When I was a lad and unmarried, I didn't know the difference. I expect when it's my time, I'll get to the gates of Heaven and she'll be waiting for me, scolding me for fussing so over her, but if I hadn't, she'd know it and be hurt." Asgarth sighed. "Must make the best of things. Spring festival's in two weeks, isn't it? In good time. We all need some celebrating."

But the next day, the duke's guard came through with some news that left the villagers even more depressed. Asgarth was furious. He growled and was so ill-tempered that Edward and Giles begged him to return to the meetings he'd forsaken since his wife's death.

Woodman and Kiffs were waiting when Asgarth arrived. Lyle scurried in moments later.

"Cyril can't come," he announced. "He's busy with his father, altering records."

"That's a kindness," said Kiffs.

"I've been doing the same since I heard," said Woodman.

"Raising the taxes!" snorted Asgarth. "Of all the most preposterous things. We're bled dry already after last winter. Where does that fool woman think we'll get the money?"

"You heard the announcement," said Kiffs. "The magistrate will take a full accounting, and each man shall be taxed according to what he and his neighbor has made this year."

"Do we have full cooperation?" asked Woodman.

"There's no way to be sure," Lyle answered. "Fortunately, Sir Leonard plans to use Mr. Cyril's records to tax the farmers. I suppose the odd tradesman or two won't be noticeable. All we have to do now is hope an honest farmer doesn't start asking questions."

"Some fool could say something wrong," said Asgarth. "Maybe we'd best warn them."

Woodman shifted. "Maybe not. We could expose a spy or two by watching to see who speaks up. Of course, that might make things awkward for Mr. Cyril, and we need the younger Cyril too much to let him be captured."

"I wouldn't worry about that," said Lyle. "When Sir Leonard asked the older Cyril for his records, he made a tremendous fuss about having burnt them for warmth while the snow was so bad. He's redoing them from memory. If there's differences, he can't be held to account for them."

"That's good." Woodman nodded. "As for the tradesmen on my street, I doubt there'll be any trouble with them. They're furious, and I've heard the others are, too."

"So is everyone," said Kiffs. "There isn't a shopkeeper in the square that isn't burning a candle or two changing records before handing them over to the magistrate."

"The farmers in my area are all saying things that could land them in prison if the duke's guard were around," Lyle said. "I've said a few of them, myself."

"What about the farmers in your area, Asgarth?" asked Woodman.

"The same. Ooph! You should have seen Murdren. It was eerie, it was."

"What?" snickered Lyle. "He actually yelled?"

"Nothing like. He went white, then pressed his lips together, and did not say one word. I don't think I've ever seen a man so furious. He seems to think Her Majesty is definitely trying to build up the army."

"What for?" asked Kiffs.

"To conquer other kingdoms," Asgarth replied. "Or so Murdren says. I wouldn't be surprised if he were right."

"Why would he think that?" Lyle asked.

"Probably because he remembers what the queen's mother did while she was regent," Woodman answered. "We were very close to attacking Karperia when King Bartholemew assumed power. The revolt came about because he did not disband the army quickly enough, which in retrospect was a very wise move. Any change in power can make a kingdom vulnerable."

"So what are we going to do now?" asked Lyle. "Besides hide what little we have."

"We wait," replied Woodman.

By the end of the week, the taxes had been paid with much grumbling. Steffan was pleased that his total was much less than he expected, but was very worried about what the extra taxation meant.

"Steffan, wait," said Ella. "It's not the right time. We don't have enough support."

"We may not have the time. Furthermore, every man who tries that ring looks like a bigger fool than the one previously. That's not a good way to establish credibility."

"Considering why the ring doesn't fit anyone else, I would think you'd have a little more faith that part of it will be taken care of when the time comes."

Steffan mused. "Your godmother, she has been very helpful. I guess I worry too much, don't I?"

"Yes, you do."

"And speaking of things to worry about, how are you feeling?"

"Quite well." Ella patted the belly that was just swelling enough to indicate eventual childbirth. "I am getting tired of looking at these four walls, especially after being snowed in here all winter. But I'd still be too embarrassed to leave."

Steffan nodded. "I know how you feel. Nobody around here seems to mind women carrying children being out and about, but I still get embarrassed every time I see one."

"It's your palace breeding. I always thought it odd that they kept everything like that so mysterious. I still can't understand why. I'm just glad my irregular bringing up wasn't quite so sheltered. Nonetheless, I feel so immodest when someone but you or the children sees me with my belly so large."

Ella remained at home for the spring festival. Steffan spent much of the week at home also. Each day he took the children into the village to enjoy the festivities and spent two evenings gambling. The first night he lost, but the second night, in the middle of the week, he won enough that he felt justified in purchasing a special treat.

The next day, after sending Barth and Alicia off to the games, with strict instructions to keep careful watch over the twins, Steffan paid a visit to the butcher shop. As usual, Isolde Dirkman and Isabelle Plainfield were busy gossiping and insulting Penelope Drusse.

"Good day, ladies," said Steffan pleasantly as he walked in. "Mrs. Drusse, I'd like to make a purchase for my wife."

"Why can't she do it herself?" asked Isabelle, knowing full well.

"She's in her time of confinement," Steffan replied. "Mrs. Drusse, you wouldn't happen to have any goose, would you?"

"No, not today."

"It's a silly tradition if you ask me," said Isolde. "Comes from being city bred, I suppose. Maybe that's why city people think they're so much better than us. They don't want people knowing they seek comfort, even if it means penning up a woman when she's carrying a wee one."

"Mrs. Drusse, what about a duck? That looks like a fine one there."

"Even if it means embarrassing her husband by making him do the shopping."

"Thank you, Mrs. Drusse. Cindy will be so surprised."

"I wonder if Cindy will go help a poor laboring woman when she's in confinement."

Steffan paused in the doorway and turned. "Mrs. Dirkman, don't the Irlichs live on your street?"

"Right next to me."

"I'm surprised you didn't notice. Cindy was over there most of yesterday catching their latest."

"Well, I'm a busy woman. I'm all alone, you know. I have to look out to my own interests, especially with taxes so dear. Not that there aren't some who change their records before the magistrate can get them."

"Happily, I have none to change. But I do remember hearing that Sir Leonard received your records later than anyone else's."

Isolde blushed. "I... I had to find them."

"I understand, Mrs. Dirkman." Steffan smiled innocently.

"All right, so I made a few changes. I've a right to keep my own money. I'm a poor widow. I've no husband to earn money for me. I must take what I can get, and keep it as best I can. And I'm not the only one doing it. This whole village changed their records, including the farmers."

Steffan shrugged. "Either way, Mrs. Dirkman,

next time I'd think twice about insulting someone for doing what you, yourself, are also doing. Good day."

Steffan left the shop, irked that Isolde Dirkman had angered him, and not sure why. The whole taxation issue was an uncomfortable one for him. Taxes were why most of his life had been so comfortable, and yet, having had to pay them, he felt somewhat guilty for living so well on other people's work.

At the same time, he also knew how necessary many of those taxes were. The kingdom needed an army to defend itself, and no matter how hard one tried to call it rationalization, the royal family was required to maintain a wealthy lifestyle, simply to retain its position amongst the royalty of other kingdoms. A good strategic marriage was a very powerful peacekeeper and trade tool, and it was hard to make such arrangements without a certain amount of status.

Steffan paused. He had resisted just such a marriage, himself, although in his case, the marriage wasn't that great an advantage. Even without strategic marriages, status was important for keeping peace. Few people would attack a kingdom with the power of wealth on its side. There were also the kingdom's subjects. Even as they grumbled about paying for their monarch's luxuries, they would not respect a monarch who didn't have them.

It was then that Steffan realized why Isolde had angered him. He had wondered why his tax had been so low. The magistrate's man had muttered something about all the wheat being lost in that area. Steffan hadn't lost all of his, but only Asgarth and the miller knew that. Isolde had said that everyone had altered their records. It seemed likely that the elder Cyril had altered his records, and Steffan unwittingly had cheated the queen of her due.

Steffan mused over that. Having been on the receiving end of the taxes, the thought of not paying what was owed was uncomfortable. Yet the tax Lanicia was exacting from her people was unjustly heavy, and would lead to war and destruction.

"There is almost no law that should not be broken for a good and just cause," Steffan's father had told him. "That is not to say that a good end will justify any means to achieve it. But there are times when the greater good requires that the letter of the law be overlooked."

That was somewhat different than breaking a law outright. Steffan could not follow a law that would lead to the destruction of his people. Even dethroned, he still felt responsible for the people's welfare. It was his responsibility, had been since the day he was born, and his father had never let him forget it.

Steffan collected his children and went home, thinking about a similar problem. He had heard the whisperings about revolt, and the possibility of removing Lanicia from the throne. Such treason was the very thing he wanted to accomplish, but with one significant difference. He was the true heir to the throne, not Lanicia, and had a right to depose her.

But what if the revolt occurred, and the people did not want him to take the throne? Could he justify taking part in such action? For obvious reasons, he had always believed in the monarchy and had never considered other forms of government. Most of the talk he had heard centered on finding another king. Yet there were a few who mentioned setting up a republic. As a monarch, himself, could he support a form of government that was opposed to the lifestyle in which he had been raised?

He asked Ella the question that evening after the children were asleep. She thought for a long time.

"Steffan, you said that your greatest responsibility above all is the welfare of people. I think the question you must answer is what is best for them? There are so many different things that could happen with a revolt. I don't think you could support a bad monarch or some other sort of despot."

"No. That would be the absolute worst. But is it just my own egotism that I think I am the best possible option?"

"Not entirely. You've spent a lifelong apprenticeship to the position, and those last few months of your father's illness, you were as good as a journeyman. I know of no one else who has that sort of training."

"I've always assumed that I should take the throne back. And if I failed it would be because Lanicia defeated me, and not that there was someone else to take it."

"There's some egotism in that, but it's understandable. The throne is your inheritance, and it does rightfully belong to you. If the revolt goes otherwise, it will be because the people have decided that another type of government would be better, in which case, you have no right to lead them. It's always possible that someone else could do your job better than you, and I think there's wisdom in being open to that possibility. But for the moment, you should fight for what is yours."

"As usual, Ella, your wisdom has outstripped mine."

Ella laughed. "Perhaps I should take the throne, then."

"Wisdom isn't all of it, my dear. There's knowledge of laws and legal workings, understanding of political and military strategy, diplomacy, taxation."

"Some of which are my greater weaknesses. Rest easy, my darling. I don't want your job. I'm too compassionate to be truly fair. That is an incredible gift you have."

"There's an idea. If we get a new government, and I'm not a part of it, perhaps I can get the opportunity to train as an advocate or magistrate."

"Perhaps you should do it now."

"No. It would be too easy to be recognized. But it is nice to consider. I don't think I could manage to remain a farmer."

Ella chuckled. "It doesn't matter to me what you are, as long as you are true to yourself."

"There's little chance of me being false with you around." Smiling, Steffan pulled her into his arms.

The duke's men arrived in the village two days later. They started at the far end, searching houses for hidden money and goods. It didn't matter if the inhabitants were home. Steffan had just entered the square when he heard the screams. His children were with the Asgarth brood again elsewhere, and Steffan had ridden into the village on Max to fetch a tool that the blacksmith was repairing.

Steffan had yet to tie Max, and he pulled the horse into a dark alley as two guards rode up to the stand where several farmers had tied their horses. With the guards in place, none of the horses' owners could leave the village. Other guards had surrounded the village. Everyone in the village was trapped and prevented from rushing home to protect their goods or warn their neighbors.

There was only one possible way out. The workings of a village's back streets are not that familiar to any but the inhabitants. While the searchers were at work at the one end, Steffan led his horse around the perimeter of the village to the mill, which sat next to a river, the other side of which was covered with thick woods. The mill was also unguarded.

Even without the swelling from the heavy snow and spring storms, the river ran fast there, and deep. With the horses captured, no man could cross, so the duke's guard had decided defending it was unnecessary. Steffan had his horse, and Max was a powerful animal.

It took all of Steffan's considerable skill as a horseman to coax the beast into the rushing stream. The water was frigid. Steffan's own fear protected him from the cold. Max just wanted to get out of the water, and if the only way out was the other side, he was going to get there as fast as he could.

A cool breeze chilled Steffan as he slid off Max's back on the other side. He walked Max through the thick tangle of branches to a point where the men guarding the village would be unlikely to see him. Steffan scrambled up onto the horse's bare back, then kicked the beast into a gallop.

They cut through Mr. Friederich's wheat fields. Steffan jumped Max over the stone wall that separated the wheat from Mr. Bosgood's sheep pasture. Even when they had gone far enough that they couldn't be seen from the village, Steffan avoided the road. Only Mrs. Pieter was home to object to Steffan riding across the fields, and she was happy for the warning.

"Asgarth!" Steffan bellowed as he rode into his own yard.

Asgarth came running from the house. "What is it?"

"Hide your money and your goods. The duke's men are raiding for the taxes."

Asgarth bolted for his house, as Steffan did for his. Ella was on her feet.

"Steffan, did I hear you right?" she asked anxiously.

"Yes. They're tearing up beds, everything. Hurry. We've got to find a better place for those medallions. You go get them. I'll get the money sack."

Ella hurried upstairs and removed from under the straw mattress the gold medallions with the jeweled insignia of their kingdom. If they were found, it would mean death.

Steffan was counting out the coins from the money sack.

"Here's a crown and a half, some silver and bits," he said, handing Ella the coins. "They should find something. Hide them under the mattress."

"But what about the medallions?" Ella asked. "Steffan, if they're taking everything apart, where can we hide them?"

"I know of a place they probably won't look, especially if it doesn't look as though we've been warned, and if they find something else hidden. Remember, they're looking for money and hidden goods, not royal insignia. Besides, we won't be here. The cherry orchard needs clearing. We might as well do that. If by some stroke of bad fortune they find the insignia, it'll be easier for us to escape then."

"The children aren't with us."

"Cover the bread as if it's set to rise, and I'll meet you in the barn."

Ella hurried upstairs to hide the money. There were two hams in the cold room that could be taken, as well as some sausage. Fortunately, there were no other jewels to worry about.

Steffan ran for the barn. The guard was not yet in view, but that didn't mean he had time to dawdle. He made the medallions into as small a bundle as possible. He looked quickly around and found what he was looking for. Bracing himself, he shoved the small sack into a pile of Daffy's droppings. Daffy kindly went to work and finished the job.

Roscoe, as usual, was out of his pen. As Steffan rinsed his hand in a pail of water kept for such purposes, he realized that the pig could be considered a fat prize indeed. Ella appeared in the doorway. Steffan grabbed some tools and sacks and hurried out of the barn.

"Call the pig," he ordered. "We're taking him to the woods with us. If I can't butcher him, I'll be damned before the duke's guard does."

"Steffan!" she chided, then called the pig.

Roscoe appeared immediately, and trotted along at

Ella's side, as they hurried to the woods.

"You shouldn't be going so hard," Steffan grumbled about midway there.

"I haven't any choice, therefore, I must take the chance. We can't risk being recognized by a guardsman. That wouldn't do the baby any good either."

Hidden by the trees of the cherry orchard, Steffan watched while Ella waited a little further in.

"They're going through the house," he told her. "I can't tell what's going on, but I don't hear anything breaking. Some of them are going into the barn. I hope Max has cooled down enough."

"Why?"

"I rode him so hard to get here, he'll be sweating, which will look suspicious, and they'll look harder. They're leaving the barn now. I don't think they have anything with them. Good. They're leaving."

As Steffan's farm was the furthest out, the duke's men returned to the village. Steffan waited a while longer as a precaution, then he and Ella returned to the house.

Straw had been flung everywhere. The rising bread dough had been slashed to pieces, as had much of the food in the cold room. All of the beds had been torn apart, with the linens and straw strewn all over the floor. Her heart heavy with worry, Ella began picking up. Steffan retreated to the barn and returned quickly.

"We're safe," he said, holding up the smelly bundle. "And good fortune was with us again. The cow pats were untouched."

"Is that where you hid them? Please, rinse them off quickly, or are you planning on keeping them there."

"They'd be too easily found if anyone really looked. No. I'm going to have to build a better place."

That evening, Steffan loosened one of the hearth stones and removed it. He dug a deep hole underneath, lined it with straw, and put most of the money as well as the medallions into it. He replaced the stone and filled the cracks in the mortar with cheap plaster.

"There," he said when done. "That plaster will be easily removed, and just as easily replaced, and this way, we don't have to worry about a raid catching us unprepared."

"That's beautiful, Steffan. Even now, I'm not sure which stone is it."

"Three in, and one up. That's not a spot that's likely to get walked on, which will make it harder to find. I don't like losing that crown and a half, but it's better than losing all of it, and our lives."

# CHAPTER FOURTEEN

Ella took a deep breath and braced herself.

"Are you sure you want to do this?" Steffan asked, not sure himself that it was a good idea. "It's getting terribly close to your time."

"I can't let that woman ruin our good name. It's the harvest. Everybody helps, no matter what. If I'm not there and Isolde Dirkman is, it will look bad."

"It will look worse if you deliver in the fields."

"That won't happen. I'll get plenty of warning."

"It's not like you to worry about Isolde Dirkman looking better than you."

"That's the problem, Steffan. It's been terrible the way she's been throwing herself at John Asgarth. Poor Berencia wasn't even in her grave six months when that woman started cooking for him, and visiting, and helping the girls. Not that she's been any help to them. Only when John is around to see her. The girls hate her, and with good reason. There are other widowers in the village. Why does she have to pick on John?"

"He is one of the most prosperous people we have and one of the most respected voices. But what does all this have to do with you going to the harvest?"

"I don't want her looking exceptionally saintly, and..." Ella sighed. "This isn't very nice, but I'm sure she's going to have something nasty to say to me, and I hope John overhears it."

Steffan laughed. "Let the man alone. I agree, it's queer that he hasn't discouraged her, but I'm certain he has some very good reasons."

"He may yet be besotted. She's not unattractive, and she can actually be rather charming when she thinks she'll gain something by it. Are we ready to go?"

"Yes. The children are waiting in the wagon."

"Oh, dear. I'm bigger than a cow." Ella took a deep breath and walked out of the front door.

The Pieter farm was being harvested first. Isolde had arrived early and taken over. The farm wives kept their distance, not quite trusting her. Ella, for her part, stayed with the wives, and steadfastly refused to take part in any gossip. Isolde approached them as they laid out the table for lunch.

"Why, Mrs. Murdren, you came out of your confinement," she said sweetly. "That wasn't necessary. You poor thing, you look as though you were ready to whelp."

Ella blushed. "Everyone helps at harvest time."

"I thought it was especially kind of her to come," said Mrs. Lieswalt. "It's not easy to do something you been taught all your life not to do."

"At least Mrs. Murdren knows where her duty lies," Mrs. Pieter added. "Unlike some who want to take up reins they got no right to hold."

"Ladies, please," said Ella. "We've much work to do."

"You're right, Mrs. Murdren," said Mrs. Pieter. "Mrs. Dirkman, we'll need you to come help us with the threshing. Mrs. Murdren, you'd best tend to the table. You'll not be wanting to thresh with your time being so close."

"But..." Ella started, then realized what Mrs. Pieter was really trying to accomplish. It wasn't very kind, but then again, Ella knew she wasn't in any condition to be doing heavy work. "Thank you, Mrs. Pieter."

It would have been unkinder yet to expose Mrs. Pieter's plan. Isolde Dirkman proved to be terribly inefficient at threshing the wheat grains from their stalks. She whirled and threw herself around in what she fancied was in imitation of the other women. Even Ella found herself chuckling over the woman's efforts.

Most of the other farmers smothered outright laughs and nudged Asgarth, who nudged back and chuckled. At lunch, Isolde made a great show of preparing a plate for Asgarth and making sure he knew which of the delicacies on it she had prepared. Asgarth thanked her and went to sit with the other men.

"She'll be wanting a ring soon," teased Mr. Lieswalt.

Asgarth merely chuckled. Later, Steffan caught Asgarth alone.

"You know, Lieswalt may have been teasing, but he's not far from the truth," said Steffan quietly.

"She already wants a ring," Asgarth replied. "Not that she's said so, of course. But I knew the first time she visited she was courting me."

"Far be it from me to tell a man to whom he should marry-"

"Who said I was marrying her?" Asgarth laughed.

"Then why do you let this continue?"

"A lot of reasons. She's a very good cook, you know. Arlette isn't bad, but she's still beginning, and her mother, God rest her, wasn't that good a cook herself. Not bad, of course, and I'll still be missing her for a long time yet. But Isolde Dirkman has a way with food."

"Cindy is also an excellent cook, and you know you and all your family are welcome at any time."

"True. But Cindy doesn't fuss over me the way Isolde does."

"She's only fussing so you'll marry her."

"Which is exactly why I won't. Heavens, man, what kind of a fool do you think I am? The day I marry Isolde Dirkman is the day I lose all the attention, and fussing, and possibly even the good cooking. I'm liking things the way they are. It's a little short on the comfort side, but I doubt there'd be much of that even if I did marry her."

"But still, it seems terribly cruel to lead her on this way."

Asgarth laughed again. "Alex, lad, look at yourself. Defending Isolde Dirkman, of all people. You'll always take the part of the poorer side."

"All right, I agree she brings it a lot of it on herself."

"She brings all of it on herself. I've made it very clear I'll not be marrying her. She's even tried tricking me into bedding her, so I'll have to." Asgarth grimaced. "Just between you and me, it was no temptation. She's a cold woman at heart, Murdren, and when you've had a warm woman giving you comfort, you want nothing else."

"So you have tried to discourage her."

"Not really. I just told her I wouldn't marry her."

"Then you shouldn't allow her to continue. She's embarrassing herself dreadfully."

"If the woman wants to make a fool of herself, it's none of my lookout."

"Furthermore, Ella is worried sick about you, and frankly, listening to you, so am I."

Asgarth casually glanced around, then lowered his voice.

"Alex, what is the one thing Isolde does more than anything else?"

"Cause trouble."

"She does a bit of that. But what she does more is talk. The woman does not stop, and she knows nothing about keeping secrets. She also knows everything that goes on in the village and thereabouts. Even young Mr. Cyril isn't a better source of news. I'd say it was through her that the duke found out we'd been hiding our goods from the taxman. In fact, it's been my job to make sure Isolde was out here where we could watch her, while we hide some of the grain sacks. How we'll get them milled with the duke's guards watching the Cyrils so closely, I don't know."

"We'd better be careful. We had two raids at the beginning of this month alone."

Asgarth nodded. "I wouldn't worry about it. There's some of us that know a hiding place that most the village doesn't know about. We won't be telling, either. But the wheat will be safe. I'll be guessing they'll take the guard off the Cyrils once they think we've brought in all our wheat. Isolde Dirkman will be certain to bring in a false figure from us. The magistrate will have to assume the others fared as poorly, and we won't be taxed so dear, or if we are, we've plenty to make up for it."

Steffan nodded. "I hate to think of Isolde being used as a pawn, but if she's willing to play the fool, then it's foolish not to use what she brings us."

"Including a few good meals. Did you try that meat roll she made?" Asgarth sighed happily.

That night, Steffan reported to Ella about what Asgarth had said. She was delighted.

"Oh, I know it's terribly mean, Steffan. But it was so lovely seeing that old bag getting her comeuppance. Did you see her threshing? Even I had to chuckle. I was trying so hard to be kind, too. It wasn't that long ago I had to learn."

"True, but you caught on quickly, and were much more graceful in the process, as several of the men pointed out to me. As far as Isolde Dirkman is concerned, it would be best to be wary of her. Asgarth may be finding her useful, but I've a feeling she'll have more trouble for us in the long run."

Ella turned thoughtful. "Steffan, why do you think John Asgarth would find it so profitable to know everything that's going on in the village?"

"I don't know, Cindy. Surely, you don't think he's a spy."

"If he was, why would he risk exposing himself to you as he did today? I wonder if something is going on. Asgarth is a well-respected voice in the village. If there were plans being made to do something, he would naturally be expected to take part."

"What are you getting at?"

"I think a revolt is being planned, or at least some

sort of resistance, and I think our neighbor is one of the leaders."

"Then our friendship is very fortunate." Steffan yawned. "I'm sorry, my dearest. I'm getting very tired all of a sudden, and we do have four more days of harvesting to do."

"You're right. Goodnight, my love."

"Goodnight."

The Lieswalt farm was the last farm to be harvested. As Ella finished washing the dishes from dinner, she felt the first pain. She noted it and said nothing. The second pain came as Steffan helped her into the wagon. She smiled and told him that they had a long night ahead of them. Steffan smiled but groaned.

As the ride progressed, Ella began to get worried. The pains were coming fast and very strong. She did her best to hide it, so as not to frighten the children. When they pulled into the yard, Ella sent Barth after the other midwife.

"Already?" asked Steffan anxiously.

"Yes!" Ella yelped as another pain took hold.

Steffan carefully lifted her from the wagon. She hurried into the house, paused in the kitchen as another pain took her, then went up the ladder to the loft. Steffan followed her into the house, carrying Alicia, who was asleep. He returned two more times with the sleeping twins, then stayed out for a longer while, unhitching and stabling Max. Ella cried when he came back in for the last time.

"Are you all right?" he called.

"Get the water and the knife and come quickly!"

"But the midwife isn't here yet." Steffan scrambled

to get the items.

"Your child is not going to wait." Ella cried out again. "Hurry! It's coming."

Steffan tore up the ladder, swearing under his breath.

"It's all right, now." He set down the pail and knife and checked her. "No! I can see the head already. It's a curse. I'm doomed to catch the rest of your children."

He grabbed the first towel within reach as Ella struggled upright and began pushing again. In another minute, the head was free, then the shoulders. Steffan gently pulled with the next contraction.

"We have a daughter," he said as the baby squawked to life.

Ella collapsed and began laughing hysterically.

An hour later, the midwife arrived to find the baby contentedly nursing, and Steffan cleaning up.

"I ought to be furious," Mrs. Markmardt said holding the infant. "This little one's cheated me out of a good fee. But she's such a lovely baby. Three hours, you say."

"From the first pain to the last," Ella murmured sleepily.

"Well, I'll be leaving you to get your rest."

"My darling, see that she gets at least some of her fee. She came. I'd hate for it to be for nothing."

"Well, at least my rest wasn't disturbed," Mrs. Markmardt chuckled. "And to be honest, I hate catching midwives' babies. They're always telling you what to do."

They named the baby Lorelei at her christening three weeks later. Widow Kinsell was one of the well-wishers who stayed on after mass to celebrate the baptism.

"I'll be sending Dora to you this week," she said after the service. "I've been aching for a fine cake with six eggs, and yours are the finest. Dora said she'd be glad to fetch them from you if you don't mind."

"No, of course not," said Ella.

"We'd be glad to have her," Steffan added.

But inside, he was puzzled. True, they had good eggs, but they weren't the finest, and for Dora to make that long walk just for eggs seemed very odd. Furthermore, why would the Widow announce it as she had?

Steffan got his answer Tuesday. Dora showed up just before lunch with a basket in hand. Ella was puzzled by her request, but went ahead and sent Dora to the barn. Isolde Dirkman wasn't at the Asgarths, so there wasn't any likelihood of scandal. Steffan was not as surprised to find that Dora wanted to talk to him alone. He invited her to sit on a bale of hay next to the chickens' roosts and leaned against the wall.

"It was the widow's idea that everyone know she wanted eggs from you," Dora explained. "She didn't want anyone to suspect anything."

"It's a little unusual for anyone to come out here for eggs, but it's been done. What is she afraid of?"

"Mr. Murdren, I've come to you because I've learned something that needs to be known, but I can't just tell everyone, or I'll get my neck stretched."

"What is it?"

"There's going to be a tax raid this Friday. The orders say march at five of the morning, which means they'll be here by dawn."

"You're sure?"

"Very sure. I read the orders myself."

"You can read."

"There's a man in the village what taught me, I won't say who. You know as well as I do how I knew him. And the widow has been making sure I keep my letters. I may butcher the language as I talk, but I read real well, and write of a fair piece, too."

"Hm. But how did you get to read these orders?"

"That. Well, I know I promised you I wouldn't, but I've gone back to my old trade. Not completely. You see, I was delivering some stitchery to the duke's palace. They've a couple housekeepers up there too lazy to do their own stitchery, so's they send it to the widow, as she does the finest around. Anyway, one of the guards, a captain, and I'm not saying who, got sweet on me. Well, we had a few laughs, for all he's a duke's man, he's rather nice, and he gets me to come to his chamber. Him being an officer, he has a private one. We drank some of his beer, him a lot more than me, and wouldn't you know it, he conks out. Dead to the world. I tried leaving, but it was after dark, and I was afraid one of the guards might arrest me if I was caught wandering around by myself. So I stayed. And there on his desk were the orders for the week. So I says to myself, Dora, there's people in the village what might be interested in what the duke's guard will be up to this week. And I read them. It was mostly who got what watch, and stuff like that. But for Friday, there was marching orders for the raid."

"Dora, that's good information."

"I'll be getting next week's orders, too, I fancy. My captain woke up without his clothes and thinking he had a finer time with me than he did. And I've got an extra pair of silver pieces."

"Dora, I don't want you selling yourself for information."

"I won't be doing that. And what's a squeeze and a kiss or two? I've done far worse for less. I'll tell you the truth of it, my captain drinks so much, even if he could stay awake, nothing would be happening."

Steffan shifted. "I don't like it."

"I'm going to do it anyway. I go up there every week. I might as well take advantage of it, and for once, do some real good."

"All right. But from now on, I don't want any contact between us. If you keep coming out here to buy eggs, then people are going to wonder, and if they find out I've got information, they'll be able to trace it to you too easily. A chance meeting or two is no problem."

Dora laughed. "Mr. Murdren, there was many a man in this village who had no contact with me, and were pretty good customers."

"Yes." Steffan blushed. "I suspect you keep secrets well also. I need you to keep one for me. As a merchant, naturally it's expected that I can read and write a little, and do sums. I'm actually better educated than that. I want it kept a secret because the fewer people know about my background, the safer my family and I are. If you read and write well, then we can leave letters in various hiding places, and no one will be the wiser."

"Oh, that will be easy. I can think of two or three

places in the church that would be perfect. I seen them going to mass, and couldn't help thinking they'd be good for such things. Oh, did I do the penance for such thoughts, too! It's a merciful Lord we have if He can make it possible for my sins to help our people."

"That He is." Steffan went through the roosts, gathering the eggs. "Here you are, then. This Sabbath, do a penance, or whatever, and show me the spots."

"That'll be easy to do, and no one the wiser."

"Excellent. Now, be careful. If your captain begins to get suspicious, or if you have to… you understand, stop. I won't have you selling yourself."

"I won't." Dora smiled. "And thank you for taking me seriously."

"We'll find out how seriously Friday morning."

Dora left almost immediately after. Steffan was pensive through lunch. He waited two days, then went to visit Asgarth just after supper. They walked out to the fields next to Asgarth's barn.

"John, I need you to help me with something that could be very ticklish, if you know what I mean."

"I haven't an idea."

"Well, I've learned something, I can't say how, but it needs to be made known, yet it must be done very discreetly."

"Oh, really? What now?"

"There's to be a tax raid on the village tomorrow morning."

"Do tell. Are you sure this is true?"

"Reasonably. It could have been changed since it was found out, and it could be my source is not accurate. But I've reason to believe neither is the case."

"Can you be a little more specific about how you got it?"

"Not really. Suffice it to say, I've discovered an ear in the duke's guard. I'm taking great pains to ensure that no one else finds out what my source is."

"That's wise of you. All right. I'll see to it that everyone is warned."

"I think it would be unwise if it were obvious that we were expecting it. Perhaps the raid should be minimally successful?"

Asgarth thought a moment. "You've a head on your shoulders, you do. Go now. I'll take care of the rest."

The raid occurred exactly as Dora had said. Asgarth had only alerted Woodman, Kiffs, Lyle, and Cyril. Monday afternoon, Asgarth convinced Steffan that he should go into the village with him that evening. Steffan returned elated.

"It was incredible!" he told Ella. "Woodman has the contacts for the entire kingdom. Cyril, with his traveling, knows everything else, and we get it first. Woodman is very close about his people, but we could stage a full-scale revolt, fully organized, in days."

"Then they are planning one."

"Not yet. They're preparing just in case right now. But the entire leadership is centered in this village."

"Why this one?"

"Because of Woodman. He and his father led the last revolt. And even better, Cindy, he wants no part of becoming the next monarch, nor does Asgarth. Kiffs and Lyle don't have the support or the ability, and they know it. That leaves only Cyril, and I'll wager he's been avoiding marriage too long to have the complete trust of the village."

"And you haven't been here long enough. There are plenty of other villages in this kingdom, and I'm sure many of them have very good leaders. I'm not saying you can't do it, Steffan, but we may have to judiciously reveal ourselves."

"Not for the moment. Right now, it's enough that I've been included in their meetings."

Ella smiled, and held him close, then got up because the baby was hungry.


The harvest festival was a merry one that year. The harvest had been good, and in spite of the taxes, there was enough for a good long winter. It was a particularly merry festival for Edward Asgarth.

During the slip step, he found himself matched with Elise Birchenweld. Tall and spindly, she was the eldest of fifteen children and considered plain by the young men of the village. Her father also made a meager living on land that was too small to really support his large family. Without good looks and little likelihood of a dowry, it wasn't expected that Elise would marry well, if at all. Instead of becoming bitter, Elise had developed a sense of humor and was a pleasant companion in spite of her solemn face. While dancing with Edward, she said something to him that made him laugh so hard, it almost broke the line. Later, he asked her to be his partner for the Raultberg dance.

Edward's fascination with Miss Birchenweld did not cool with the winter. He spent more time at the Birchenweld home than he did his own during the long snow-bound months. It was no surprise to anyone when John Asgarth managed to buy a large piece of land next to his farm.

"Well, of course, he's been planning to buy it for a long time," Isolde Dirkman told Isabelle Plainfield toward the end of winter. "Edward's been of marrying age for a year or two now. I'm surprised John didn't buy it sooner."

"But what of Elise Birchenweld?" asked Isabelle. "She's so poor. Everyone knows Berencia made Asgarth promise to see that his children married well."

"He hasn't handed over the land yet. My guess is that he's trying to tell his son he'd better find a better bride, or look what he's missing. I can't imagine what that boy sees in her. If she had looks, I could understand not worrying about a dowry. I told John he's looking for trouble if he endorsed that marriage."

But John Asgarth did endorse the marriage and before the snow melted, the contract was made.

# THE FOURTH YEAR

## CHAPTER FIFTEEN

By late spring, Edward's upcoming marriage was all anybody had on their minds. Steffen couldn't help laughing as Alicia, now six, talked non-stop about the coming party. Barth, who had just turned eight, kept practicing and practicing the Raultberg dance and the slip step. James and Nella, who had turned four the November before, were busy trying to imitate their older brother, while Lorelei grew and was able to roll about the farmhouse floor.

But Ella had, perhaps, the greater task. She had become Edward's confidante, and spent many an evening listening to him tell her his plans and how it all had come about, over and over again.

"I've been plowing all my life," Edward told Ella one evening before the spring festival while Steffan and Asgarth were at their meeting. "But it certainly is different when you're doing it to support your own, instead of just helping your father. Of course, I'm working the land Giles will get when Father passes on or gets too weak to work his own. When and if Giles gets married, we'll share it until father's time comes, or maybe just until the girls are married off. Gen's not even thirteen, but Arlette should be getting calls soon."

"Oh, I've heard there are a couple young men who blush when her name comes up."

"Arlette's going to be a hard one to please. She says she's not to be faulted for wanting to fall in love. What's going to be embarrassing is that Meg is already sweet on Matthew Heislman, has been for a long time, and he's well suited and just as sweet on her. I know he's been talking to Father."

"The last I heard from Arlette is that she doesn't mind one bit if Meg is married before her. Arlette says she'd rather never marry than not fall in love."

"That's a foolish way to think. Granted, I've been lucky. Who'd have thought Elise would be such a treasure. I was a fool, I was. A plain girl, what good could she be? I'm so glad I was wrong. Sure, I'm getting ribbed because my wife will be taller than me. But can you imagine how tall our sons will be?"

Ella laughed. "And what about your daughters?"

"Fine statured women, every one of them. Oh, Mrs. Murdren, it's a fine thing to be in love, I tell you. Did I tell you, when I asked Elise if she'd mind if I asked her father for her hand, she cried? Got down and wept, she did. Said she never expected me to do that, what with her being so poor and all. Cause Father promised my mother we'd marry well. I told her that what my mother meant was to see that we married good women who loved us, and if she loved me, then I'd be marrying well, indeed."

"There are many who can't say that much," Ella said, trying not to laugh because Edward had, indeed, told her Elise's reaction to his desire to marry her several times already.

"Well, Elise just cried harder after that." Edward shifted and blushed a little. "She said I was the finest gentleman in the world. I couldn't have felt better if I were the crown prince."

Ella laughed aloud.

"I guess it is kind of silly," said Edward, suddenly sheepish.

"Not in the least." Ella paused. "It just brought back some memories, some very special ones."

"Did you cry when your husband asked for your hand?"

"Actually, no. It was rather awkward. I didn't have any family, then, and I left my guardian just after Alex and I met. Alex on his part found me again and assumed we would marry, which wasn't a bad assumption. I had assumed the same. I was so happy to be loved, and to love someone."

"That's how I feel. I can't wait til June."

For Edward, it was a long wait. But for Steffan and Ella, it seemed as though the spring months flew by. Steffan would never be a good farmer. He knew it and accepted it. But he was finally feeling reasonably competent. Nor was money so close. The good harvest and prior notice of the tax raids had left Steffan with enough money that at the spring festival, he paid a visit to Widow Kinsell.

"I want my wife to have a silk dress," he told her. "Her birthday is the first day of July. What would it take to get it for her?"

"Enough silk for a fashionable dress would cost you at least three gold crowns," replied the Widow sadly. "Then you'd have to add in the trims, and the stitchery."

"I can't afford the three crowns." Steffan sighed. "I wanted her to have something soft."

"Now I've an idea, Mr. Murdren, if you wouldn't find it too embarrassing."

"What?"

"Silk bloomers, and a camisole. They'd be nice and soft against her skin, and you'll be pardoning me for saying so, but a silk dress would look awful foolish around here, even for Sabbath."

"I guess it would. But she needs a new dress. She has two work dresses, and they're both falling apart, and her Sabbath dress isn't that nice. She could work in that one, as easily as not."

"How much have you got?"

"A crown and a half."

"That's a fine bit. I can make her a nice pretty dress for Sabbaths, and some nice silk underthings, so she can feel pretty even in her work dress."

"Then I'll trust you to take care of it. I've no head for styles or fabrics. But it must be pretty. It's frivolous, but she deserves better than she has."

The widow laughed. "And it's a fine husband you are for doing something about it. Off with you, now. I'll have it all ready for the first of July."

Steffan left, feeling that he had accomplished a great deal. At last, there seemed to be hope. Not the least of it was the meetings he'd been attending.

One Monday after the spring festival, Cyril rushed into the back meeting room at the tavern, his face flushed with excitement. Steffan and the others were already present.

"I've just got back!" Cyril gasped and sat down. "And have I got news! It's all over the local villages. The queen plans to put one of her own in every village in the kingdom. He'll be charged with keeping the peace."

Woodman looked over at Steffan. "That confirms what you've been telling us."

"What?" Cyril glared at Steffan.

"The duke's guard has been instructed to find a room for a queen's guard," Steffan said. "They're not sure when he'll arrive, but he is due sometime this summer."

"This is a disaster," Kiffs groaned. "How are we going to meet?"

"We'll have to find a better hiding place," Cyril said.

"I don't see what difference it makes," Steffan said calmly. "Everyone knows we meet every Monday night to play dice. We may just have to actually play dice some nights."

Woodman nodded. "Murdren makes a good point."

"He always makes a good point," Cyril grumbled. "At least, I knew it was happening other places."

"And we're grateful, Cyril," Asgarth said. "Now, do we want to let this guard in one of our homes?"

It was generally agreed that would not be a wise move.

Steffan returned home that night feeling better and better. True, Cyril was obviously feeling threatened, and with some justification. But with the information Steffan had been getting from Dora, and his own knowledge of politics and strategy, he'd made quite an impression on the others in the group. If Asgarth and Woodman wanted none of the leadership, then it would be easy for Steffan to step in, Cyril notwithstanding. He might not even be forced to reveal himself.

As June approached, the village was filled with excitement. Edward Asgarth and Elise Birchenweld were not the only couple getting married. In fact, there were quite a few more than usual. The first Saturday of June, the church bells pealed continuously. The second Saturday was Edward's day. After the early mass, the families and friends followed the happy couple to the house Edward had built with his father, with the neighbors helping.

Ella had helped prepare the feast with Elise's mother. The tavern musicians came and played as everyone ate. Games were played, with foot races for the children, target games for the older boys. Then some of the younger husbands began wrestling matches. Cyril spotted Steffan and decided he was young enough.

"Mr. Murdren, I'd like to challenge you to a match," he said loudly.

The eyes of everyone in the party flew to Steffan.

"I'd don't care for combat games," he replied. "Thank you for asking."

"What combat?" Cyril pressed. "It's only a friendly wrestling match."

The group fell quiet.

"It's kind of you to ask, but I'd prefer not."

"What? Are you afraid of being beat?"

Steffan paused. He was afraid of looking too good. Wrestling was yet another manly art in which he'd been trained. Worse yet, he knew what Cyril was trying to accomplish. Still, it had been many years since Steffan had wrestled, and given the crowd, he would probably look worse by not accepting than being beaten. Steffan stood, and stripped off his jacket.

There was a roar of approval from the guests. They formed a ring on the grass around the two. Cyril was smiling, but he was not entirely friendly.

The two men crouched and warily circled. Steffan dove first, caught Cyril's leg and tripped him. Cyril rolled on top of Steffan, fought to pin his shoulder, and lost. Steffan bounced up. Cyril followed, and they grappled standing up for a minute. Steffan pulled Cyril's legs from under him with a quick twist, then fell on top of him. Seconds later, Cyril was soundly pinned. The guests cheered. Steffan helped Cyril up, shook his hand, and returned to the tables to continue the feast.

Cyril got soundly teased for losing. He accepted it with easy grace, then won two other matches. Lyle sat down next to Steffan.

"You're in trouble now, you know," the older man said. "Cyril is our best wrestler."

"I know, and he can stay the best wrestler," Steffan replied. "I don't particularly care to take part."

"He wasn't just wrestling, you know."

"I know what he was doing. He's looking for glory and the role of leader, and I can't say I don't know how he feels. I'm his strongest competition, and it's worse because I'm a newcomer. I've a feeling when everything falls together, whoever lands on top will have done so by a close margin."

The musicians began playing again, and Steffan

got called to join in the Raultberg.

Everyone was gasping and laughing, then Cyril stood up and coaxed the musicians to play something different.

"It's called a waltz," he announced. "It's very easy, sort of like a polka, only slower. The rich people and the city folk have been doing it for years. Murdren, you're city bred. Surely you know how."

Steffan silently cursed. "I'm not very good at it."

"Let's have a go at it anyway," said Edward. "Cyril, you show us how."

Cyril's instructions were quick but thorough, and the waltz was easily mastered. Steffan danced at first with one of the other women, since he and Ella knew how, and could teach others. Ella could, at any rate. Steffan just barely managed it. Cyril called for the waltz again, and Steffan insisted on dancing with his wife.

There was something special about dancing with her. She was light and pretty. Steffan was again fascinated by her beauty and her love. Ella smiled, gazing only at him. She had danced for the first time in his arms, and the sweetness of that first dance lingered every time after. As the music swept to its close, Steffan twirled Ella a couple times, then bowed as she made a deep curtsy. They blushed as the rest of the guests applauded. Ella ran for the cover of a nearby table, and Steffan followed.

"Ah, that's sweet," sighed Widow Kinsell to Cyril. "They've been married a good while, and they're just as in love as our newlyweds."

"Not everyone is that fortunate," grumbled Cyril, and stalked off.

A little ways off, he found Arlette gathering plates and singing old ballads.

"Pretty song, Miss Asgarth," he said coming over.

Arlette blushed. "I'm sorry. I do it so much, I quite forget I'm singing."

"You're getting to be quite a lovely young woman.

"Thank you, Mr. Cyril." Startled, Arlette ran for the house.

Cyril smiled to himself, then went to find Asgarth. He found the older man at the stone wall between Edward's land and his own, gazing over at his own house.

"You know, Asgarth, I've been noticing your oldest daughter," Cyril said.

"Have you, now?" replied Asgarth, distracted.

"I'm beginning to think I might be missing something by not being encumbered. I'm thinking I might want to pay a few calls on Miss Arlette, with your permission, of course."

"Hm."

"Don't you like the idea?"

"I don't know yet."

"Well, I've got a good inheritance coming to me. And when I'm traveling, she can come with me for a while, at least. Then there's my mother. They've always gotten on very well. There are worse fates than being a miller's wife."

"As long as Arlette marries a good man, who loves her, he can be a tinker, for all I care. I'm just wondering if you might be thinking that since Alex Murdren has a good wife and children, you'd best be getting one, too."

Cyril paused. "That may indeed be true. I really

don't know. But I am lonely, and your daughter is a very fine young woman."

"I suppose I've no right to keep you from calling on her, then, as long as she wants you to."

"Certainly. I wouldn't try to any other way. Thank you."

Asgarth nodded, then peered down the road. "Who's that coming?"

"It looks like a duke's guard, but we've had no word of a raid."

The lone horseman was a tall thin man with a sleek mustache and sleeker mannerisms. He was wearing the uniform of an officer in the duke's guard. Asgarth and Cyril went back to the group. It fell silent as the horseman turned into the yard and dismounted.

Steffan and Ella worked their way as inconspicuously as possible to the back of the crowd.

"Do you know him?" she whispered.

"No, but he could know us." Steffan closed his eyes and willed the horseman's eyes away from them.

The man looked over the group with deep satisfaction.

"Well, what have we here? A wedding? Excellent." He paused, then affected a quick bow. "Permit me to introduce myself. I am Lieutenant Filfeldt, of Her Majesty's royal army, late of Duke Desmond of Raultberg's guard. I have been stationed here by Her Majesty to keep the peace. I recommend that you look upon me as just another neighbor." There was a pause. "Well, carry on." He waited. "Carry on! Musicians? Play! Where's some food? Is this not a wedding?"

Someone found a plate and put a little food on

it. The musicians began a tentative version of an old folk song. Slowly, people began quietly conversing. Lieutenant Filfeldt swaggered through the crowd.

"Let's have a dance!" he called and grabbed the nearest available female arm.

It was Ella's. Her heart pounded in terror as he spun her to face him.

"Why are you so glum?" Filfeldt demanded. "Isn't this a wedding?"

"Yes." Ella swallowed. "But we are not accustomed to having our celebrations intruded upon by total strangers."

"You speak well, and not with the accent of this region." He looked at her carefully.

"I was raised in the city. My husband and I came here when his cousin left us his farm."

"Ah. Let us begin, then. Musicians, a lively dance."

They danced a polka, with other couples reluctantly joining in. Two dances later, the lieutenant decided he'd had enough.

"I hate to tear myself away from this lively gathering, but I'm afraid I've other neighbors to meet," he announced. "I look forward to being a part of your little community. Good day."

He made a quick bow, then patted Ella's seat. Steffan stood up and faced the man.

"Sir, you have the right to force yourself upon our celebration. But you do not have the right to take liberties with my wife. I expect that it shall not happen again."

The lieutenant smiled. "I am the queen's personal representative. I have her full permission to do anything

I wish."

He reached out, but Ella was not there. He looked again at Steffan.

"Farmer, my authority is greater than any you think you have by virtue of your voice in this village. Do not cross me, as I am quite prepared to deal with any and all treason. You have been warned. I am the queen's personal representative. I am also your neighbor. Whatever happens to me reflects directly upon Her Majesty, and shall be dealt with as such."

He walked over to his horse, mounted, and rode off towards the village proper. The wedding guests waited until he was out of sight.

"Well, he certainly knows how to dampen a party," said Edward, jovially.

The new Mrs. Asgarth suddenly giggled. "Maybe we ought to let our guests go home, and go to bed."

One of the young men laughed aloud and whistled. Edward stood through a round of bawdy teasing, and then the party resumed once more.

That night, Steffan was awakened by the sound of sobbing. Ella moaned again, thrashed, and cried some more.

"Ella?" Steffan gently shook her.

"No, not my babies!" she cried.

Steffan shook her again, and she fought him.

"Ella, wake up!" He shook her harder. "You're dreaming! Wake up!"

Ella opened her eyes. "We're home."

"Yes. You were dreaming. What did you dream?"

"That they'd come for us. It was horrible. We were sleeping here, like always, and they burst through the door. They had the children chained together, then they grabbed you, and I couldn't stop them. Oh, Steffan!" She broke down in sobs.

"It's all right, Ella. We'll be all right."

"But what if that lieutenant recognized us?"

"I'm sure he didn't. I was watching him very closely. There would have been some sort of a reaction. Here, I'll hold you now, and let's try and sleep."

But Ella could not close her eyes. Every small little sound made her heart pound with fear. Steffan got up three times to prove to her that what she heard was not murderers sent by the queen. But even as he reassured her, Steffan wondered himself.

Monday night, he went with Asgarth to the tavern, as usual. The others were waiting, with dice and coins on the table, as they had planned earlier that spring. The precaution proved sound. They'd been talking for a few minutes when the knock came. The dice game started.

Lieutenant Filfeldt walked in wearing the same satisfied smile he'd worn at the wedding.

"A dice game?" he asked.

"It is our custom," replied Woodman quietly.

"Then might I join?" Filfeldt pulled up a chair and sat down. "Just groats, eh? Ah. That's right. You're not rich men. I am not either. Here's my coin. Whose roll is it?"

Kiffs reached over and took the cup. Within four rolls, it was the lieutenant's turn to roll. He won the toss. He rolled and won again. Steffan stretched and stood.

"I think I shall take my leave," he said.

"Why so soon, friend?" asked Filfeldt.

"I don't care to lose any more money."

"You decide that on two rolls?" Filfeldt rose menacingly. "Perhaps it is that you don't like playing with me."

"If you say so." Steffan turned to go and casually bumped Filfeldt's arm.

The extra dice clattered onto the table. Without a word, Filfeldt gathered his dice and left. In the silence, Steffan sat down.

"You bumped him on purpose, didn't you?" said Asgarth.

Steffan shrugged. "I dislike cheaters, and I particularly dislike them when they are commissioned to keep the peace."

"That wasn't a wise move," Cyril said.

"It doesn't matter," said Woodman. "We shall have to find other times and places to meet."

"I think not," said Steffan. "We've made it obvious that we are regular dice players. If we change our meeting, then he will know that we've something to hide. What we must do is find a better warning system."

"Then let us disband this meeting, and think on that this week," said Woodman.

# CHAPTER SIXTEEN

The night of the first of July, Ella got into bed feeling depressed and sullen.

"You seem unhappy," Steffan observed with a sly grin.

"It's nothing," she replied.

"Oh, yes, it is."

"Please, Steffan. It's all right. I'm just being silly is all."

"Why? Because for the first time since we've been married I've forgotten your birthday."

"You did forget?"

"Close your eyes." Steffan placed a large bulky paper-wrapped package in her lap. "Now, open them."

"What on earth..." Ella tore open the paper carefully. "Oh, Steffan, it's beautiful." She held up the dress as best she could. "And there's a new petticoat here, and bloomers and they're silk! Steffan, how in Heaven's name did you get the nerve to buy these?"

"Well, it wasn't my idea entirely. What I wanted was a silk dress. I couldn't afford it, so Widow Kinsell suggested these, and I had to admit it wasn't a bad idea. I've wanted you to have some finery for so long. It isn't much."

"Steffan, it's wonderful. I shall feel so elegant with my new silk underthings, and those gossipy old ladies needn't know about what a woman of the world I am.

But why did you wait til tonight to give them to me?"

"I thought it would be best to wait until the children were asleep. After all, it wouldn't be proper for you to model your lovely new top and bloomers with them around, now would it?"

Ella chuckled. "Do you really want me to wear them?"

"For a little bit." Steffan moved in and kissed her.

"If I'm sick next month you are going to catch it."

"I'll gladly accept all responsibility."

Ella happily wore the new dress the following Sabbath. It was such a success, Isolde Dirkman was still talking about it almost a week later. But then, she'd had to take some time to find out a few things first.

"He had it made for her," she told Isabelle Plainfield in the butcher shop, as usual. "Widow Kinsell did it, and I heard she made silk bloomers, too."

"I thought it odd that he was talking to the widow last spring festival," Isabelle replied. "Not that they aren't good neighbors. But what is a man going to talk to the widow about?"

"The man is disgusting. He brings her beer. He brings her dresses."

"I've heard he loves her," Penelope volunteered.

"He's paying for a guilty conscience is what he's doing," said Isolde firmly. "That's why he went to the widow. He was visiting Miss Dora, he was, and so are half the men in the village. She's gone back to her old trade, you know."

"I know," said Isabelle. "But you have to credit her for lasting as long as she did."

"The widow was a fool for sending her up to the

duke's palace. All those lonely soldiers with plenty of silver and nowhere to spend it. Why the time she spends up there, and all the richer for it, you can mark me on that."

Penelope waited until Isolde decided she could make more mischief elsewhere. As soon as she and Isabelle left, Penelope removed her apron and got her basket.

"Drusse!" she called into the back. "I've got to do my shopping."

"Don't be long about it!" his drunken voice returned.

Penelope went first to the widow's house and was told that Dora had indeed gone to the duke's palace on her weekly errand, and probably wouldn't be back until mass the next morning. She returned to the shop. Instead of going in, she went around back and upstairs to the rooms that were rented out. She didn't knock, but went in and shut the door.

"Who's there?" asked the sleek voice within.

"Just me," she answered.

"Come on back. I'm only shaving."

"In the middle of the day?" Penelope dropped her basket and went into the bedroom.

"Must look good for this evening." Lieutenant Filfeldt dried his face. He was standing bare-chested in front a mirror with a half-filled basin. "There's nothing that lends authority like a well-shaved chin."

Penelope ran her hands over his chest. "I think I've found your spy for you."

"Mmm." Filfeldt purred, equally pleased by the news and the affection. He kissed her long and hard.

"So, who is it?"

"Miss Dora, Widow Kinsell's apprentice. She goes up to the duke's palace every week to deliver stitchery."

"She's been doing that for over a year. What makes you so sure that she's the spy?"

"According to Isolde, she's gone back to her old profession, and I know for a fact that she never comes back from her trips until the next morning. It's a three-hour walk each way. Why would she be staying the night when she wants to be at church the next morning?"

"She needs to deliver some information?"

"Perhaps, but I think not. She seems truly devout or at least wants everyone to think that she is. That would be very important if she didn't want anybody to know that she's got a good customer in the duke's guard."

"How is she getting the information to the rest of the village?"

"I have no idea. Isolde says that half the men in the village are seeing her again, but I think that's exaggeration. She was always very good at hiding her connections. That's why Isolde finally took to watching Dora's doorstep. Now, it'll be almost impossible to say."

"If she were writing notes, I could make a guess. Even then, I'm not entirely sure he's got that much education."

"Mr. Murdren? It's possible, but I doubt it. They don't come into contact with each other often enough. Nor are they avoiding each other."

"If she were leaving notes, it wouldn't matter. But given her speech, I seriously doubt she can read. Not many here can."

"We don't need to." She reached up and embraced him.

He chuckled. "We'll have to wait for a moment. I've got to send a message to the duke's palace."

"As always," sighed Penelope bitterly. "Duty before pleasure."

"But, my beauty, I will make it up to you."

Filfeldt quickly put on a shirt and his uniform jacket checked to be sure that all was right, and left the rooms.

Steffan was puzzled and worried when Dora did not appear in church that Sabbath. There wasn't much he could do. Asgarth noticed his concern, and given Dora's absence, deduced the rest. Quietly, he made a few discreet inquiries to no avail.

The news was announced Tuesday. The young seamstress' apprentice had been caught going through the papers of one of the duke's captains. The trial was set for the next day, but no one doubted the verdict.

Steffan spent many long hours trying to decide what to do. He was prevented from making a rescue attempt by Lieutenant Filfeldt. The Lieutenant was watching everybody, but Steffan in particular. Steffan knew the Lieutenant suspected him of receiving Dora's information but had no proof. Furthermore, the Lieutenant was looking for a way to work his revenge on Steffan. Catching Steffan at rescuing a spy would bring him much joy.

Dora was convicted on Wednesday and ordered to hang Friday morning at dawn. Thursday, Lieutenant Filfeldt was called to the capital city by the queen. It was a summons he could not ignore, much to his dismay.

That afternoon, Asgarth went over to see Steffan. He found him in the barn.

"Alex, we're having an emergency meeting." He stopped. "What are you doing?"

"What does it look like?" Steffan answered, reaching for more soot. He applied it carefully and evenly to Max's white flanks.

"You're going to go after her tonight, aren't you?"

"I should never have let her continue. It was too dangerous."

"Well, that's what we're meeting about."

"You'll have to meet without me. I've got to time this just right. I'm leaving in a couple hours."

"You can't go alone!"

"Alone I have the best chance. They'll be expecting a much larger party if anything." Steffan paused. "And I know those dungeons, certainly better than you or anyone else here could."

"Now I know why you hide from the duke's guard." Asgarth nodded, drawing the obvious, but wrong, conclusion.

Steffan went back to coloring his horse. He knew the dungeons because he had played there as a child, unknown to anyone. He had also discovered an ancient secret passageway, long forgotten. It had been built centuries before as an escape for the duke's family in case of a successful attack. Steffan had to hope it was still forgotten. And if it weren't, he knew of another way into the palace.

"And what are you going to do with her when you've got her out?" Asgarth asked.

"I'll take her to Leiderkeit. I have friends there."

Ella rushed into the barn. "I've got it. Mrs. Schmidt is wondering why I'm making fancy cake this time of year, and Mrs. Kinsell gave me the pins in an envelope. Oh. Mr. Asgarth."

"What are you bringing?" Asgarth asked.

"Some things I'll need," said Steffan quickly. "Asgarth, you once told me there was a hiding place for our grain that no one knows about. Could people hide there?"

"Yes, easily. Who do you want to hide?"

"My family." Steffan cast a grim glance at Ella. "If I'm not back by two hours before dawn, I want you to take them there. Then, when it's clear enough, help them to the Leiderkeit border. Cindy can find our friends from there."

"I'll gladly do it. And in the meantime, I'll be praying that I won't have to."

"Thanks."

"Is there anything else I can do to help?"

"No."

Asgarth took the hint and left. Steffan finished with Max, then followed Ella into the house.

"Were you able to get ink and a quill?"

"Yes. I'm afraid I stole them, though, from the Widow, no less. If she could know, I'm sure she wouldn't begrudge us. I happened to meet the priest and confessed it, and he said there was no sin anyway."

"Good. Where's that sealing wax you use for your preserves?"

"Right here."

"Excellent." Steffan took the parchment Ella had purchased for her "cake", trimmed the point on the quill, and wrote. After the ink was dry, he folded it and dripped hot wax on the opening. He pulled the ring from his pocket. It was a meaningless seal to any but his most intimate friends. He set it in the wax, feeling terribly restless all of a sudden. He put the parchment in the envelope and sealed that also.

When the wax had hardened, he put the envelope into his jacket pocket. Ella was weeping.

"I'm sorry. You're the only one who can go," she said. "But I'm so frightened."

"So am I. At least you'll be safe."

"I don't want to be safe. I want to be with you. If it weren't for the children, I wouldn't let you go alone."

Steffan softly kissed her lips. "Ella, darling, I know I'm leaving you the harder part, but I feel as if I'll be back. It's a foolish chance, otherwise. Yes, there's risk, but not so great. Even for Dora, I couldn't risk an impossible scheme that would end in my certain demise. It wouldn't do her any good, and I have a responsibility to fulfill."

"I am going to be a nervous wreck until you get back."

"And I will be back." He kissed her again. "If only because I've not yet had my fill of your love."

Ella smiled in spite of her tears. "You're being silly."

"And you are enjoying it."

The shadows had lengthened, but the sun was not yet down when Steffan led Max from the barn to the woods. It was a long walk around the village through the trees. Only after he was well away from any property owned by anyone he knew, did he leave the woods and make for the road. It was dusk by then. Steffan mounted Max's bare back and kicked the horse into a fair run.

Two and a half hours later, the dark covered Steffan's approach to the duke's palace. The opening to the passage was along the river bank, next to a small pool. Steffan stopped at two such pools before finding the spot. He left Max tied up with a nose bag, after listening for any signs of guards. It wasn't likely. Even after Lanicia had taken over, the guards rarely patrolled the woods at night.

Steffan slid into the passage, then replaced the branches over the rotting wooden door behind him. The passage reeked of mildew and age. Slowly standing upright, Steffan lit a small candle. It took almost an hour to get to the palace end of the passage. The door there opened into a small room, hidden behind the huge fireplace of the great hall.

The huge drafty old great hall dated back to the times of knights and ladies. It was rarely used anymore. Steffan listened through a small crack for a long time to be certain that no one was there to see him emerge. Thanks to the chimney, all sound traveled to the hidden room. Still, Steffan worked slowly, willing away anyone to see him as he removed the brickwork at the back of the fireplace.

The room was empty and filled with eerie shadows and ancient wall hangings. Steffan silently replaced the bricks, then slid along the back wall toward the servants quarters. The door leading to the dungeons was in a forgotten hallway, not far from the main kitchen. The servants never went down that way, claiming that spirits usually walked there. Steffan had never met any but felt the usual tingle as he entered the forbidden hall.

The door to the dungeons bore a huge iron lock. Steffan pulled his steel hoof pick from his pocket. His friend, Lord Chester, had been the son of a locksmith when Steffan had elevated his status to Baron of Fin Reache so that Chester could marry Steffan's cousin Marcella. Steffan had never abused the knowledge his friend had shared and was again finding it useful. The lock clicked open. Steffan took it with him and slid along the walls again.

There were few torches lit along the cell block. The guards had no reason to go there. The cells were of stone, and immune to escape. The guards' greatest concern was those who would try to enter from the outside. The occupants of the cells were all asleep as Steffan looked in. Dora was in the end cell.

Somewhere in the building above, a clock tolled out eleven o'clock. Steffan sighed in relief. The guards would not come by again until midnight if the schedule was still the same. There was no reason to assume it had changed.

Steffan picked the lock on the wooden door and opened it silently. Dora was asleep in a pile of straw and wearing a huge manacle around her waist. Steffan shut the door and went to work on the manacle lock. Dora stirred. Steffan clapped his hand over her mouth.

She looked at him, afraid to believe that she was awake.

"When do the guards come by next?" Steffan asked whispering.

"Eleven-thirty," she answered.

"Damn! We haven't much time."

Steffan twisted at the manacle again. The lock popped open. Dora rose, and Steffan frantically grabbed at the chains. They clanked on the stone floor. The two froze. Silence.

Motioning, Steffan showed Dora how he wanted her to remove her top dress and stuff it with straw. She obliged. Steffan tried not to look her way, as he put the manacle around the bundle and threw the straw about so it appeared she'd used it as her covering. Then he removed his jacket and had her put it on.

They slid out of the cell, and Steffan relocked it. Silently, they returned the way he had come. They had just entered the forgotten hallway when loud howling echoed through the passage. Dora stifled a screech. Steffan locked the door to the dungeons. The howling got louder and came right at them. Steffan was so startled, he forgot to will it away.

The source of the unearthly cries was a man. He was older with gray hair, and gaunt face. His shirt was half out of his pants, and his eyes burned with terror. He came running down the hall and crumpled at another door nearby. Steffan pulled Dora out of the way as the man went past.

"He's coming for me!" screeched the man.

"Father?" called a woman's voice. "Father, please come here. I've got something special for you."

She entered the hallway and stopped as she saw Steffan. She was not unlike him in coloring and facial structure, and recognition shone in her eyes. Before she could recover, Steffan had his hand over her mouth.

"Yes, you know me," he said softly. "But I need

your silence. We all do, for our lives' sakes. Do you understand?"

She nodded. Steffan removed his hand and gestured at Dora. They went past the woman towards the great hall.

"But-" the woman started.

Steffan whirled. "Not a word!"

He pushed Dora ahead of him to the great hall. Dora remained silent while Steffan got them into the passageway.

"We can talk quietly now," he said about halfway down.

"Who was she?"

"Someone who knows me."

"But who?"

"It doesn't matter. She won't betray us."

Dora fell silent. Steffan cursed the meeting. His cousin Marcella would not betray him deliberately. But she would tell her husband, and Chester had a talent for rash behavior. There was nothing to be done about it, however.

At the river, Steffan made sure the bank looked the same as it had before, dragging a branch behind him to cover the footprints. Max was still waiting. As Steffan untied the nose bag, bells from the palace sounded the alarm. Dora went pale.

Steffan remained calm. One good look at the palace told him that the guards were assuming Dora was still in the palace. Perhaps that was Marcella's help. Steffan didn't know or care. The guards would be after them soon enough. Quietly, he led Dora and the horse through the woods to the road. There, they mounted.

Steffan kicked Max into a dead run.

He took a circuitous route that got them to the village about an hour before dawn. His house was empty. Although he was glad Asgarth had kept his promise to hide his family, Steffan sighed, knowing the pain that Ella felt. At least, the pot on the hearth was still warm. He directed Dora to find one of Ella's old dresses and put it on while he quickly washed and dried Max.

The sun was rising when Giles Asgarth came running up.

"You're back!" he exclaimed. "We've got to hurry and get the others here and Miss Dora hidden before the duke's guard comes through. They're searching everywhere."

Giles led them to the hills at the back of his father's farm. There, behind the overgrown brush, was a group of caves. Inside the largest, Ella held Lorelei and tried not to cry. When she saw Steffan, she yelped, and almost dropped the baby trying to get to him. He accepted her first embrace, then helped Asgarth remove his children and belongings back to his house. Giles remained in the cave to keep care of Dora.

When the duke's guard arrived at the house, Steffan was in bed.

"He's sick," Ella explained. "He's had a fever all night. It broke just a little while ago. You can see how sweaty he is."

Frustrated, the guard couldn't see anything that denied her story, and angrily stomped off with his men. Steffan spent the rest of the day in bed.

# CHAPTER SEVENTEEN

The next morning, Lord Chester duGrackel, Baron of Fin Reache, returned to his wife, the Lady Marcella, at her father's palace in Raultberg.

"Hullo, love." He kissed her, then threw his riding gloves on the table next to the sofa in their private apartment.

"How fares your holding?" she asked.

"As well as anything these days." He sighed, swung her into an extended embrace, then stumbled over the sofa. "Is there any way we could pack up your father, and move back home? I do so prefer my cozy thirty room manor to this drafty old ruin."

"It's an idea. I'll have to check with my sister first."

"I'll give good odds she'll agree to it, as long as it wasn't my idea. Anything that keeps me out of the way seems to please her. I hear there was some trouble here last night."

"That." Marcella sighed deeply. "It's bad enough the guard keeps prisoners here. You may have heard that they caught that young girl, the seamstress, spying. She was scheduled for execution this morning. I protested, of course, but you know how much good that does. Last night, she escaped. They think one of the guards must have helped her. All the locks were intact, so the reasoning is that the person must have had keys."

"Why do I get the feeling you suspect otherwise?"

"I know otherwise. Well, not about the keys. He could have had them. Father had a bad night last night. He got away and ran off down that haunted hallway. I went after him, and there she was, the prisoner that escaped, and the man that helped her." Marcella paused, somewhat frightened. "The man was Steffan."

"As in King Steffan, my friend and your cousin?" Chester gaped.

"Yes."

"Are you saying a ghost rescued that girl?"

"It wasn't a ghost. It was Steffan. He's alive, Chester."

Chester shook his head. "You could have been imagining it. That hallway is terribly strange."

"I'm not. If I'd seen a ghost, or if my imagination was at work, I would have seen him as he was. He was different. He was wearing a beard, and he was dressed in rags practically. The girl was wearing an old farmer's coat. It must have been his. They found her dress in the cell. But the shirt had Ella's embroidery on the collar. You can spot that cross pattern a mile away. And his eyes. It was Steffan, Chester. I know my own cousin."

"He's alive." Chester sat down in wonder. "What about the others?"

"I can only guess that they're alive also. He put his hand over my mouth before I could say anything, and wouldn't let me speak. He said 'I need your silence. We all do for our lives' sakes.' He must be in hiding, and the girl didn't know who he is."

Chester got up and began pacing. "Of course. Lanicia's too powerful for him to just announce himself, and the people he can trust are too few to support him. But why didn't he surface right after the accident?"

"He or Ella could have been ill, or injured, or one of the children. He'd want to be sure of their safety before doing anything like oppose Lanicia."

"Well, that's irrelevant now. How do we go about finding him so we can get him back where he belongs?"

"Chester, be careful. He doesn't want to be revealed yet."

"So we stir up a few rumors. At least tell his mother."

"That much I'll agree to. The poor woman has suffered so much already. But the rest, Chester, we can't. He ordered me to silence. I will obey him as my sovereign."

"We should still find him." Chester flopped onto the couch. "He rescued that seamstress. That would mean he probably knows her. I'd say it's even money he's somewhere in that village she came from, the one below us some miles away. The question now is how to get down there and find him?"

"The question is how to do it discreetly. My sister would be very eager to dispose of him if she could do it without anyone knowing."

Chester thought for a moment. "You know how your father keeps saying the coffins were empty? Do you think your sister knows they were?"

"I can't say." Marcella sighed and sat down next to her husband. "I haven't told her what all Father's been ranting about. Either way, I'm fairly sure she sincerely believes Steffan and his family are dead."

"It would be very hard, even for her, to justify her actions if she didn't believe it."

"And she's very frightened they're not."

Chester lapsed into thought.

Ella returned to the cave later that afternoon with a large basket of food.

"Here we are," she said, dropping it on the floor. She handed Giles a wine skin. "Giles, will you please fill this with some water?"

"Certainly, Mrs. Murdren." He took the skin and left.

Dora stared at Ella sleepily.

"I just woke up," she said. "I wanted to tell Mr. Murdren how grateful I am for him rescuing me."

"He likes doing things like that, but I'll convey your thanks." Ella pulled an envelope from her dress. "He didn't get a chance to give you this. You should hide it. We've arranged for Giles to accompany you to the Leiderkeit border. From there, make your way to the capital. It should be easy enough to get there. It's not that far from the border, and the people tend to be friendly, or so I've heard. King John holds general audiences once a week when he's there. He travels a bit among his own. Go to a general audience, and present this envelope to him. It was given to my husband years ago, as a letter of introduction. Alex saved it, at first because he wasn't dealing much with Leiderkeit at the time, and then because he wanted to see if things would work here first. They're working, so we don't need it."

Dora took the envelope. "That's one fancy seal. Who's it from?"

"A dead king. Now, hurry and hide it before Giles comes back. It's better that no one knows certain people called us friends once."

"I know. We all thought he's just fallen from favor with the queen. But Mr. Murdren knew those dungeons awful well. It must have been hard on you when he was arrested."

Ella just nodded and didn't correct her.

Giles returned soon after. Ella told him about taking Dora to Leiderkeit, and he readily agreed. The two left that night under the cover of darkness. They traveled by night, staying off the road, speaking little. During the day, they slept, taking turns watching. By midnight of the fourth day, they reached the border.

"I can go the rest of the way now," Dora said. "It's been very kind of you, Giles."

"Oh, I like a bit of adventure," he grinned bashfully. "Not that we've had much. You'd best be going."

"Right."

There was a pause, then Giles reached over and generously kissed her mouth.

"You're a fine woman, Dora," he sighed. "I might've thought of marrying you, but this spying business, it's given you a bad name."

Dora laughed. "On with you, Asgarth. You sure you don't want all of me?"

"It's tempting, but I'd be doing my future bride wrong by it. Thanks anyway."

"Thank you. Thank all of them for me."

"I will. Goodbye."

"Goodbye." Dora took one last look, then scurried

through the trees.

It took her another day's walk to reach the capital. It was a fine city filled with stately houses, ancient cathedrals, and many people. She found a small inn and paid for a room with the money she'd found in the food basket. After a long sleep, she awoke the next morning, cleaned herself and her clothes as best she could, and sought out the palace.

King John was giving a general audience that afternoon. Dora begged, pleaded and almost sold herself to the guard for a guarantee that she would have an opportunity to speak with the king. As it turned out, she needn't have worried. The audience hall wasn't terribly crowded. Audiences with the young, popular king were common, and only those who had a need usually attended.

Dora decided that John was rather handsome, though not in the way she favored. He seemed intelligent and good humored as he listened to his people. Mid-way through, Dora was signaled, and she made her way forward.

Curtsying as she'd seen the other women do, she pulled the envelope from her dress.

"Majesty, I'm not a fine lady, and not from your country, but friends of mine said I should seek you out, and give you this letter."

"Thank you." John motioned, and a guard took the letter from Dora and handed it to the king. He froze when he saw the seal. "Miss, if you don't mind, I'd like to deal with this matter after the audience is over. Would you kindly wait here until I am able to give this the time it deserves?"

"As your Majesty likes, sir." Puzzled, Dora followed another guard's signals and was seated near the front of the room.

John did his best, but his attention had fled. The seal was too obviously his friend's, a friend he'd thought dead for some years. How had a letter bearing it come into the hands of this poor uneducated girl? Unable to concentrate, he adjourned the audience early and led Dora to a private study.

There, he sent the guards, clerks and other royal hangers-on away.

"Where did you get this?" he demanded.

"It was given me." Dora began to get frightened.

John didn't notice. He broke the seal, and then the one on the letter itself.

"To John, King and True Sovereign of Leiderkeit. Greetings," the letter read. "The bearer of this letter has proved to be hard-working, honest and worthy of trust. Consider it a personal favor to me to grant whatever aid is requested. Your friend, as ever, Steffan, Royal Prince, Heir Apparent."

"This is incredible." John pulled another piece of parchment from a drawer and compared the two. "If this is not genuine, a master was at work. You said a friend gave you this."

"She did, on her husband's word. It was his. He was a merchant what fell from the queen's favor. His wife said he got it years ago and saved it, expecting to come here some time. Only he fell from favor with the new queen, so he waited to come here because he had this farm from his cousin, and it's paying, so I got the letter. I was in a bit of trouble, and it seemed better if

I came here."

"It says here you're honest." John smiled mischievously.

"Oh, I am! I was just helping the village. You might have heard. Taxes was just awful heavy, and the duke's guard, they was raiding the village to get the slack, because we kept hiding our money and saying things weren't as rosy as they were. 'Tisn't a nice thing to do. I know that. But them taxes weren't right, and they was using them for the army, they were. So I found a way to find out when the raids was coming, and I told the right people."

"You were spying."

"Only to help my people!" Dora fell on her knees. "Please, they said you was a kind man, and that letter says you got to help me."

"Have you read this?"

"No. It was sealed when I got it. But why would they give it me if it didn't say that?"

John chuckled. "I'm not about to condemn you for spying on an evil queen's servants. Especially when I'm intent on spying on her myself. I'm merely concerned that you might be spying on me."

"Why would I do that? I was sent here for help."

"And you wouldn't admit to being a spy, yourself, if that were truly your purpose. No. I believe your story. This letter puzzles me, though."

"Mr. Murdren is a fine gentleman. Well, he has gentleman's manners, he does. He says he's better educated than he wants people to think, and he sure knew them Duke's dungeons. I think he escaped from there himself. He sure never wants to be seen by a duke's guard."

"This is the friend who gave you the letter?"

"Well, his wife did, on his word."

"Has he any children?"

Dora laughed. "I know what you be thinking. It couldn't be the young king. They have five children and had four when they come to us. Them younger two, well, when they came, they're twins and was awful young. But we counted, and they'd have to been started before the accident, and the queen would have known to look for a larger family, and she didn't."

"That makes sense." But the letter didn't. John put it aside for the moment. "I suppose we can tend to your problem. I assume you're unmarried. Do you have any trade?"

"Stitchery, Majesty. I did some of the finest in the village."

"That's an excellent skill. My brothers enjoy wearing all the latest styles, and their wives are worse. I suppose if we can teach you to speak properly, and dress you up a bit, you might make a fine lady in waiting."

"A lady? Me?" Dora giggled. "I can try, Majesty. I can read, you know."

"Excellent. Let me send for my best tutor, and we shall see what you can do."

John went to the door, sent Dora off with one of the guards to the woman he wanted, then returned to his desk to ponder the letter. The envelope and the paper weren't worn nearly enough for the letter to be as old as the girl had said they were. Yet the script was unmistakably Steffan's, as was the personal seal. The odds against a person finding that seal after the accident, knowing it for what it was, and then being able to forge Steffan's cramped scrawl were astronomical. So were the odds against his being alive. If he were, Lanicia had been unaware of the impending arrival of the twins. Something terrible had happened during that accident that was sufficient to drive Steffan into hiding. John wondered how best he could find his friend and help him.

Giles returned to the village somewhat faster than he'd left. He arrived just in time. Lieutenant Filfeldt was beginning to get suspicious. The lieutenant had arrived back at the village late Saturday night. He'd heard in detail about the rescue.

No one in the village could say who had done the deed. Mr. Murdren had been ill with a fever the whole time. Asgarth had sworn to that. Several others had sworn to Asgarth's presence at the tavern well into the night. All the other likely troublemakers were vouched for. Filfeldt was furious.

He tried to get the Murdren boy to say anything but that his father had been ill, but soon realized he'd only terrified the lad into silence. He questioned several other village boys. They couldn't tell him anything. He grilled Edward Asgarth, who remembered settling the Murdren livestock for the night because Mr. Murdren was too ill. Then Filfeldt realized that he had not spoken with Giles Asgarth, or that he'd even seen Giles Asgarth for some time.

Wednesday morning, he rode out to the Asgarth farm.

"Isn't he in the barn?" Arlette asked innocently. "That's where he said he'd be this morning."

"He is not there."

"He's probably run off to see some sweetheart. That's Giles for you. Always chasing the girls."

No one in town had seen him, but one young woman said he'd been there earlier that day. She didn't know where he'd gone. Wherever Filfeldt looked, Giles had just left, or had left some hours before, or hadn't been around.

Filfeldt continued his search for two days more, as he could. Several villagers decided they needed him to settle their differences immediately, and almost a full-scale riot broke out in the square Friday morning. Filfeldt was disgusted when he couldn't jail anybody for starting the fight, and there were too many people who had been fighting to arrest them all.

Giles appeared Friday afternoon, and Filfeldt questioned him to no avail. It was an utterly unsatisfying conclusion to the search.

# CHAPTER EIGHTEEN

The last days of summer turned unbearably hot. The air was thick with moisture. The afternoons took on a dead stillness as everyone remained in the shelter of their houses as much as possible. Ella patiently stitched a new shirt together for Barth, as Steffan held children close to him and told them their history. They could hear Arlette Asgarth's voice across the road as she sang of new love fading and a lover's betrayal.

Arlette was doing some baking and decided that outdoors had to be cooler than next to the ovens. She sat on a bench in front of the house, leaning against the wall in the little shade available. She sewed as she sang, working on a shirt for her father.

Down the road a ways, coming towards the village, a lone man walked. He was dressed in rags and carried a fair bundle on his back. As he got closer, Arlette's interest picked up. He was rather handsome, and out of the bundle poked what appeared to be a fiddle. She continued singing as if she hadn't noticed him.

He stopped at her gate and listened for a moment. His eyes were full of lively good humor, and he smiled. Suddenly, he hopped onto the wall and pulled out his fiddle.

"What are you doing?" Arlette gasped.

"Accompanying you, if you'll spare me a moment to tune," he replied, plucking at the strings. He settled comfortably into his precarious seat and crossed his legs. "That's a very pretty song you're singing, and one of my favorites."

"You know it?" Arlette was intrigued. "There are not many around here what know the old songs. My grandam taught them to me, and I learned some others along the way."

"The same way I learned. There. All tuned." He rosined his bow quickly and struck a chord. "Is that too low for you?"

"Not at all."

"Then, let's start again."

He played a few notes, and Arlette began the mournful song again, with the stranger joining in on the chorus. He held the fiddle in the crook of his arm, and not under his chin, so he could sing. Arlette was enchanted, and the stranger no less so.

In the house across the way, Steffan noticed the fiddle music first.

"Who could that be?" he asked.

"Probably some wandering musician," said Ella, turning a seam.

"That's not just any wandering musician." Steffan stood anxiously and peered out the window.

"His voice does sound familiar." Ella paused. "Steffan, that's King John's voice. What's he doing here?"

"Accompanying Arlette at the moment." Steffan left the window, thinking. "He's probably spying, and possibly looking for me."

"But, Steffan, you wrote that letter so he'd have no reason to believe you were still alive."

"Who knows what brought him here. He was always the fanciful sort. He's been wandering all over his kingdom dressed as a poor musician since he was fourteen. It used to infuriate his father. But no one knows more about what's happening among his own people. He's probably heard about Lanicia's army plans, and wants to know how much support she has."

"And poor fortune has brought him here."

Barth sighed. "So why is it so bad if he knows us?"

"Because, my son, it's possible he could give us away accidentally," replied Steffan, suddenly realizing he was gripping Barth's shoulder a little too firmly. Steffan looked out the window again. "He seems absorbed at the Asgarth's for the moment. I recommend we avoid him."

Across the way, Arlette smelled her bread starting to burn and ran into the house. John followed.

"It should be all right," Arlette said, pulling the loaves from the oven. "They're just a little over brown." She shut the oven door. "Oh, dear. I left my sewing outside."

"I'll fetch it." John hurried outside. He returned, very interested in the collar that was being worked. "This is a lovely pattern."

"It's a new one I'm trying. Mrs. Murdren, across the road, she taught it me."

"Murdren?" John looked across the road. "Do tell."

Arlette suddenly became wary. "And what is your name, and what are you doing wandering through here?"

"I'm a musician." He bowed elegantly. "John of Leiderkeit is my name."

Asgarth stalked in the back door. "A musician, are you?"

"Yes, Mr..."

"Asgarth. You look a bit well-fed to be one who plays for his pennies."

"Ah, but Mr. Asgarth, I am a fiddler extraordinaire." With a flourish, John fitted his instrument under his chin and played a lightning quick jig.

"That's good enough." Asgarth gazed at him. "What's your interest in the Murdren family?"

"I came on behalf of a friend who might want to help them." John smiled.

Asgarth snorted. "Murdren's a fine fellow, and you won't find me helping him to his doom. Now, be off with you."

"Papa!" begged Arlette. "He don't mean any harm. I'm sure he don't. Please? Might he stay and have supper with us? Surely you might get to find if he's a bad man or not in that time."

Asgarth looked John over again. "All right. I suppose it's better you're here where I can keep an eye on you, than over there making mischief."

Arlette was beside herself with joy. She sang for the rest of the afternoon while John played the fiddle and sang with her. Meg and Gen came back from the village near supper time, and John kept them entertained with sleight of hand while Arlette prepared the meal. Giles came in prepared to be cool and aloof towards the stranger but was quickly won over by John's charm.

The only person who remained less than

enthusiastic about John was Asgarth, himself. He could see John was a good man, better educated than one might think of a wandering musician, and every so often finer manners would briefly appear. Whenever the subject of the Murdrens came up, he was truly interested and completely without malice. The children told him how the family had arrived, and what they were like. John kept nodding as if he expected the Asgarths to say what they did.

Arlette was the most animated, and the most taken with the stranger. The more Asgarth thought about it, the more he realized that was what irritated him about John. This thought, in turn, irritated Asgarth even more.

John smiled at Arlette with distinct fondness. She smiled prettily back. Gen, Meg, and Giles noticed, and nudged each other, stifling their giggles.

"That was an excellent meal," John said as he finished eating.

"Better than you've ever done, Arlette," teased Giles. "I wonder why."

Arlette glared at him, as Meg and Gen giggled. "Mrs. Murdren's been helping me, and you know it."

"You do all of the family's cooking?" John asked her.

"Since her mother passed two winters ago, God rest her," Asgarth replied with distinct jealousy.

"Oh. I'm terribly sorry."

"One has to go on," said Arlette with a little shrug. "It will happen to us all someday."

John smiled warmly. "You do quite a job, filling your mother's shoes."

"She has to," teased Gen. "Poor Papa wouldn't survive. You won't see him making bread like Mr. Murdren does in a pinch."

"He does?" John was definitely amused.

"He doesn't have three fine grown up daughters," warned Asgarth jovially.

His girls laughed.

"How many daughters does he have?" asked John shrewdly.

"Three, but they're small yet," Asgarth answered.

"Lorelei's still a baby," Arlette said. "She won't be one 'til September. And Nella and James will be four in November."

"Four?" John mentally counted. "How old are the older two?"

"Lucas is eight, and Grace is six."

"That's perfect." John grinned.

"Almost too perfect," said Asgarth, gazing again at his guest. "Are you thinking Murdren might be the lost king?"

"One hears the rumors."

"Even in Leiderkeit." Asgarth shook his head. "I wouldn't think it of the Murdrens, though, even with their fine manners. Murdren's no farmer, and the ages of the children are curiously close, but it's just coincidence."

"How can you be sure?"

"I used to wonder, but I started watching Cindy. She wears a wooden wedding band. And she was no newcomer to cooking and keeping house. You can tell. She's been working all her life, and no fine lady or princess has been doing that."

John held in his laughter. Steffan had confided in him the state in which he'd found his wife. There were those in the city that knew, but few of them would admit it. Poor Steffan, working a farm, baking bread for his family in a pinch. John sighed over the tragic waste of his friend's talents.

Meanwhile, there were the decided charms of Arlette Asgarth to investigate. John knew he shouldn't. She was far too sweet and pleasant to indulge in what would most likely be a casual dalliance. Still, John found it hard to help himself.

Music filled the Asgarth house well into the night. Edward and Elise came up from their house and joined in the merriment. Asgarth finally sent John with them to sleep at their house.

The next morning, John was up with the sun. The house across the road was beginning to show the usual signs of life on a country morning. He was too far away to make out her face, but the stature of the woman who emerged and headed for the barn with a pair of buckets was not unlike Ella's.

He waited until the morning chores were done, both at the Murdrens' and the Asgarth's, then wandered over to the Murdren yard. He stepped in at the gate and was rewarded with a tremendous squealing and grunting. The pig that appeared was huge and menacing. John stepped back onto the road and pondered another course of action. He waited until he saw Barth head for the barn with a pail. The pig hurried after his young master.

With the pig thus occupied, John made his way to the back of the house. The man he saw patiently weeding the garden had Steffan's coloring and build, even if he was somewhat thinner. He was in his shirt sleeves, due to the hot weather, and did not seem unhappy.

"Who would have thought after all these years to find you peacefully weeding a garden?" said John quietly.

Steffan started and looked up. There was a moment as he recovered from the surprise.

"There are those who would be shocked to find you playing your fiddle for your supper," he replied.

"True. But I do it by choice. I wish I could say the same for you, old friend."

Steffan shrugged as he stood and wiped the dirt from his hands.

"You are here looking for me then."

"Yes. You will be happy to know that Miss Dora is well and has become quite a lady. She's been teaching my brothers' wives the gentle art of stitchery, and has not a few young men looking her way."

"That could prove interesting. I trust she has remained virtuous?"

"The very pinnacle." John sighed. "To see you like this. Steffan, it brings tears to my eyes and the bile to my throat. If only attacking Lanicia wouldn't bring her the very support you need."

"I'm collecting it, little by little."

"You'll be an old man at that rate!"

"It's not nearly as bleak as all that. We're better organized than you might think. I can't say more, lest I betray confidences. It should be interesting."

"It's disgusting. Look at you."

"An honest day's work never hurt anyone, as you've frequently pointed out to me."

"Yes, a day's work. And, no, it's not that what you're doing is beneath you. It's the waste of your talent. Steffan, you were born to rule, and a better head for it, there isn't anywhere."

"Does Lanicia's avarice frighten you that much?"

"It does in some ways. But forgive me. You are my friend. Your concerns are my concerns. You'd be equally worried about me."

Steffan smiled and threw his arm around John's shoulders.

"I would. All those years. You were my only equal."

John tripped Steffan. "That's what you thought."

The two men roared with laughter as John helped Steffan up. Ella heard the noise and came out of the house to investigate.

"Oh, dear," she sighed when she saw John.

"It's not to be helped, my darling." Steffan shrugged merrily. "He came looking for me."

"Did Dora guess or something?" Ella asked.

"No!" John shook his head. "It was that letter you gave her. It was too new, and the wax. You used to use much finer, my friend."

Steffan sighed. "It was the best I had. I should have known you'd notice."

"Well, rest assured. Your secret is safe with me, on one condition. That you come to me when you need help. If you're going get back on the throne, you'll need weapons and a reasonably adept army. I can supply both, and help you smuggle it in, so it doesn't look like I'm attacking."

"You're too kind, John," said Ella. "Now come into the house and we'll share our own meager hospitality."

John stayed through the Sabbath but spent surprisingly little time with Steffan and Ella. Monday morning, he had to leave. Arlette Asgarth walked with him down the road a ways.

"I don't know if I should promise my return or not," he sighed.

Arlette sniffed. "Why do you have to leave?"

"Arlette, you know I'm better situated than I appear. That's how I knew the Murdrens. He's content to continue as he is, and I'm content that he's content. I have responsibilities elsewhere. I'd take you with me, but I can't right now."

"I'm trying to understand. These past few days have been so nice. I've never met anyone who knew how I felt about singing and such."

"Nor have I. I can't tell you how much it hurts me to leave you here. I shouldn't have spent so much time with you in the first place." He paused. "How well do you know your letters?"

"I can read a fair bit. Not well."

"Have someone teach you to read better. I understand there's a widow in the village that's well-learned."

"Widow Kinsell."

"Yes. My hand's a fair bit difficult to read, but it will be better than nothing, won't it?"

"You mean write letters to me? I'd adore it. I could even write back."

"Don't count on anything. Relations between my kingdom and yours aren't the best. If the borders are closed, there won't be much getting through."

"I understand. John, you're the kindest man I ever met."

"And you are the sweetest woman I've ever known." Throwing all caution to the winds, he took her face in his hands and softly kissed her lips.

They stood that way for several minutes, then John turned her back towards home.

That night, Steffan teased Asgarth about the wanderer as they walked to their weekly dice game and meeting.

"Well, he's gone," Asgarth growled. "And all the better."

"How's Arlette taking it?"

"Well enough. But she's not happy about it. You say he's an old friend of yours?"

"Yes. He took quite a risk coming here, but I expect it will be profitable in the long run."

Asgarth snorted.

They were the last to arrive. They had barely said hello when a small bell jangled from above the doorway. The dice cup and coins appeared on the table and the men made ready to play. Filfeldt wandered in, sniffed because he could see no sign that anything but a dice game was going on, then left.

Lyle chuckled. "Thanks be for that bell of yours, Cyril."

"We still need to be cautious," said Woodman. "He's anxious to catch us doing something wrong. Kiffs, I believe you have something for us tonight."

"I do. As regards Penelope Drusse. Now, I been wondering about her since the lieutenant moved into the rooms above her shop. Granted, he's the type will take what he wants. But after Dora's arrest, I heard from Widow Kinsell that Penelope was there that Saturday asking after Miss Dora. She must have heard Isolde Dirkman talking about Dora's weekly trips, and went to find out what she could. Last week, I let Isolde hear something about some money hidden out by Likkel pond. Then I saw Penelope visit with the lieutenant, as any landlady might. But the next day, the duke's guard were at the pond."

"So Penelope Drusse is our spy." Lyle sighed.

"Somebody had better tell Isolde Dirkman," said Cyril.

"I wouldn't," Steffan replied. "She would merely regard it as another attack on her, and the people she associates with, and Penelope would be sure to hear about it."

"True," agreed Woodman. "At least we know better than to let Isolde know anything in the first place. We can't do anything about Penelope, but be aware of her. Cyril, you just got back from Greenwalt. What's the news from there?"

"Interesting. I was selling flour to the duke's manor there. The Duke of Greenwalt is a fine man, you know, and his sister, the dowager queen, she lives there, too. Anyway, they needed all the extra flour because Lord Chester and Lady Marcella were visiting. They do that often. Lady Marcella's the dowager's niece, and they're close. Now, the dowager's been a pretty sad lady these past few years, what with losing her husband and her son and his family inside of a month. But the servants are talking about how since His Lordship arrived, the dowager's been just as perky as ever. Well, the rumors been flying again that King Steffan is really alive. So's the servants asked the dowager if she's heard word from her son, but she says he's as he is, and there's naught she can do about it. The servants say that don't mean a thing and keep hoping. To my way of thinking, he's dead, and if he isn't, why hasn't he revealed himself before now?"

"Lanicia is too powerful," said Kiffs. "He'll need a whole army to take the throne back from her."

Steffan chuckled. "We may have one, provided of course that His Majesty is indeed alive and well. As you know, we've had a musician from Leiderkeit over the past week, and you all know that he knew me before my unfortunate fall. He is not without power and influence in Leiderkeit, although he has none here, thus his costume. He has promised us weapons and training in their use. He is close to the king, and we can trust that promise."

"We'll have our revolt!" Cyril laughed out loud.

"Not yet," hissed Woodman.

Steffan nodded. "I agree. We must establish a firm leadership. Without that, there will be chaos, and we will be vulnerable to attack from without."

"Why would King John want to help us?" sniffed Asgarth.

"I asked my friend the same," Steffan answered. "A great deal of it stems from the king's worry that Lanicia will attack Leiderkeit. He doesn't want war any more than we do. There is also a more personal side. King John was a great friend of our own king when they were boys, and later as men. His Majesty feels a debt of friendship to the people who oppose Lanicia, and who would support the return of King Steffan."

Woodman sighed. "Perhaps we should consider that. The rumors do not cease, and it seems they are worse than ever. What if the king is alive and wants his throne back?"

"We should help him," said Asgarth without hesitation. "His father was a wise ruler, and he ruled in his father's name for several months before the old king died."

"They say he was as good a man as his father," said Cyril.

Woodman nodded sadly. "I guess we should help King Steffan back. It would appear that's what everybody wants. But should we topple Lanicia, and find King Steffan is indeed in his grave, what will we have for a new leader? Murdren is right. We need that established before we organize how we're going to do it."

"You're hoping for a republic, aren't you?" asked Asgarth.

"I can't say I'm not," Woodman answered. "But by my own principles, if that's not what the people want, then I must abide with that."

"We've always had a king or a queen," said Lyle stubbornly.

The others nodded, except Steffan. Woodman looked at him.

"Murdren?" he asked. "What do you think?"

"I honestly don't know," Steffan replied. "I'm inclined to side with those who favor monarchy. Present monarch excluded, this kingdom has not done badly by it. Yet what I know of the concepts of a republic I find intriguing."

"They are at that," said Kiffs. "But they don't work in practice. The Romans went back to monarchy."

"I say we think on it," said Cyril. "I'm in favor of a monarchy with a new king, myself. But since we are divided, we should consider the others' views, so we can be agreed again."

"A very wise conclusion," said Steffan.

"True," Woodman said. The bell jingled again. "It's going to be a long night."

Coins switched places. The talk remained centered on the dice. Filfeldt did not enter right away, and when he did he was already disgusted and left quickly.

# THE FIFTH YEAR

## CHAPTER NINETEEN

Time's march was unrelenting and ever constant for the poor man as well as royalty, Steffan reflected as he plowed his fields for the fifth time.

The children were growing more rapidly than seemed possible in so short a time. Had Lorelei really left her swaddling clothes behind so quickly? And yet, at a year and a half old, she ran rather than walked. The twins were now four and young children rather than older babies. Indeed, James and Nella had joined the evening lesson times and could recite their letters. Steffan smiled, thinking about listening to Alicia, who had just turned seven, read and work sums. Barth, soon to turn nine, was reciting more and more of his history and beginning to tell tales of his own.

There had been a fair harvest, not to mention money from Ella's midwiving, the eggs they sold, the extra vegetables from the kitchen garden, and the breeding fees from Roscoe, still the biggest pig in the village. Their clothes were ragged, and there weren't many extras, but living wasn't quite so close, and there was enough food on their table.

That winter had been mild, and the spring storms somewhat wetter. As Steffan plowed and watched

Barth leading Max, the horse, on, he wondered if he'd ever get his furrows as straight as Asgarth's. It didn't really matter. Steffan's wheat grew just like anyone else's. Perhaps it wasn't quite as tall or full, but he had gotten a good enough return from that last harvest that Ella had splurged and bought Steffan a saddle for Max as a Christmas present.

The best part was that Steffan's leadership was well established among the dice players, as the meeting had come to call itself. Cyril frequently tried to best Steffan, and only looked more foolish for his pains. But he took his losses with good humor and found he had to admire Steffan as much as envy him.

With the seeding more or less done, and spring festival due soon, Steffan went into the village early one Monday afternoon to pick up a few items needed by Ella, and to get payment from a farmer on the other side of the village whose sow had whelped fifteen piglets by Roscoe. Having achieved his errands, he was walking through the square near the butcher shop when he happened to meet Cyril, and the two men stopped and chatted amiably.

The shrill screams cut their conversation short.

"It's coming from the butcher shop," gasped Cyril.

He and Steffan ran off that way and followed the cries to the back of the building. The door to Lieutenant Filfeldt's rooms was open, and Penelope Drusse burst out, holding her bodice shut and warding off the blows from her husband behind her. She paused at the top of the stairs, Mr. Drusse struck her again on the ears, and she tumbled down the stairs.

Steffan and Cyril ran to her side as Mr. Drusse

came tearing down the stairs after her. Steffan gently checked for Penelope's injuries while Cyril held back her husband.

"Give her to me!" Mr. Drusse yelled. A crowd collected. "She's mine, she is! I caught her! Adulteress! I caught them together, and she's mine. I've my rights."

"You've no right to beat anyone," said Steffan as he helped Penelope to her feet. "If she's truly an adulteress, then hand her over to the law, and make a claim against her and her lover."

"I'll make a claim!" Drusse struggled harder yet against Cyril.

"Hold now!" Cyril pushed the furious man back against the stairs. "Murdren is right. You can't go beating your wife. If you've a claim against her, do it through the magistrate."

"What's going on here?" demanded Lieutenant Filfeldt, coming down the stairs. He was fully dressed and perfectly sleek.

Drusse dove at him. "Thieving son of a-"

Cyril clapped his hand over Drusse's mouth as he pulled the man back from the stairway.

"It would appear that this man has a claim against you and his wife," said Steffan.

Filfeldt looked the group over. "I believe there's been a misunderstanding."

"You would say that," growled Penelope. "After all we've been to each other."

"Are you saying this man is your lover?" asked Cyril.

"Yes, I am."

"This is preposterous!" Filfeldt replied with a

sarcastic laugh. "It never happened."

"And of course your word is better than Mrs. Drusse's," said Steffan.

"I'm not sure what she expects to gain by such an accusation," said Filfeldt. "Perhaps freedom from her husband. He has been known to be unkind to her."

"Mr. Drusse," said Cyril, "If Filfeldt denies that he was your wife's lover, and if she cannot name another, then you can't claim she's an adulteress if she had no one to commit it with."

"Then give her to me!" Drusse grabbed at Penelope.

"No!" Penelope dodged behind Steffan. "Mr. Murdren, you've got to help me!"

"I'm afraid Cyril's right," said Steffan. "And we shall have to hand you back to your husband. Unless the lieutenant might care to consider the following. He is a personal representative of the queen, and as such can do as he pleases. There is no way you can be considered an adulteress if the lieutenant has insisted you bestow your favors on him in the name of the queen." Steffan turned to Filfeldt. "Which is it, sir? Shall we give the woman back to the dubious mercy of her husband, or will you step forward and generously accept responsibility for her crime?"

"Why don't you do the same?" replied Filfeldt.

"Mrs. Drusse did not flee from her husband through my door," Steffan answered. "Nor am I exempt from Mr. Drusse's just retribution by virtue of the queen's patronage."

Filfeldt glared at Steffan for a long time.

"You will pay for this, Murdren," he said softly.

Then he turned to the crowd. "I am innocent! But to protect this poor woman, I will accept responsibility for her crimes against her husband, and will see to her care." He turned back to Steffan. "Will that suffice?"

"More than adequate." Steffan smiled bitterly. "A worthy way out."

Filfeldt stalked off, up the stairs to his rooms. Cyril took Drusse with him to the tavern, and Isabelle Plainfield took Penelope with her. The crowd broke up, gossiping over the scene, analyzing every detail.

Two days later, Penelope suffered a miscarriage. The next day, she was found hanging from one of the trees near the mill. There was no doubt that it was suicide. She'd left a note, badly written but unquestionably hers.

Steffan received the news late that afternoon and became extremely depressed.

"It's tragic, my darling, I know," said Ella as he held her in bed that night. "But what else was the poor thing to do? According to Drusse, the baby had to have been the lieutenant's. She'd lost her name, her husband, her lover, even her baby. I'm not saying she should have killed herself, but I can understand it."

"Oh, it's easy to understand. What truly angers me is that low excuse for a human being will not suffer one bit for it."

"Well, not now, maybe not even in this life. But the lieutenant will suffer for it sooner or later. And if we are to be truly honest, Penelope was responsible for her share. The poor woman was so unloved, she knew nothing but to hate even the few kindnesses that came her way. She scorned it as pity and was glad to sell us all out as her revenge. The poor thing."

"I wonder how many more lives that man is going to drag down into ruin before he's through here?"

"I don't know. But there has been one blessing in this whole event."

"What?"

"He's been avoiding you. After you left him no opportunity to look even partly respectable, he will not face you."

"Mm." Steffan shook his head. "He may be avoiding me, but I'm sure he's planning some trouble for us. That kind does not know what forgiveness is."

"Then we shall be on guard. But it's no use spending all your time worrying about what he might do. Just take care to stay out of his way, and do not give him the least opportunity to arrest you."

"That sounds a lot easier than it will be in practice." Steffan sighed and laid his head on her breast. "You're right, Cindy. This whole affair has been dismal, yet he's defeated me if I let fear of him rule my life."

"Are you looking for a little comfort?"

"Yes. Thank you for sparing me the trouble of asking."

Ella chuckled and pressed him closer.

Shortly after the spring festival, she became sick. She was not happy about it, but not angry at Steffan either. He was overjoyed, as usual, and sympathetic. He and Alicia took over the cooking cheerfully, as being around any food except broth and day-old crusts sent Ella running for her bucket.

Lieutenant Filfeldt continued to avoid Steffan, and as Steffan expected he would, brooded and plotted. He was called back to the queen early in June but made it clear he would return to the village.

The timing was perfect as far as Giles Asgarth was concerned. He'd been quietly courting Berta Lyle for over a year. Lyle announced the impending nuptials at the spring festival, and on the last Saturday in June, Giles and Berta were married, and happily settled down with his brother and Elise in their house. Elise announced that she was with child, with the baby to be born sometime late that next winter or in early spring.

The summer rolled along pleasantly, with warm but not hot weather, and a few storms. The harvest was fair, and Steffan was again pleased with himself. There was nothing to mar the harvest festival except for the return of Lieutenant Filfeldt, and a new levy of taxes.

The snow came somewhat early that year. By the last week of November, the village was covered with a thin blanket. The news that the Duke of Raultberg had died caused little comment beyond the rumor that the duke had been found frozen stiff outside his palace without a stitch on his body. Steffan found himself believing the rumor, although he refused to say so.

However pleased Lanicia was by her father's convenient demise, it did lead to a division between herself and her youngest sister. The queen had never liked Chester. Unable to bear him any longer, Lanicia stripped Chester of his land and title. Marcella protested, and in the ensuing argument, Lanicia banished both her and her husband.

As the news went through the kingdom, unrest and fear grew. If the queen would show no mercy to her own sister, who would be safe?

"I believe the time is right to start preparing for a revolt," said Woodman solemnly the Monday evening before Christmas. "It will have to be done slowly, so as not to attract attention. I have letters indicating readiness, but we need someone who will take Lanicia's place on the throne. What we need to do is arrange a meeting whereby representatives from all the provinces can come and discuss what government we shall have and choose the man who will lead us. We shall obviously be the leaders of the meeting, and quite probably the leader shall come from among us."

"Then we'd best choose our man," said Cyril eagerly.

"I would recommend we wait on that," said Steffan, although his heart was pounding with excitement. "It will take time to organize this meeting, and to be truly fair to the other provinces, we don't want to bias them with our choice before they've had a chance to present theirs."

"Coming from you that's exceptionally just," said Lyle.

Cyril snorted. "It's not been decided yet."

"Your ambition has been noted," said Woodman.

"And his hasn't?" Cyril replied self-righteously.

"I make no secret of the fact that I would like the throne," said Steffan. "Nor should you, Cyril. It's nothing to be ashamed of. It is merely a question of what one's motives are. Do you truly want to be of service to your kingdom, although it is admittedly heady and rich service? Or are you looking for glory? I'm sure there is a desire for both in you, and there's no reason there shouldn't be. I must examine my motives all the time. Being king may involve a lot of power and wealth, but it also is a tremendous responsibility, one that cannot be abused. Why else are we here?"

Cyril sighed. "It's to your advantage that you say these things. But I cannot fault you because you're right."

Woodman chuckled. "I must say that the same is true for an elected leader, should I get my wish, and we pull together a republic."

"I'm sorry, Woodman." Cyril shook his head. "I'd as soon lead a republic as a kingdom, but the talk I've been hearing is that they want a kingdom."

"I know," sighed Woodman ruefully. "Perhaps someday."

Steffan smiled, still unsure how he felt about it. Ella wasn't sure where she stood, either, and thus was no help at all.

"We're too biased, Steffan," she said that night. "We were raised under a monarch, and that's what you are. Probably the best thing to do is to wait and see what the people choose. Although, I have a feeling they're going to want a king. Most of the talk I've heard is wondering when King Steffan will come back."

"They don't entirely believe I'm dead, do they?"

"I find it hard to believe." Ella smiled mischievously.

Steffan laughed, and gently pulled her next to him. She was too great with child for him to play as hard as he would have liked.

Christmas passed peacefully. But three days later, trouble erupted in the worst way. It started innocently enough. Several children were playing on the drift of snow that had piled up next to the magistrate's house,

Barth among them. Lieutenant Filfeldt rode up on his horse and smiled with satisfaction.

"You, beasts. That's the property of the queen," he commanded. "Have you no respect? Off of there, immediately!"

The children froze in terror.

"Get off! Now!" Filfeldt spurred his horse and hit the children with his riding crop.

They scattered. One, a cripple, couldn't move as fast. Filfeldt began beating the boy. Barth ran back.

"Stop it!" he cried. "Stop it, sir! He can't move that fast."

"And who are you, you little vermin?" Filfeldt turned all his wrath on Barth. "Ah, yes, Murdren's son. I might have known you'd turn on your better." He reached down and caught Barth by the neck with both hands. "That's what happens to those who turn on the queen. That's what happens!"

Filfeldt shook and squeezed, then threw Barth against the snow drift. The body lay still and lifeless.

# CHAPTER TWENTY

Ella's cries burned themselves into Steffan's memory and would haunt him for the rest of his life. He stood breathless as he watched his wife rocking with grief as she held their son's body. Then the rage filled him. Three men had to hold him back, he never knew who. He broke down into sobs and knelt next to Ella, their grief blending together, blurring the next few hours.

They had other children to care for, whose grief was no less great. Even Lorelei, who was only two, knew that her brother was gone. Lost and confused, she stumbled along with the stricken family, wondering why her parents had forgotten her.

They left Barth in the church to be prepared for burial. Sleep seemed impossible that night, yet the grief had exhausted Ella and Steffan so much that they fell into blessed unconsciousness as soon as they got into bed. The next morning was so empty, Steffan felt as if he could not breathe. Ella wept some more, then collected Barth's Sabbath clothes for the funeral. Elise and Berta Asgarth came to prepare breakfast and help with the children, as did Arlette, Meg and Gen. Gen, in particular, took special care of Lorelei, knowing how in times of grief, the youngest child could be overlooked.

Ella refused to leave her children, so the whole group went to the church to make the arrangements.

Steffan stayed behind. The livestock needed tending, and he hoped to lose some of the anguish in his work.

Roscoe triggered the rage again. Steffan heard the pig snorting around the side of the house, and the fury grew. The pig had been bought to be butchered. Its life had been spared, but his son's had not. Steffan grabbed the long knife and went after the animal.

It had moved to its pen and was dismally rooting up some earth next to its trough. Roscoe knew that Barth would not be coming to feed him anymore. He knew the sadness in the house and was listless and uninterested even in his favorite pastime. The pig looked up at Steffan.

He stood with the knife in his hand. Barth's young voice once again defended Roscoe, and the silent tears once again slid out from the squeezed shut eyes. Across the years, Barth's weeping once again tore at Steffan's heart.

The knife dropped, and tears filled Steffan's eyes.

"I can't do it," he told Roscoe. "My son is killed, and I can't do it. You should be ham!" The anger faded. "It's not your fault. But the man whose fault it is shall pay for this. I don't know how, but he will."

Before the others returned, Steffan removed the hearthstone and pulled out Barth's medallion. It was getting late, but he walked into the village anyway. He met Ella and the others on the way and told them he'd be back soon.

The old priest had to light a candle when Steffan walked into his study.

"I take it you have a special request."

"Yes, Father." Steffan pulled out his pouch. "I

don't know how much it costs. I haven't much, but I don't want my son in a pauper's grave. I want him to have his own, with a marker."

"I understand," replied the priest, who had heard many of the family's secrets in the confessional. "You keep your money. I can't take it from a murdered child's father."

"Thank you." Steffan handed over two gold pieces. "Take this anyway for the marker. Good stone isn't cheap."

"As you wish, then."

"Is he still in the chapel?"

"Yes."

"I'd like to visit for a few minutes, if I may."

"By all means."

The priest led Steffan to the church door and left him. After honoring the Sacrament, Steffan went to the little side chapel where his son lay wrapped in a white linen shroud. Almost numb, he undid the sheet, then took the medallion from his pocket. His hands trembled as he slipped the chain over the head and around the poor misshapen neck. He bent and kissed the cold forehead, then quickly re-knotted the shroud.

He and Ella were numb through the funeral the next day. Later, that night, they were finally able to talk.

"I feel as if I've failed you," Ella said, sniffing. "We've been so distant, and when we've needed each other the most."

"If there was any distance, it's most likely my fault. I can't believe what this has done to me."

"I thought I was strong, that I could take anything. But I hurt now worse than I've ever hurt before. Oh,

Steffan, you've got to be careful. If I lost you, I don't think I could bear it."

"I know." He pressed her close to him and wept with her.

Barth had been dead a week when Steffan felt as though he could face the lieutenant with a reasonable amount of calm. He still brought Asgarth, Edward, and Giles with him to the magistrate's house. Filfeldt was waiting, as were two young boys.

The boys told what had happened with frightened but sure voices. Then Steffan watched in shock as Filfeldt questioned them, and undermined everything they said.

"It's simple," Filfeldt told the magistrate. "The boys were confused. That slope was dangerous. I was trying to warn them, and they took offense. The Murdren boy came at me and shied the horse. It was an accident that he fell under the hooves."

"There were no hoof prints on that body," said Steffan with calm anger.

"Then he broke his neck in the fall. I can't be held for that."

"Queen's representative or not, you cannot murder and expect that even she will protect you."

"But it wasn't murder, Mr. Murdren. It was an accident."

"I'm sorry, Mr. Murdren," said Sir Leonard. "The boys' testimony was so confused, I am forced to disregard it as unreliable. The death will be recorded as an unfortunate accident."

Filfeldt smiled his satisfied smile. "It is regrettable, and I offer my condolences. But, Mr. Murdren, perhaps if the boy had been taught more respect for his queen, this might not have happened."

"He had more respect for the monarchy than you could possibly understand," said Steffan. He turned to the magistrate. "This is not justice."

"I'm sorry, Mr. Murdren. My hands are tied."

"Come along, Alex," Asgarth whispered in his ear. "You'll get nothing here but more grief."

Steffan allowed Asgarth to lead him out of the house and to the road.

"His hands are tied," Steffan spat out venomously. "Tied by a thieving queen who stole her crown. It was almost murder that got her to her throne. No wonder her servants can escape punishment for it!"

"Easy, Alex. We'll find a way, and he won't escape," said Asgarth.

Steffan didn't hear. "She almost got us once. Now, she's gotten my son. I'll be damned if she's going to get the rest of us." His gesture was as unconscious as it was imperious. "Leave me. I want to be alone."

He stalked off down the road. Asgarth held Giles back.

Steffan went first to the barn and readied the wagon. Then he walked into the house. Ella was sitting and staring into the fire as she held Alicia and James. The other two girls were napping in their bedroom.

"Start packing," Steffan ordered.

Ella looked up. "What happened?"

"The magistrate ruled it an accident." Steffan piled the kitchen equipment onto the table.

"But why are we leaving?"

"We're going to Leiderkeit. It's safe there."

"What about the revolt?"

"They'll have to have it without me."

"You can't do that!" Ella stood, her eyes blazing.

Steffan faced her. "I have no choice. Do you want the rest of your children murdered?"

"You're giving up."

"I don't know yet. Right now the important thing is your safety."

"The important thing is your duty. Your first responsibility is to your people!"

"And I have failed it. I can't even get justice for my son with witnesses to the deed!" Steffan returned to gathering kitchen utensils. "Get packing."

"No!"

"It is my wish. You will obey."

Something inside of Ella went dead. Listlessly, she did as her husband directed. Steffan was too numb and too angry to notice. They left early the next morning before the sunrise, bringing along Daffy and Roscoe, and a few chickens.

Four days later, they crossed into Leiderkeit. Steffan bought some parchment, sealing wax, quill, and ink, and wrote another letter. The Earl of Ebenwalt was a little confused by the letter of recommendation.

"I've had it for a long time," Steffan told him. "I left His Majesty's service to help with some family matters shortly before the old king's death. After that, it seemed better to avoid mentioning it."

"Why have you come to Leiderkeit?" asked the duke.

"The family matters have been settled, and the climate in my kingdom is not entirely hospitable. I thought it better to begin again someplace else."

"Well, Dame Fortune is smiling on you at this moment. My stable master has recently died. His boy is trying, but he's really too young to manage the entire place. I tried one other man, and he proved to be dishonest, which was very upsetting." The earl looked at the letter. "A recommendation from Prince Steffan, I mean King Steffan, however old, means a great deal. I hope you will find the position adequate. It comes with proper uniforms and a cottage for you and your family. How many children do you have?"

Steffan swallowed. "Four, with another due soon."

"Quite good. And some livestock, too, I understand."

"I have my own horse, a cow, a pig, and a few chickens."

"You may make room for them as you see fit."

"You are most generous, my lord."

"Thank you. I don't mind doing well by a good man. I'm confident you will prove to be such."

"Thank you, my lord." Steffan bowed and left to settle his family in their new home.

Ella didn't react to the news of Steffan's position. She hadn't reacted to much of anything since they had left. She mostly slept or stared, not responding when anyone spoke to her. Steffan decided it was her grief and the strain of the coming baby, and helped Alicia with the tasks that Ella was suddenly too sleepy and tired to do.

They'd been there almost a month when Ella's face suddenly tightened. It was close to dinner time, and Steffan had just entered the cottage after a long day in the stables. The stable boy, Carl, was there, as he usually ate dinner with the family. Steffan's heart filled with an intense fear he'd never known before.

"Are you in labor?" he asked Ella.

"All day now," she whispered. Her face tightened again.

"I'll fetch the doctor!" Carl bounced up and ran off before Steffan could tell him to.

The midwife arrived first and clucked worriedly when she saw Ella. Steffan paced, while Alicia put the other children to bed. The doctor arrived soon after, and Steffan was left with Alicia to pace and wait.

At two in the morning, Carl was again sent on an errand, this time to fetch the local priest. The baby was alive but sickly, and his mother wasn't doing much better. She managed to nurse the infant, but that was all. The priest arrived promptly.

"What name do want to give the child?" he asked Steffan.

"Darling?" Steffan looked over at Ella. She was asleep. "Let's name him Steffan. Steffan Bartholemew Lucas James."

"A good long name. Pray God he lives up to it." And the priest baptized the baby, then blessed Ella, and left.

Steffan reached over and touched his new son's neck.

"Oh, my son. You were conceived because I was depressed, and you've been born into a house of sorrow. I don't know what kind of life I can offer you, but I beg you to keep yours. Another loss would kill us."

"Papa?" Alicia walked up sadly. "Is Mama going to be all right?"

"I don't know. We've got to keep praying and hoping."

"Why does she sleep all the time?"

"Because she's very sad, and it's hard enough to give birth when you're happy. It's been very hard for her."

"It's been hard for me, too."

"I know, my dearest child." Steffan held her. "But I've been very proud of the way you've been helping out. You've made it easier."

"Thank you, Papa. I love you."

"I love you, too, my darling."

He put her to bed wondering where the life in her had gone. She'd always had her mother's brightness. But then, Ella's light had dimmed also. Steffan slid into bed and held his wife's sleeping form close to him, trying to will into her that missing light.

Miles away, and a week and a half later, John Asgarth looked at the deserted farmhouse, and again shook his head. He understood what had made them go. But the departure had hurt and disillusioned him far worse than he could have imagined.

Searching for some sort of answer to a question he didn't know to ask, he went again across the road, and into the house. The dust had settled over the two months, dust that Cindy would have never let inside had she been there. Anger mounted in Asgarth, not so much at his neighbor, but at the evil that had driven his neighbor away. There was a loose brick on the mantelpiece. Suddenly infuriated, Asgarth threw it at the hearth.

There was a hollow sound, the brick rolled over, and one of the hearthstones bounced. Asgarth looked at it more closely and noticed the plaster that had fallen out of the cracks. Carefully, he lifted the stone and peered inside the hole. There was a small cloth bag laying on a bed of straw. Asgarth drew it out.

The medallions sparkled in the thin sunlight. Asgarth read the names on the back, although he didn't have to. The boy's was missing; Alex had probably managed to bury it with him. The others had been left. Since there was no hope of regaining what was his, there was no point in keeping the identification.

Asgarth sat back on the hearth in wonder. All that time, and always so cautious. No wonder the man leaned towards a monarchy, and yet he was open enough to consider a republic. The waste caved in on Asgarth yet again.

Outside, another pair of refugees got down off their horses and looked about.

"It doesn't look like there's anyone home," said Lady Marcella, the breath escaping from her mouth in clouds.

"This is the place according to King John," her husband replied. "They're probably all gathered around the fire, exchanging memories about the palace. Let's just go on in and surprise them."

"I don't know. Oh, all right. Chester, I just don't know how I'm going to manage this."

"The same way Steffan has." Chester opened the door wide. "Surprise!"

The surprise was mutual. Asgarth bounded to his feet. Chester and Marcella gazed at the dust and desertion. Chester recovered first.

"Perhaps we have the wrong house." He stopped as he saw the medallions in Asgarth's hand. "Where did you find those?"

Recognition formed in Asgarth's mind. "Lady Marcella, Lord Chester, I..."

"Not anymore," sighed Chester. "Come here, darling, have a seat."

"Where are they?" Marcella asked.

Asgarth shrugged. "They left. Right after the start of the year."

"They left?" repeated Chester. "Where did they go?"

"Maybe they went back to the city to get back what was his," said Marcella suddenly smiling.

"I doubt as that's it," said Asgarth. "They had good reason to go. I think it was towards safety."

Chester took the medallions. "You know who we're talking about, don't you?"

"I knew them as the Murdrens. Obviously, they weren't."

"King John of Leiderkeit sent us here," said Marcella. "I've known for a couple years now that he was alive. When we were banished, we went to John. He told us the same, and sent us here."

"But why didn't he know they'd left?" asked Chester. "If they were in trouble, I'm sure they would have gone to John." Chester looked again at the medallions. "One of these is missing." He looked accusingly at Asgarth. "Where's Barth's?"

Asgarth lowered his eyes. "Buried with the boy."

"You mean Barth's..?" Marcella couldn't finish.

"It's why they left, I expect," Asgarth continued. "The way he was talking that day, that could be the only reason. The boy was murdered by one of the queen's servants. We tried to get justice from the magistrate, but Sir Leonard ruled the death an accident. Murdren got very angry and swore that the queen wouldn't get another of his. The next morning, they was gone."

Chester sank onto the kitchen table bench. "His heir and pride. Now, what do we do? Maybe we can find him, and talk him into coming back. Do you have any idea where he went?"

"He once told me to send his family to Leiderkeit if something happened to him," said Asgarth. "He said he had friends there."

"Yes. King John, who doesn't know he's there."

"Let's write him anyway," suggested Marcella. "He might be able to find them for us. John has a way of doing things like that."

"That makes sense," said Chester. "Let's see if we can find some paper and ink."

# CHAPTER TWENTY-ONE

King John shuffled one last time through the papers on the desk of the Earl of Ebenwalt. John had always considered the Royal Review of the landed gentry in his kingdom his least favorite task. However, he'd uncovered more than one cheater, proving that the Review was necessary. Ebenwalt had always proved honest, which made the task easier, even if John could not get away with overlooking it altogether.

"Well, your affairs are in order, as always," John said pleasantly. He noticed a piece of parchment with familiar handwriting. "What's this?"

"A letter of recommendation, Sire," answered the Earl. "I thought it a little odd, but it seemed in order. It's not false, is it?"

"Hardly. New paper again, too. At least he's using better wax. Who gave this to you?"

"My new stable man. A fine worker, name of Alex Murdren."

The name rocked John. "What's he doing here?"

"Do you know him, Sire?"

"As a matter of fact, I do, though what he's doing here, I can't imagine."

"He's managing my stables, and doing a very good job, in spite of his wife doing poorly. The most the stable boy can get out of them is that they've suffered a tremendous loss recently."

"It would have to have been. I'd better deal with this immediately." John rose, trying to keep a steady grip on his worry about his old friend. "And alone. You will see to it?"

"Immediately, Sire."

"Excellent." John hurried out of the study.

He knew the Earl's estate intimately. It took him only a few minutes to reach the stable man's cottage. He knocked and entered without waiting for an answer. Alicia was at the fireplace ladling out soup for her younger brother and sisters.

"Oh!" she gasped, then smiled weakly. "You're the musician man that knows us."

"Yes. Is your mother about?"

"In there. She's asleep."

John went into the room. "Ella?" He waited. "Ella?"

She did not respond. John sighed at her pallor.

"That's all she does anymore," said Alicia sadly. "Sleeps and feeds the baby. Sometimes she'll take some broth."

John looked around. "Is Barth with your father?"

"No." Alicia sniffed. "He's dead, sir."

John reeled. Suddenly the flight, the dismal house, Ella's illness made sense.

"Where's your father? In the stables?"

"Yes, sir."

"Excellent." John put his arm around Alicia and squeezed. "It'll be all right, little one. Your mother will get better, I'll see to it."

He left and went to the stables. Steffan was picking a rock from the hoof of the Earl's prize stallion. His back was to John as he worked. John was forced to smile. The normally skittish stallion was calm in Steffan's hands.

"It's odd how the Murdren family suddenly turned up here, isn't it?" said John.

Steffan started but stayed calm enough to finish the job at hand. He turned slowly.

"Your Majesty." His head lowered.

"Don't you dare get on your knee to me. We are equals."

"We were equals." Nonetheless, Steffan remained erect. After a moment, he led the stallion back to his stall. "Fortune has turned her face from me, and I'm willing to accept that."

"You've given up."

"Call it what you will. I have a family to keep, and I'm going to do the best I can by them."

"I was at the cottage. Alicia told me about Barth."

"Then you know why." Steffan finished grooming the stallion and locked the stall door shut behind him.

"You're going to let the boy die in vain?"

Steffan turned on him. "What do you know about it? You haven't got a family. I've got to protect what I've got left."

"And how many other children are going to die because you won't oppose Lanicia?"

"They were doing fine without me."

"They'd be doing better with you."

"I can't." Steffan paused, then picked up a shovel. "I'm sorry, John, but I can't. You don't know what it is to lose your child."

John shook his head. "I do know, Steffan."

"You've never been married."

"That doesn't prevent fatherhood, unfortunately. I was young, and my father insisted that it be kept quiet." John leaned against a stall as Steffan sat down on a bale of hay. "I more or less fell in love with a chambermaid. We got caught off guard one day before either of us knew what to guard against. We had a little daughter. Lillia. She was such a beautiful girl. We gave her mother a good estate, nicely close so I could visit often. Lillia and I adored each other. Then about three years ago, there was a sleigh accident." John paused to get his grip back. "She was gone, my beautiful little girl. Her mother asked for some money and left. She couldn't bear being kept by me any longer, in every way a wife, but never able to marry. I lost both of them."

Steffan closed his eyes. "Barth was murdered by the queen's representative. I couldn't even get justice for him."

"Maybe not at that time you couldn't. But you will get it, if only you don't give up."

"John, my wife is barely alive, this grief has torn her apart so. How can I risk doing that to her again?"

"Ella is a strong woman. Don't you see, Steffan? She's given up because you have."

"I don't know." Steffan wandered over to the pig pen. He looked morosely at Roscoe. "We bought this pig to butcher. He was Barth's responsibility, and Barth couldn't let him go when it came time for butchering. He'd taught this pig tricks, to come on command. He loved this pig. The day after Barth died, I tried to butcher it. I couldn't do it, any more than I could the first time." Steffan slammed his hand into the wooden slat. "Damn it, John! Doesn't this pain ever go away?"

"No. For the rest of your life, there will be a hole. But time does ease it. I'll be here for a few days yet, probably through the Sabbath. Go ahead and ask for me at the house."

Steffan nodded.

John left and paid a quick visit to the local bishop.

"This is an honor, Your Majesty," said the man.

"Actually, I've come to ask you a favor. I understand you'll be preaching at this Sabbath's mass."

"Yes, Your Majesty."

"Please feel free to refuse if it's not appropriate. I won't go interfering with God's work. But if possible, I'd like to hear a sermon on responsibility."

The bishop smiled. "I had already planned to preach on just that subject, Your Majesty."

"Excellent. I shall look forward to it with relish."

John left and found himself whistling merrily. It didn't become a monarch, especially one of his standing, but he decided he didn't care.

Steffan remained deep in thought for the next two days. The problem was, John was right. But so was Steffan's responsibility to his family's preservation. Ella wasn't doing well as she was. Steffan shuddered to think what would happen to her once the baby no longer required her milk. But the children were all well, and alive, and not in any real danger. As he sat outside the cottage in the evenings, he noticed the lights of the Faer Folke in the trees and couldn't help wondering why they hadn't been able to save Barth.

Steffan went to mass that Sabbath both out of habit and because Ella would have expected it of him.

He stood at the back with his children and squirmed through the whole sermon. Afterward, he got the children home and retreated to the stables to think.

John was waiting for him.

Steffan sighed. "With Your Majesty's permission, I'd like to be alone."

"Enough with the deference nonsense. We are equals, we shall always be equals. And I'm not letting you alone until you face up to the responsibility you were raised to face."

"I'm facing it already, John. What do you want me to do? Sacrifice Alicia, and James and Nella. Do you want me to cut out Lorelei's heart right here, and throw little Steffan on the pyre?"

"What kind of a man are you? You've changed, Steffan. The man I knew would have gladly given his life over for his kingdom."

"My life, yes. But must I give over my children's lives? They didn't ask for this to happen."

"Neither did you. What's happened to you? You've let fear rule your every move. That's not you, Steffan. You used to have the courage to stand up to bullies, to fight for those weaker than you. You had pride. You were strong. You were a man who could call himself king. Now, you're nothing. You're hiding behind your children because you think you've failed when you couldn't get justice for your son on the first try. That's not the man I knew. Now you're no better than the worm who murdered your son."

Steffan's rage burst out of him in an explosion. John barely had time to put up his arms against the rain of blows. He pushed against Steffan and got thrown across the stable for his effort. Steffan's fury poured out against the walls, against the stalls where the horses stamped and neighed in fear. Steffan tore the tools from the ceiling. Bales of hay went flying. Steffan found one that had remained intact and punched and punched until his knuckles bled, and the fury drained out of him.

Weeping, he collapsed. John came over and knelt beside him.

"I was never allowed to be angry as a child," he said softly. "It would have been too undignified. And Heaven forbid if I should ever weep. When Lillia died, I tore apart the royal kitchen."

Steffan sniffed and nodded.

"Feel better?"

"Yes. Finally." Steffan wiped his eyes and sat up. "It still hurts. But you're right. Ella was right. I've got a responsibility to that kingdom, and I can't let that woman continue her destruction."

"There is such a thing as faith, you know."

Steffan thought of the lights in the trees and realized that he had been helped in the all-too-perfect timing of his friend's arrival.

"And that is what I must rely on for my children's safety."

"I can keep them here if you like."

"I don't know. I'll have to ask Ella. I have a feeling she won't want to leave them, and she will refuse to stay without me."

"You've started a good tradition that way. I wish I could find a woman with that kind of intelligence. Let me rephrase that. I wish I could find a well-born woman like that. Your neighbor's daughter is bright enough." John chuckled. "You do realize, dear friend, that I must get you back on your throne. Then you can elevate Arlette's status, and I can marry her, and finally live as happily as you."

"Happily?" Steffan snorted and looked about him at the mess he'd made.

"Everyone has their valleys. You'll manage to be happy again. That was the one thing that struck me about your little house on the farm. You were happy in spite of the poverty about you. You've suffered a great loss. But you've still got a great deal left. More than even I have. Fortune hasn't turned her face from you. She merely blinked for a moment."

"It was a pretty devastating moment."

"But think how much stronger you're going to be, how much more wisely you'll be able to rule your people. You've lived their pain. You know what their struggles are. Why do you think I spend so much time playing the fiddle in rags?"

"John, you are a greater friend than I ever thought possible."

"You've always been one to take everything on yourself. Help up?" John stood and offered his hand.

"Yes, thank you." Steffan took the hand and pulled himself upright.

"You should have come to me."

Steffan smiled. "I should have. They say afterthought is a wonderful counselor."

The two men laughed and embraced. Steffan quickly swept the mess into one corner, then helped John replace the tools. When they were finished, John turned to Steffan.

"I've got to get back to my palace, now. Send me word through this Earl when you need arms."

"I will. I'd better get back to Ella." Steffan paused. "Thank you, John, for everything."

"You're welcome to it. It's what I owe you. When my father died, I almost did, too, for fear. I was always a rebel, never content with the way things were. You wrote me a letter at that time. I still have it. It gave me the courage to accept my responsibility. We're back to that again, aren't we? Thanks to you, I was able to channel my rebellious energy to constructive ends. I've been a better king for it, and all because you had the courage to share your fears and hopes with me. If I can help you, what am I doing but paying off an old debt?"

"I never knew that letter meant so much."

"You do now. I'll be seeing you, hopefully, next time wearing better clothes."

Steffan laughed. "And a crown on my head."

John left the stable, whistling again. Steffan took a deep breath.

He entered the house and went to his wife's bed. He gently shook her.

"Ella, please wake up. We've got to talk. We're going home."

Ella stirred.

"Ella, wake up, darling. We're going home."

Ella's eyes opened. "Steffan?"

"Yes, dearest. I owe you an apology."

"Why?"

"For not listening to you. You were right. We have to go back, and I've got to do my best to recover my throne."

"Oh, Steffan!" Ella held him as tight as her weakened limbs would hold.

Then the tears came. They lasted a long time. Alicia came in with a worried frown, followed by the others.

"What's wrong?" Alicia asked.

"Nothing anymore," said Steffan. "This is the good kind of crying, the kind that means healing. Come here, children, we've been sad too long."

Alicia got little Steffan from the cradle, as Nella, James, and Lorelei joined their parents on the bed. Alicia crawled into the group and they held each other close.

"Papa, Mama, I think Barth is still with us," said Alicia.

"Yes, he is," said Ella. "He's with us in our hearts."

Steffan and the children spent that night packing. Ella spent her time trying to get her strength back. After so much sleep, she couldn't anymore, but the lack of food had left her too weak to stand for more than a few seconds. So she started eating. Steffan gave her weak broth and bread first, but soon she was craving eggs and ham and beef joint. Steffan indulged her as he could.

The next morning, Steffan told the Earl that he was leaving. The Earl wasn't pleased, but the King had asked as a personal favor to release Steffan, and the Earl could not refuse. He gave Steffan a generous severance stipend and wished him well. Steffan returned to the cottage, where Alicia was packing a few last minute items.

"I'll be done in a minute, Papa," she said.

"Leave that for a moment," he answered and put his arm around her shoulders. "We've got to talk."

"Yes, sir." Alicia looked at him with grave eyes that were also so bright and so much like her mother's.

"Alicia, you were so small when the accident happened, and we had to go into hiding."

"Barth told me about the palace, though, and what a wonderful place it was."

"Well, we're going to try to go back. Not right away. We'll be going back to the farm first. That's where I have the most support."

"You mean people who like you."

"Yes, and who will say they want me to be their king. If I am successful, then a tremendous responsibility becomes yours at the same time."

"Why?"

"Because you are now my heir. You are my oldest child. In the past, it has been the oldest son, but that's what started this whole problem. Your great-grandfather chose your grandfather over his oldest daughter, and she was very angry, and passed that anger to her own daughter, who is Lanicia."

"So I will be queen after you?"

"Yes. From now on, you must remember that. It will be a wonderful blessing and a curse. I will help you, Alicia. I will teach you all the things my father taught me, and you will learn to be a good queen, just like my father taught me how to be a good king."

Alicia thought for a moment. "I'll do my best, Papa."

"And your best will be wonderful." Steffan smiled

and swallowed as he held his daughter.

In a terrible way, it was better that Alicia ascend the throne. Alicia had more of her mother's gentleness, and her father's ability to analyze. Steffan still felt the loss, but could, at last, find the faith to trust all would come out to the better.

# THE SIXTH YEAR

## CHAPTER TWENTY-TWO

The family arrived home early in March. They celebrated Alicia's eighth birthday during the journey, as it had been forgotten in the weeks before. On the last leg of the journey, Ella suddenly sighed.

"Something wrong?" Steffan looked up from the road and Max's back.

"I'm just hoping you haven't lost your support."

"So am I. If I have, I'll just have to get it back. It shouldn't be that hard. One of John's generals caught me just before we left. We're carrying weapons in the wagon, and more are on their way."

"That sounds so ugly, weapons." Ella shifted baby Steffan as he slept in her arms.

"It does, but as one of my fellow dice players pointed out, I'll need a whole army to get back the throne from Lanicia. There may yet be a way to do this without bloodshed, but we'll have to appear sufficiently menacing."

Ella nodded. Over the past four days of the journey, she'd gotten most of her strength back, even if she tired more quickly. The hurt continued to burn within her, and any hint of her lost son brought tears to her eyes. At least she and Steffan were able to talk out their pain. The pain would still be there, probably for the rest of their lives, but it was time to start looking forward.

They arrived at the farmhouse in the middle of the night. A final light snow fell, laying a soft glowing blanket over the roofs and sleeping fields. Ella held little Steffan closely wrapped in her arms. The other children slept under an improvised tent in the back of the wagon. Alicia held five-year-old James and Nella, while Lorelai, now three, snuggled up close to James.

Max pulled into the yard almost on his own. Steffan reined the horse in, then helped Ella and the baby from the seat. After checking the children, Steffan pulled the cradle from the wagon and followed Ella to the front door.

"It's locked," she said, puzzled.

"Maybe I did leave it that way." Steffan went through his pockets. "I believe I have the key somewhere."

"Here it is." Ella produced the key from her own pockets.

"Thank you." Steffan fitted the key in the lock, but it wouldn't turn. "What is going on?"

"Steffan, that's smoke coming from the chimney."

"Who's in there?" Steffan pounded on the door. "Open up in there!"

Steffan pounded harder.

Upstairs, in the loft, Marcella sat up in bed. Chester awoke also.

"Who's that?" she hissed, fearfully.

"Open up, I say!" The pounding came harder.

"That voice." Chester bounded out of bed and

slid on his dressing gown. "Who's calling?"

"The man who owns this house! Now, open my door!"

"They're back!" crowed Marcella.

She quickly put on her dressing gown and followed Chester down the ladder. He unlocked the door and admitted Steffan and Ella. Steffan gaped.

"What are you two doing here?" he asked.

"Didn't John send you?" Marcella asked. "I sent him that letter to find you."

"He said nothing about a letter to me," replied Steffan. "He only told me that he'd sent you two back to this village."

"Darling, we'd better get the children in," said Ella.

"Of course, my dear, and the animals need stabling. Chester, come help." Steffan set the cradle by the fire and left.

Ella quickly found some clean straw, put it in the cradle, and laid the baby down.

"So this is the new one." Marcella peered lovingly over the infant. "We'd heard you were with child. There's a gossipy old bird in the village that said it was unthinkable that you should be made to travel when your time was so near."

"Isolde Dirkman." Ella smiled softly. "I wasn't that near, and for all Steffan knew, it wouldn't be long before the rest of us were butchered."

"Boy or girl?"

"A little boy, perhaps to make up for his brother. Steffan gave him his own name. At the time, he didn't think he'd be using it again."

"Oh, Ella, what pain you've suffered." Marcella put her arms around Ella.

Ella patted Marcella's arm. The woman had been barren, and her grief over never having a child was equally profound.

"In some ways, I envy you," Ella replied. "I would almost rather not have had Barth than to feel this hurt. But at the same time, I'm glad for the memories I do have. It's strange. I keep wondering if I felt this hurt when my father died, or if I was too young to understand, or if it's been so long I've forgotten. This pain is the worst I've ever known. But I also know I can live through it. Steffan and I have even been able to laugh again."

Steffan and Chester came in carrying James and Lorelei, while Nella and Alicia shuffled sleepily along next to them. Ella went to prepare the beds, and give her children one last kiss good night. Steffan and Chester returned some minutes later and announced that the wagon was in the barn, and the animals were settled.

"That pig might even stay in his pen, for once," said Steffan.

Ella had brewed a hot pot of tea and was pouring it into bowls.

"So how did John find you?" asked Marcella. "We sent a letter asking him to when we found you'd gone."

"It was an accident that he found us," Steffan said. "He found a letter of recommendation that I'd written for myself, and asked about it. I'm not surprised he didn't say much about you. We had little time to talk, once other matters were cleared up. But what happened to you? Why did you come back?"

"It was only rumor that we were actually banished," said Marcella. "My sister only said she would be happy if she never saw us again. So we thought it would be expedient if we left the country, and we went to Leiderkeit. Of course, we went straight to His Majesty. John was terribly sweet. Then, it was almost a month ago, John was in one of his moods, and insisted on having a ball, and that we attend. We were the guests of honor, along with this older duke who had recently taken a new bride. I looked at her and was thoroughly confused. I knew I'd seen her before, and couldn't think where. When I finally remembered, I nearly fainted. I saw her once, in a corridor of my father's palace, the haunted one. She was with a man who clapped his hand over my mouth and ordered my silence."

"Dora?" Steffan looked amazed, then turned to Ella.

"That was her name," said Marcella.

"Dora?" asked Ella. "And she's married a duke?"

Ella looked at Steffan, and the two of them burst into laughter.

"Just before we left, they announced that she was newly with child by him," said Chester. "What's so funny?"

"She was such a common, coarse little thing," gasped Ella. "Not that she wasn't very nice, but a duchess..."

"Well, I told John about how I'd seen her, and that I was certain she was the same girl," Marcella continued. "And John confessed that he'd done quite a bit of lying. But since she and the duke were deliriously happy, it didn't really matter, and he was certain he had any number of undesirables in his family tree also. He also said that Dora had told the duke all about her former life, and the duke didn't mind one bit."

"A very open-minded man," chuckled Steffan. "I'd like to meet him."

"You don't understand," Ella added. "Dora used to be... It's not at all proper, but she was a prostitute. She gave it up and was the seamstress's apprentice when she was arrested. But to think that she's a duchess now. I'm so happy for her."

"She is happy," said Marcella. "But to continue, talking about Dora led us onto another subject, and John finally dragged it out of me that I had seen you, and that I knew you were alive."

"You told my mother, didn't you?" said Steffan.

"Of course. We couldn't let her continue to suffer. There wasn't much that we could tell her. But it was enough. Steffan, you should have seen her. She'd been so gray and dismal since the accident. Some days it was all she could do to get out of bed. When we told her, it was as if she'd come alive again. She said you'd be back, she knew it."

"I'm glad you did. I probably should have sent word, but I don't know how I could have done it."

"Let's get back to John," said Chester. "Once John knew that we knew you were alive, he told us the rest, about how he'd been to see you. Discreetly, he said. How he managed that, I don't know."

"He has his ways," Steffan replied.

"Anyway, he told us that we should go back and help you gather your support, that the time was ripe for you to take back what was your own."

"So, just to be certain, I wrote a letter to my sister," Marcella cut in. "And I told her that I wanted to live in my own kingdom, but that we would live by my husband's work, as simple folk, and that she need never know we were there, only we didn't want to come back and find a price on our heads. Well, we got back a letter that said, of course, there wasn't a price on our heads, but if she ever set eyes on us again, there would be."

"She'd had to revoke the banishment because she was losing support," said Chester bitterly.

"So John told us exactly where we would find you, and here we are. Except you were gone."

"Well, it was and it wasn't a necessary departure," said Steffan. "I had some business to settle with myself first. And we've got our first weapons. I'm just hoping we can avoid using them."

"So reveal yourself," said Chester. "You've got this entire village behind you, and everyone else is behind them. I've been playing dice, too, my friend. Your neighbor Asgarth insisted I come because of my noble background. We'll need their support, too, you know. The people are ready for you to come back."

"Not quite ready." Steffan paused. "There is more involved than you or any of them know. We will wait, Chester. I know now that the time will come, but it will have to do so without any pressure, and by the definite consent of the people. Be patient, we will yet succeed, but it may not be in the way we expect."

They went to bed soon after that. Chester and Marcella insisted on giving Steffan and Ella their own bed back and slept on hastily made straw mattresses downstairs. Ella slipped close to Steffan as they made themselves comfortable.

"Are you leaning towards a republic, my love?" she asked.

"No. Not really. What I want is to be chosen leader, or king on my own merits, and not my name. It was one of the things I found so special about you, those first two times we met. You didn't know who I was and liked and loved me because of me. Anyone can hide behind a name."

"And now I have that much more confidence in you. But what if you aren't chosen?"

"Then I shall have to shave the dice a little and see if they'll still accept me. After that, if they don't, then the throne was not meant to be mine. I did my best, and I shall have to go into another field of endeavor. Don't worry, Ella. Whatever happens, my success at living is not dependent on whether or not I am king."

"I'm glad. I think you are now truly ready to take the throne. It's what I said at the beginning of all this. You can't be dependent on your situation to make you happy. You must make yourself happy, then there is no situation that can overcome you."

"We've certainly learned that the hard way. Let's get some sleep. Dawn's almost upon us as it is."

John Asgarth first noted Roscoe rooting about in the front yard. It was a little late when Ella came out of the front door and went to the well.

"Hullo!" Asgarth bellowed ecstatically.

Ella looked up and smiled. "Hello to you, John. How are you this morning?"

He came running over. "Well, indeed. When did

you return?"

"We got in late last night. We didn't know we had houseguests."

"I thought I heard some noise over there. His Lordship's been locking up. He don't trust the queen."

"Do any of us? He told us he was a locksmith and quite apologized for locking us out. It seems our friend in Leiderkeit sent him to us. Alex had talked to our friend about the situation here, and King John actually wanted His Lordship to come and help us oppose the queen." Ella smiled, then bent her head to catch the bucket of water. "I'm so glad the well didn't freeze over."

She didn't see the puzzled frown on Asgarth's face. He'd been wondering how he would face the Murdrens if they returned. He still kept the medallions secret, as had His Lordship. Apparently, His Lordship and Her Ladyship hadn't told the Murdrens what Asgarth knew. He found it hard to see them and anything but Alex and Cindy. She seemed content to leave it at that. Perhaps he should also.

"You're looking rather drawn," he admitted sadly.

"Yes. I was ill for a good while. But I'll be filled out in no time. Since we weren't here for the winter, our cold room is still pretty full."

"And the new one?"

"A boy. He's been named Steffan. A good name, don't you think?"

"Yes, it is. Elise is still waiting. Hers should come any time now." Asgarth paused. "I don't know as I've a right to ask."

"You have every right, given what Alex and you

are involved in. He needed to escape for a while, to recover. When we fell from favor, it was always his greatest fear that his children would be wiped out."

"But you're back now."

"He can't escape what he's part of here, either." Ella smiled and took Asgarth's arm. "Come on in. I know he'll want to say hello."

The greeting was enthusiastic. Later, in a quieter moment, Asgarth reassured Steffan that he was much wanted by the dice players. Woodman confirmed it that Sabbath after mass. Monday night, Steffan attended the meeting.

He was greeted with enthusiasm again and thanked the group warmly for it. Then the business began.

"The worst thing that's happened is the conscription into the queen's army," said Kiffs. "So far, she's only taken young unmarried men. But the married ones are getting nervous, and there's been a lot of weddings recently."

"We could use it to our advantage," said Steffan. "We can help them carefully create dissension and unrest among the men. A divided army cannot stand."

"An excellent suggestion," said Woodman. "Murdren, you also need to know that we've arranged for a special meeting with representatives from all over the kingdom. It will take place during the middle of the spring festival."

"Good." Steffan nodded.

"We're choosing our leader then," said Cyril. "And then we will revolt."

"With all respect, neighbors," said Steffan carefully. "That is the absolute worst time we could do it. Choose a leader then, definitely. But not start a revolt."

"You want to fight a revolt in the winter?" asked Asgarth incredulous.

"For this revolt to be successful, and to reduce the risk of another kingdom taking advantage of our vulnerability, we shall have to strike a quick, firm blow, and establish ourselves almost immediately. Admittedly, it would not be a good idea to base our entire strategy on that. We do have to be prepared for the possibility a long fight, as well. That is precisely why we should wait for the harvest. Then we will have food stored away, and be ready for anything. In the spring, our stores are depleted, and our crops are still in the ground. It's going to be very hard to fight a revolt and farm at the same time."

Asgarth laughed hard. "Wouldn't you know it'd take the worst farmer in the district to tell us something we should have known ourselves."

Woodman chuckled. "Well, you can't blame me. I'm a tradesman. I think we will still choose our leader this spring. He can use this summer to further establish himself. There are two men being presented by the other provinces. I wasn't sure if we'd have a man to present." He looked at Steffan.

"You do have Cyril," he replied, more casually than he felt.

Cyril shook his head. "I thought about what you said the last time we met. Damn you, Murdren. You were right. I tried to lead this group a couple times, and I knew I couldn't as well as you. I willingly concede to the better man."

"Are we agreed then?" asked Lyle. "Kiffs?

Woodman? Asgarth? Your Lordship?"

"On one condition," said Chester. "That should King Steffan present himself, you will agree to follow him."

"That seems fair," agreed Asgarth.

"My Lord, may I ask why you want this agreement?" Steffan asked.

"It is time I told the truth." Chester looked straight at Steffan. "I happen to know for a fact that His Majesty is alive and in hiding while he draws together the support he needs to regain his throne."

Asgarth put his hand over his mouth.

"If that is the case, then at such time as His Majesty makes himself known, I will gladly give him my complete support," said Steffan. "I can do no less."

Asgarth choked. "I will do the same, and encourage everyone else to, also."

"Same here," said Kiffs and Lyle at the same time.

Cyril nodded. "Of course I will. That's what everyone wants, isn't it?"

They all looked at Woodman.

"If we must have a king, I'd rather he were one of our own," he said slowly. "But if King Steffan reveals himself, and if he has the support of the people, then I will do as they wish. I firmly believe that a republic is what's needed to prevent what's happened with Lanicia. But the people must choose their own government, and if they want a king, then I must support that. So, are we also agreed that we shall present and encourage the acceptance of Alex Murdren as our leader in this fight against the queen and her injustice, in the event King Steffan does not present himself, as I truly believe he will not?"

The others voiced their approval, and Steffan calmly smiled and graciously thanked them, then went home and shouted out his joy.

# CHAPTER TWENTY-THREE

Elise Asgarth had just as much reason to be glad of the return of the Murdren family as her father-in-law. While Steffan met with the dice players, her labor started. Ella went over soon after Steffan returned home. It proved to be a difficult time, with tearing and bleeding. Several times, Ella was certain that Elise was done for, and tried everything she knew to save Elise and the baby. In the end, Elise survived, and the baby was a fine, big girl. The doctor arrived in time to tell Ella what a good job she'd done.

The next day, Steffan hitched Max to the wagon and brought Asgarth, and Chester into town with him. Chester wanted to find a space in which to live and work, even though as he said, it would be a temporary situation. Asgarth went with Steffan to buy extra seed from the Cyrils to add to what had been saved from the previous harvest.

The miller had set up space in the marketplace, as usual. The farmers banded together in convivial knots while each waited his turn to make his purchase. Steffan bantered casually with the others, feeling easier than he had in months. A voice broke in that completely shattered his mood.

"So, you've returned," it said sleekly. "We had all thought you'd left us for good."

Steffan looked everywhere but at the speaker.

"Good day, Lieutenant. I hope all is well with you."

"Well enough."

"No lost sleep?"

"Not a wink."

"That's good for you. I've heard it told some men can sleep through anything."

"Murdren?" called Cyril, the elder.

"Two and a half sacks," Steffan called back.

"That's a lot," observed the lieutenant. "You must have done quite well to be able to afford all that."

"It's all I have. Graves are not cheap, you know." Steffan walked over and gave the coins to the younger Cyril.

"Please accept my condolences on your loss," said Filfeldt, following.

"I accept and will convey them to my wife."

"That's very generous of you. I must say, you've been very decent about this."

"Lieutenant, I am a man of peace. I have reconciled myself to my son's death. Violence against you, or anyone else will not bring him back."

"Very noble sentiments. I can appreciate that. Well, neighbor, a good day to you."

"Good day to you, Lieutenant." Steffan swallowed, wondering how much longer his own nobility would hold out.

As the Filfeldt left the square, the murmuring rose.

"The nerve of that man confronting him."

"Notice how many witnesses there were? That one's not taking any chances."

"You've got to give Murdren a lot of credit. I would've squeezed his eyes out before he'd spoke three words."

Asgarth stepped up next to Steffan. "Couldn't look at him, could you?"

"It's entirely possible I would have killed him if I had." Steffan let out his breath. "And I do like to think I am a man of peace."

"Anyone can be angry, and you've got more right than most. But it takes a strong man to be angry, and be civil to his offender."

"I appreciate the encouragement. But if I ever see that self-satisfied smile again, I don't know if I could stop myself."

"Well, I wouldn't worry about you meeting him alone." Asgarth grinned.

Steffan laughed. "I doubt he'll be that foolish."

Steffan never met Filfeldt again without a large crowd around. It was a small village, and their paths were bound to cross periodically. Each time they met, they were polite to each other. Steffan began to suspect that Filfeldt was hoping Steffan would attack him, or give him some excuse to fight back. Steffan strengthened his resolve, and even when Filfeldt needled him, he remained cool and deferential, which in turn strengthened his position among the villagers. Even Isolde Dirkman had to give Steffan credit for his polite attitude. Gradually, it got easier for Steffan to speak to the lieutenant, and soon he was even able to look at him without burning up with rage.

Barth's birthday was a hard day for everyone in the family. Ella tried not to but found herself crying several times. Steffan was plowing, and showing James how to guide Max, and pick out the rocks from the field. James was as old as Barth had been that first spring. Steffan had to hold his eyes shut several times that day.

As the spring festival drew near, Steffan got tense. Chester tried several times to get Steffan to agree to reveal himself at the meeting. Steffan refused, insisting that he knew what he was doing. At home alone, he wasn't so sure.

"What if I lose it?" he said to Ella the night before the meeting. "I will have to reveal myself then, and then how will I live with knowing that it was only my name and not my ability that got me to power?"

"I wouldn't try answering that question now, Steffan," Ella replied with enduring patience. "You and I both know that whatever happens, you will be able to accept it, and continue on."

"I've heard the other two are both good men, Ella. They could both do an excellent job."

"But you could do a better job, and you should tell the people what virtues you have that these two other men don't."

Steffan grimaced. "That kind of bragging is not in my nature. Woodman says I'm being foolish. It's not hubris to acknowledge your good qualities especially in a situation like this."

"He really wants you to have it, doesn't he?"

"He says I'm open to new ideas, and that's important. The poor man wanted a republic so much. I feel bad that I can't bring it about for him, and yet I can't go against what I am.

Ella laughed. "At least you've answered that question for yourself. Now, get some sleep. You have an important night ahead of you tomorrow."

It was a critical night for Steffan. Everything depended on what he would say to the thirty men gathered at the mill. Guards were posted everywhere, and their families were all at the festival, so it was hoped that Lanicia's spies wouldn't notice all the extra people in the village. Ella waited with Steffan as he listened to the other two men speak.

They were good men. Steffan had no qualms about that. Yet, as he listened, he could tell that he could do a better job. It wasn't pride. It was a simple fact. So, when it was his turn to speak, that is what he said.

"It is not in my nature to go about explaining my virtues. If they were not self-evident, to speak of them would make me a liar. But most of you do not know me or know me only by reputation. These two men who have spoken to you are worthy men. I would be proud to follow either one of them. However, I know that I could be of better service to you and to our kingdom. Like me, these men have lived your lives, your struggles, your pain, and your joy. But as you know, I became a farmer rather late in life, so even as I have lived your life, I have lived another. The man you choose tonight will not lead only you, but our nobility as well. In my former life, I dealt with nobility. I know them, as I know you. These two men are very wise, but there is more to running a kingdom than wisdom. There is knowledge of military strategy and trade and commerce, of which I have personal experience. There is also justice, for our king is as often a judge as a leader. There is no man, woman or child in this village who will go the magistrate before coming to me. Yes, our magistrate is not entirely honest. But I know of no one here who settles more disputes than me. All of my varied experience, wisdom, and justice is what I now offer to you, to be of service to you and to all our people."

There was no clapping or cheering. It had been agreed there wouldn't be any lest it create suspicion. Steffan was excused with his two opponents to wait outside while Asgarth, Woodman and another man from the city supervised the vote. Ella waited with him, easily as tense, but trying to remain calm for her husband's sake. Steffan appeared calm, but his tension and worry leaked out as he flexed his hands continuously.

Chester approached, irritated. "You should have revealed yourself."

"No, I shouldn't have. We would have had to take Lanicia on right away, and this is not the time of year to do it."

"What if they choose someone else?"

"Then I will call for a second vote based on all the facts."

Chester snorted.

Woodman and Asgarth emerged from the mill and approached. The other two candidates and their wives came over, as well.

"Well?" Chester asked, anxiously.

Woodman shrugged. "We were able to call it with a show of hands. It was overwhelming."

"And...?" Chester pressed.

Woodman put his hand on Steffan's shoulder. "Your Majesty."

"You mean I did it," said Steffan, still holding his

breath.

"Oh, my love!" Ella ecstatically embraced him.

Steffan contained his excitement with the lifelong habit of dignity.

"They're waiting for you," said Asgarth, nodding at the door.

Steffan went inside to face the crowd. "I most graciously thank you. We've many months before the final confrontation, therefore I would ask that any status you have given me be forgotten for the moment, except in the case of orders. I will remain your fellow and neighbor. If you were to approach me any differently, then surely it would be noticed, and possibly by the wrong people. I still have a family to protect. We will be sending messages, arms, and training to you. For the moment, let us return and celebrate at the festival. Thank you, once again."

Chester waited as the other men filed out. As Asgarth made ready to go, Chester held him back.

"Did they know about... You know, when they voted?" he asked softly.

"They had no idea," replied Asgarth with a soft smile. "I've told no one."

"That's all to the good, I guess. He won't let me say anything. He ordered me not to, and he knows I'll obey."

Asgarth chuckled. "He knows what he's doing."

At the festival, Steffan was so relaxed and happy that he only marginally fumbled through the slip step, and danced the Raultberg with Ella, as happy as he was on the night they had first danced. A waltz was called, and he watched her bright eyes as they slid around the floor together, again lost in her beauty and warmth. Her eyes filled as she felt his love, and she knew no triumph could be sweeter than this one, for they were able to share it, as they had their sorrow and their work.

"Are we still truly partners?" she asked as they rode home.

Steffan studied the reins on Max's back and listened to hoof falls, the creaking of the wagon, and the stirring of the children in the back.

"Yes," he said finally. "As we danced tonight, I knew I would you need you more than ever. You have the wisdom I lack. They may have chosen me tonight, but they also chose you without knowing it, and that's to their loss. Ella, I can't do this without you. I need your counsel. So we are truly partners, and we shall rule together."

"It's not that it matters. You told me when we arrived here that we were partners in surviving, and now that we're going back, I wondered how that would change."

"I wonder, too. It won't be the same. It will probably be better."

"That we knew from the start." Ella chuckled and laid her head on his shoulder.

Even in the wake of triumph, Steffan knew the final test was still to come. Lanicia was sure to deny him, even as he revealed himself. If the army chose to side with her, it would mean hard fought battles and the possibility of losing after all. As the months passed, and clandestine training progressed, Steffan worried. The people had none of the discipline and ability of Lanicia's well-trained troops. Steffan feared for a long winter.

"We must strike the blow quickly, and I must establish my leadership before as many people as possible," Steffan told the meeting one night right before the harvest.

Lyle suddenly chuckled. "I once suggested this years ago, when you first arrived here, Murdren, and it seems like a good answer. Have him try the ring. Lanicia will be there to see it."

"As will her most powerful supporters," agreed Woodman. "If we capture them, then it doesn't matter if the ring doesn't fit."

"It's to our good fortune that Lanicia has planned that special festival for the harvest," said Cyril. "Even if she's hoping to unite us against Leiderkeit. It's been announced that she will indulge any man who wants to try the ring, just to prove that King Steffan is really dead."

"Do you think he'll try to reveal himself then?" Kiffs asked, suddenly worried.

Steffan smiled. "I don't see how it will matter, as we've all agreed to give him our support should he do so."

Chester coughed and got sound kicks from both Steffan and Asgarth.

The harvest was a merry one, at least outwardly. A current of uncertainty ran through the villagers, as each wondered whether that harvest would be his or her last, and if so, would it be because one had found glory or a grave? Steffan particularly had cause to question his future. Knowing full well that the revolt could ultimately fail, he still drilled Alicia and the twins in the proper forms of behavior for royalty. The twins thought it great fun and had to be reminded that they were still in hiding. Steffan drilled Alicia the hardest.

"This is miserable stuff," she complained one evening in October. "Why must I learn all this nonsense?"

Steffan chuckled. "Because you are my heir, and eventually you will rule our people. You must remember that their welfare, from the highest duke to the lowest commoner, is your responsibility."

"But I don't want it to be."

"I know, Alicia. Believe me, I told my father the same thing when I was just about your age. However, it's what we're born to, and we can't ever forget it. I tried. That's why we went to Leiderkeit, and why we're back here now." Steffan pulled her into his lap. "I know it's hard, darling. But you'll soon find there are a great many privileges to be had. It's just that with privilege comes responsibility. Now. Back to work."

It was miserably hard work, and Steffan sympathized. But it had to be done. The special harvest festival that Lanicia had called was fast approaching. Every village was expected to send as many of its people as could be spared. Admittedly, most of them were sending members of the new rebel army.

Lanicia was well aware that the army existed. In fact, she had arranged the harvest festival in hopes that an uprising would occur, which she would quickly and firmly put down. The difficulty was in knowing how well the commoners were organized, and how many of them there were. And in stopping those infuriating rumors that her blasted cousin was still alive, and waiting to take back his throne. The harvest festival would be the last time she'd allow anyone to try the ring. After the festival, the ring would be melted down. Lanicia would see to it herself, and anyone who protested could be hanged.

Two days before the twins' birthday, Giles helped Steffan pack his wagon in the barn.

"It's a good thing the Lieutenant was sent back to the city," Giles said, strapping blankets to the wagon's sides.

"There are enough people going to the festival, you and the children wouldn't have been missed," said Steffan. "We would have said you were lost in the shuffle. The only advantage to having the Lieutenant gone is that you'll all be in Leiderkeit before the festival starts."

Giles chuckled. "Meg is mighty miffed that Father's sending her with us."

Ella laughed as she entered the barn. "You can hardly blame her, Giles. She finally gets betrothed, and she has to leave her beloved Matthew behind."

"Damn and blast!" bellowed Asgarth's voice from outside. He burst inside. "Damn and blast! Giles, you had something to do with this. Don't tell me you didn't."

"What, Father?" Giles was genuinely puzzled.

"Murdren, what about you?"

Steffan looked at Ella, then back. "We have no idea what you're talking about."

"Meg! The fool child ran off and got married this morning."

Giles burst into laughter. "That's grand, it is! No,

Father. I had no idea. I swear!"

"Neither did we," said Ella.

"It's an interesting turn of events," said Steffan. "Are she and Matthew going with the children?"

"Ha!" Asgarth snorted. "Why do you think she did it? She says she didn't want to miss any of the excitement in the city. She and Matthew are going to the harvest festival."

Giles' sigh escaped him. He hadn't wanted to miss the excitement, either, even though he knew how dangerous it could be. His older brother, Edward, had reluctantly offered to be the one to take Steffan's children, and his sisters, Arlette and Gen, to Leiderkeit, which meant that Edward's wife, Elise, and their baby, named Berencia, would have gone, too. But Berta was several months with child, and Giles didn't want her to risk the harvest festival. It had been decided that missing wives would be too conspicuous, and no one was likely to believe that Berta was staying in confinement. So Giles became the driver, with Berta riding along, and baby Berencia.

The final preparations were tense. They would be leaving early the next morning. Just before he sent her to bed, Steffan pulled Alicia aside.

"I wish I didn't have to send you," he told her, as he held her before the fire.

"Did I do something wrong?" she asked.

"No, darling. You've done wonderfully well. You should remember that." He sighed. "I have to send you to Leiderkeit because the revolt may fail. Alicia, someone must remain behind to carry on and do what's best for our people. Lanicia won't. I can trust you to do it. You've learned an awful lot in these past few months, and I'm very proud of you. You're very young to have such responsibility, but I'm confident you'll be able to manage it. That's why I must send you and your brothers and sisters to Leiderkeit."

"To King John, our musician friend."

"Yes, darling. You'll be a princess, there, and you must remember to act like one."

"And make sure James and Nella do."

"Yes. But be kind about it."

"I will, Papa."

"You will indeed, my darling." Steffan squeezed her.

Later, after she was asleep, he wrote a letter, and sealed it, then sealed another package. The next morning, he gave the letter and package to Giles.

"Keep the letter hidden until you are in Leiderkeit," Steffan said quietly. "If you should be captured, see to it that it's destroyed. As for this package, see that it is put into His Majesty's hands only. If it should be opened by anyone else, say that you found it, and are looking to sell what's in it."

"We're going to the king, himself?"

"My friend, the musician, insisted upon it. His Majesty knows you will be coming. He just doesn't know when."

Giles looked the envelope over. "A letter, with a real wax seal, too. That's pretty fancy, Mr. Murdren."

Steffan smiled. "A merchant needs to read and write. It's addressed to His Majesty. Don't leave the palace until he has it."

Giles nodded. There were plenty of tears and

embraces before the wagon was loaded with the children. Ella swallowed and buried her head in Steffan's shoulder as the wagon pulled away.

"They won't have any trouble," said Steffan to reassure himself as much as Ella. "They're well-prepared. They know what to say if they're stopped by Lanicia's army."

"I know."

The rest of the week passed slowly. Steffan remained preoccupied with preparations and plans to the point where his own packing for the festival was left until the morning they were to leave, and Asgarth had to do it for him. Ella kept checking and rechecking her bags and was still certain she had forgotten something.

"It shall have to remain forgotten," said Steffan as he settled Ella into the back of Asgarth's wagon the morning before the festival was to start. He sat down next to her. Elise and Edward rode on the seat with their father.

Ella smiled. "Well, Your Majesty," she whispered. "This isn't quite the triumphant entry we had assumed you'd make."

"I expect not. But, Your Majesty, it is a sweeter one."

Softly, he kissed her lips. The wagon lurched forward.

# CHAPTER TWENTY-FOUR

The journey to Leiderkeit was long and tense. As they neared the border, the twins began squabbling, and little Steffan and Berencia were fretful. Giles hied Max to a trot, hoping to be in Leiderkeit before sundown. Shortly after lunch, a patrol of horse soldiers stopped the wagon.

"Where are you going?" demanded the captain.

"To Leiderkeit," said Giles.

"Haven't you heard our queen's edict about the harvest festival?"

"We have, sir." Giles hoped he sounded more confident than he felt. "We'll be headed that way soon. But first, we've got to deliver these orphans to their relatives in Leiderkeit, so as not to be taxing Her Majesty with them."

"Orphans, eh?" The captain ran a critical eye over the crowded wagon. "All right. Be off with you."

The patrol went on. Everyone in the wagon who was old enough sighed in relief as Giles started Max again.

They were stopped once more at the border as twilight fell. Giles explained once more about the "orphans," and the guards let them pass. Giles hied Max to a trot and no one really breathed until they reached an inn some miles away.

The next day, they reached the capital and went

straight to the palace. The wagon was admitted without question through the palace gates. Giles left Max tied up in the courtyard. The guards showed them into the palace foyer, where they were stopped by a finely dressed man with an aristocratic, arrogant air about him. He looked over the group with obvious disapproval.

"And what is your business here?" he asked, his voice soft and hissing. "There is no public audience today."

"I've a letter to deliver to His Majesty," said Giles, holding out the envelope.

The man took it, looked at it, and sniffed. "I'll see that he gets it."

Giles swallowed. "I was told to wait until His Majesty has it."

"It's as good as done." The man smiled, and it was clear that they were dismissed.

Giles turned.

"Wait," snapped Alicia.

The others stared as the small girl planted herself in front of the man.

"Grace, no," hissed Berta.

Alicia ignored her. "Sir, that letter is urgent, and we are to wait for a reply."

"My dear little girl," said the man. "His Majesty is very busy with matters of state. You could be waiting a long time."

"And why are you so certain that letter is not a matter of state, or that His Majesty would want you to wait to deliver it?" returned Alicia.

The man was nettled. As the king's secretary, it

was his duty to keep undesirables from His Majesty. On the other hand, his sovereign was noted for odd quirks, and unseemly preferences.

"Very well, then," he said, reluctantly. "I will attempt to deliver this, and you may wait. But I warn you, it will take a while."

The secretary had them shown into a drawing room and disappeared. Both of the babies decided they were hungry right then. So while the others nervously prowled about the fine room, Alicia and Berta fed the infants out of the bottles they had prepared.

King John was quite involved with his minister of farming when the secretary knocked. John bade him enter.

"I thought I told you I was not to be disturbed," said the king.

"Pray forgive me, Your Majesty, but there is a group of peasants who insisted that I deliver this letter right away. They are waiting for a reply."

Irritated with the man, John took the envelope. "Arnault, they are our people. We do not look down our noses at them. It is also your duty that I when I say I do not want to be disturbed, I am not disturbed. Our guests are to be treated with respect and made comfortable until I can look at this."

John was about to toss the letter onto a table when the seal caught his eye, and he caught himself. Grinning, he opened the envelope.

"Forgive me, Lord Cresy," he said to the farming minister. "I must look at this now. Arnault, I apologize. You were right to bring this to me." John read the letter, muttering happily. "They are here. And Arlette..." John looked over the rest of the letter quickly. They were mostly Steffan's instructions in case of the worst. John decided he could study those at his leisure. He chuckled. "Well, Arnault, how many times have I told you not look down on those less fortunate? Let this be a lesson, my good man. Our guests are nobility from our neighbor's kingdom. They've been in hiding since Lanicia took over, which explains their poor appearance, and their rough manners. In fact, until I personally can assure them of their safety, we must not let them know that we know their true identities. It would be too frightening otherwise. I must continue with Lord Cresy for now. I want you to see to it that they are bathed, and given new clothes that are more fitting for royal guests."

Arnault kept his sigh to himself. "Yes, Your Majesty."

"They can wait for me in my private drawing room when they are done dressing. Except for the one they call Arlette. Have her wait in my study. Eh, discreetly. We don't want to frighten them."

"Yes, Your Majesty."

Arnault had the servants lead the guests to their baths and changing rooms. Fortunately, two of John's brothers and their rather large families lived in the palace, so there were clothes for the children. Giles felt very shy about taking a bath and had no idea what to do with the cravat. The manservant pretended not to notice and tied it for him. Five-year-old James thought all the fuss was a terrible nuisance. The highly polished floors of the long hallway were just perfect for sliding on and the temptation was too strong. He did not appreciate the reprimand from the manservant.

Neither Arlette or Gen had forced themselves into corsets before. They thought it quite romantic and elegant until the maids pulled the strings taut. Berta had to laugh. Her belly was far too large for her to be wearing a corset. A lovely India cotton gown was found for her. The hairdresser finished with Arlette first, and she was led to the study.

She gazed at the books in wonder. There were so many of them.

"Arlette?" asked a soft voice.

She turned. He had come in through another door and stood behind a tall, comfortable chair.

"John." She smiled. "I was hoping I'd find you."

"You're even more beautiful than I remember."

"Thanks to this fine dress, I am. I've saved all your letters. They were purely marvelous."

"Yours were just as wonderful." John came out from behind the chair.

"Oh, no," sighed Arlette.

"What's the matter?"

"You're so fine. A gentleman. I was afraid you would be."

"But why?"

"I'm a commoner. I thought you might be a commoner who had the king's ear or a member of a council. But a gentleman. You can't marry a common girl like me."

"And who says you are?"

"But..."

"Nobody here knows how you were born. In fact, they think you are a noblewoman who's been in hiding these last six years."

"What about Giles, and Berta, and Gen?"

"They, also."

"And what's going to happen when it's found out that it's not true?"

"Who's to say it won't be true come the end of next week? Your father is great friends with your king, and His Majesty is not one to forget friendship."

"I don't understand."

John took her hands. "You will, Arlette. And it doesn't matter, anyway. If anyone should question your birth, let them. They will not question me."

"You do seem sure of yourself." Arlette giggled.

John chuckled also, then kissed her mouth. Arlette returned the affection.

"Such passion," John sighed as he held her. "And as much as I would like to continue this, we must greet the others."

"I suppose."

John took her hand firmly in his. She did not know the worst about him yet, and he wasn't sure how to tell her. Tea was being served in the private drawing room. James was trying to put on his best "royal" manners, but John could see that the boy would have much preferred playing. Nella eyed the piano, and Lorelei helped herself to the plate of sweetmeats, stuffing little cakes in her mouth as fast as she could. Giles, Berta, and Gen were nervous wrecks. Berta kept hissing at the children to be careful, and to keep the babies away from anything breakable.

Only Alicia appeared calm. John doubted that she felt it. But Steffan's training had left its mark on her.

The servants bowed as John entered.

"You may be dismissed," he told them.

"Yes, Your Majesty."

John felt Arlette's hand pull, and he tightened his grip. She did not escape.

"Your Majesty?" gasped Giles.

"I'm afraid so," teased John.

Giles scrambled to one knee, while Berta and Gen made awkward curtsies. John pulled Arlette next to him and got a firm grip on her shoulders. Alicia, James, and Nella stood at attention and properly inclined their heads.

"It's all right," John announced. "Get up, everyone. I'm glad you've arrived safely."

Giles recovered himself, more or less. "Oh. Your Majesty. The children's father, Mr. Murdren, he asked me to put this into your hands only."

John took the sealed package. "Arlette, darling, would you please sit there while I open this?"

"Yes, Your Majesty," she replied in a tiny voice.

"You and I are going to have a long talk very shortly," he told her as he struggled with the sealing wax and parchment. "Ah. I know what this is." He pulled the sparkling jeweled medallion from the package. Giles gulped. "I expect that this was entrusted to me so that it might be returned to its owner in complete safety. Princess Alicia?"

"Yes, sir," she answered.

"But her name's Grace," blurted out Gen.

John nodded. "Yes. Alicia Grace Adriana Marie deGrudesberg." He put the medallion around Alicia's neck. "Surely you didn't think her name was really

Murdren?"

"We'd no reason not to," stammered Giles.

"Then the ring..." Berta gasped. "But he never revealed himself."

"He will soon enough," said Alicia. "Until then, we must wait."

"Well said, Your Highness," said John. He looked about the room feeling very pleased with himself.

The feeling lasted but a moment. For all Alicia had assumed the correct posture, hearing her true title for the first time had unsettled her. James and Nella seemed more bored than daunted and about to get into mischief. Lorelei decided that if her brother and sisters were standing at attention, perhaps she should, too. Gen, Berta, and Giles trembled and remained standing without the faintest idea of what to do.

John sighed. "Well, as you are all nobility in hiding-"

"But we're not," Arlette sobbed.

"My dear, I have said we will talk later."

Giles took a deep breath. "Begging Your Majesty's pardon, my sister's right. We're just common folk, ex—except for the children."

Baby Steffan squawked as he tried to pull himself up on the tea table. Little Berencia cried with him. Alicia gave John a quick nod and tended to the babies.

"You are also the sons and daughters of a favorite in King Steffan's court," said John. "So you have been in hiding these many years and have forgotten your fine manners. You can learn them again."

"But–" began Arlette.

"If I say it is so, who is going to argue?" said John.

"For now, you are my guests, and so that you do not feel so embarrassed, I will send for my finest tutors. Until then, enjoy yourselves. Arlette, you will come with me?"

"As Your Majesty wishes."

With an even deeper sigh, John led Arlette from the room. Behind them, Berta burst into hysterical laughter.

John looked at Arlette. "Come. We will go to my private garden, and there we will forget about titles and rank and just talk."

Once sheltered among the plants, Arlette's tears flowed freely.

"Now, tell me what is grieving you," said John, softly holding her.

"You're king."

"I thought we were going to forget about titles."

"I can't. I'm just a poor farmer's daughter, and I thought I fell in love with a wandering musician."

John softly hummed an old ballad. "The truth is, Arlette, you did, with unfortunately a musician who happens to have a throne he can't seem to escape, but one who loves you very, very much, who needs your gift of song, because you are the only one who understands."

"I can't be no fine lady."

"If a fine lady was what I wanted, then I would have been married years ago. I want you, Arlette, and no one else."

"But what about..."

John shrugged. "So we tell a few stories. And when my good friend regains his throne, they'll mostly be true. As I said, your father is a good friend of your king's, and Steffan is not one to forget his friends. I have good reason to know that."

"Do you really want me?"

"Yes. Do you really want me?"

Arlette sniffed. "I want my fiddle player, the one who wrote me those marvelous letters."

"Can you forgive me for being more than I told you?"

Arlette nodded. John bent his head to her lips. They kissed for several minutes, then joined the others as they waited.

The waiting was almost as bad in the city. Steffan and Ella arrived after the festival had been going for several days. They shared a room in the new inn which bordered the marketplace with the Asgarths. Saying that it would be safer to supervise from there, Steffan remained in the room, as did Ella. The others found it puzzling but did not question it.

The final day of the festival was to be the biggest. Lanicia had arranged to preside over the celebration from a platform set up at the end of the marketplace. That morning, Steffan presented Ella with a silk dress.

"The ladies of our village asked if they could do something special for me," Steffan explained. "I told them that it was my greatest wish to see you in a beautiful silk dress. So they got together and made this."

Ella began to cry. "My love, thank you so much. They must have worked so hard. All this summer we worked to make you a fine new military suit."

She fetched the new suit, with its elegant braid, and fine wool. Steffan smiled and kissed her.

They had to share a bath. Steffan longed to soak, but Ella was waiting, and they would be called for soon. They were dressed and ready long before eleven, the hour the queen had said that Alex Murdren should try the ring. The rebels knew it only as the signal. At ten-thirty, Asgarth knocked and entered.

"I suppose I should beg pardon for coming in before you let me," he said sheepishly.

"It's your room also." said Steffan.

"Yes, but in half an hour, you're going to be my sovereign."

"You will always be our friend," Ella said.

"You do look regal enough." Asgarth grinned, then sighed. He pulled a small velvet bag from his coat. "You left something back at your house. I saw you send your daughter's with Giles, and I didn't see yours with your things. So I brought them along."

"That's what I forgot," groaned Ella.

Asgarth handed over the medallions. Steffan looked at them with a sinking heart.

"You knew," he said softly.

"I found them when you was gone last winter."

"Damn! And I thought I had won on my own merits."

"Your Majesty, I wouldn't be thinking like that. His Lordship knew, but he knows you. I never said a word even to my own family. They have no idea." Asgarth suddenly chuckled. "I can't wait to see the looks on their faces when that ring fits. Isolde Dirkman says she wants to be right at the platform to see the queen get her comeuppance when the rebellion starts."

Ella burst into laughter. "It's mean to laugh, but it will be fun to see her."

Steffan smiled, but without mirth. "I'm sorry, Asgarth. I thought that you were supporting me because you believed in me."

"What makes you think I don't? Alex Murdren, or whatever name you were born with, if you weren't the man I wanted over me, those medallions would have been in the bottom of the river, with no one the wiser."

Steffan nodded, finally reassured. The palace tower clock struck the quarter hour.

"It's time we went," said Asgarth.

Steffan nodded. He and Ella put on long cloaks, with deep hoods which they pulled low over their faces. Outside, in the crowd, the wind suddenly caught Ella's hood and pulled it back. An older woman gasped when she saw.

"Either I've seen a ghost, or Lanicia's doomed this time," she croaked.

"Don't be silly, woman," her husband chided.

"Now you know why we didn't leave the room," said Ella to Asgarth, smiling as she replaced the hood.

Getting through the crowded square was time-consuming. The last stroke of eleven was dying in the distance when Lanicia stood.

"It seems that this latest fool has lost his nerve," she announced.

The crowd of courtiers and councilors also on the platform whispered and tittered among themselves.

"No, he hasn't!" bellowed Asgarth. "Make way!"

The crowd pulled away from the two cloaked

figures and allowed them to mount the platform. Something about them struck terror into Lanicia, although she was too well-bred to show it.

"I understand you wish to try the ring," she said when the pair arrived. "Well, you're too late. I said eleven, and it is past that."

Steffan removed his hood, as did Ella. Lanicia contained herself admirably, but there were several betraying gasps on the platform already.

"Am I, cousin?" Steffan said with a grim smile. "Lord Cedric, bring the ring forward."

There were was dead silence in the square. There were those who knew the ring would fit. Even with a beard, their king's face was recognized. For many more, the ring was not an issue. It was the signal, and though their leader was behaving a little oddly, they knew he would choose the perfect moment.

Lord Cedric's eyes were full as he bowed before Steffan.

"Stop that, you fool," screeched Lanicia. "He's just another impostor."

Steffan picked up the ring. Ella held her breath. Brief visions that this was all a dream, and that she would wake up back in the farmhouse, flitted through her mind, with the even more disturbing fear that the ring would not fit after all, and they would be defeated. Steffan glanced back at her and smiled. The same thoughts had burst across his mind, too.

Slowly, holding his hand where all could see, he slid the ring onto the third finger of his left hand, then gave his hand to Cedric.

"It fits!" the old man cried.

In triumph, Steffan raised his left fist as the crowd thundered. Isolde Dirkman, standing at the front of the platform as promised, gaped and fell silent. Woodman gazed at Steffan, wounded and betrayed. Lieutenant Filfeldt slipped off the back of the platform and ran. A minute later, Steffan signaled for silence.

"He's an impostor," Lanicia cried desperately. "Don't you think I would know my own cousin? I don't know this man!"

A slow rumble of doubt rippled through the crowd. Steffan pulled his medallion from his suit.

"I wear the same medallion as she," he announced, pulling Lanicia's from her dress.

"It's a forgery," Lanicia insisted. "I do not know you, or this woman with you. I'd know my cousin."

"And I know my son," said a woman's voice from the side of the platform.

The dowager queen walked around to the front and up the stairs.

"Poor Lanicia, don't fight it anymore," she said, the tears streaming down her face. "Everyone knows who I am, and why would I claim a son that is not my own?" She turned to Steffan. "You are the child I bore, the boy I raised, and the man who will do your father proud."

"Mother, how did you get here?" Steffan asked softly.

"Chester brought me."

"He's an imposter," screeched Lanicia. "My captains, seize him!"

There was an awkward pause. A shot cracked, and splinters flew near Steffan's foot, as a ball buried itself in the wooden platform. Ella screamed.

"Enough," shouted Steffan. "Men! Show your arms!"

There was a short scuffle as guards were disarmed or surrendered their weapons. Infuriated, Lanicia grabbed a pistol and aimed. Ella caught the movement out of the corner of her eye. Terrified, she dove. The shot went wild. A captain wearing the colors of Gittlesmarkt, the duchy that had been Ella's before her marriage, leapt to the platform and pinned Lanicia. Steffan turned and helped Ella up. Slowly the ruckus in the square quieted.

Steffan looked it over and smiled. "Cousin, it doesn't really matter whether you believe me or not. My mother has identified me, and I've got the crown anyway." He turned back to the crowd. "Who will follow me?"

The crowd roared their approval, including the guards and the rest of those on the platform. Ella whispered in Steffan's ear. He nodded.

"Lord Everett, Lord Timothy, Lord Siefert, I need you here." Steffan pointed at the people he wanted. "Cedric, notify the bishop and collect the jewels of office. I will be crowned this afternoon. Woodman, Asgarth, Cyril, I need you here."

Cedric scurried off as the men Steffan called scrambled to face him.

"Remember what Everett's like," Ella hissed.

"You're right, my love." Steffan said to her, then turned back to the men. "I need a sword. Asgarth, Cyril, Woodman, kneel now. We need to act fast, as you know."

The three men knelt, puzzled as Steffan took from Lord Everett the ceremonial sword that he'd been wearing.

Steffan lightly touched each of the kneeling men on each shoulder.

"From this day forward you three are Sir Ernst, Sir John, and Sir James, knights of this kingdom, pending the right and proper assignments of holdings and titles. Now rise."

Cyril grinned, but Woodman looked shocked. Steffan pointed at Cyril, as Ella pulled Woodman aside.

"I hope we can rely on your friendship," she said softly.

"Cyril, you and Lord Timothy will draft a letter to the surrounding kingdoms," Steffan continued.

Woodman nodded at Ella, confused. "I swore I would support him."

"I know it's a terrible shock, and not in keeping with your principles." Ella glanced over at the two nobles. "Everett may be very smart about military matters, he's the commander of the army, you know, but he's a fool when it comes to titles. He won't listen to anyone without one, and Steffan needs people he can trust working with that pompous idiot. We can't let our borders become vulnerable during the change of power."

"I want it very clear that I am in control," Steffan was saying, "That I am not looking to expand my borders, but that I will defend them without fail." He sighed. "That's one good thing about Lanicia building up our army. You will start immediately. I expect the first draft after the coronation. Sir Ernst, Lord Everett!"

"Yes, Majesty!" Woodman nodded and smiled at Ella as he went to face Steffan.

Steffan smiled apologetically at Woodman, then gave his commands.

"I want our borders secured. There is to be absolutely no aggression. This is merely a precautionary measure. I will leave you two to decide on how best to distribute the troops. Go now. I will want a report immediately after the coronation. Lord Siefert, you will help Lord Cedric with the details of the coronation, that it be carried out properly, but by two o'clock this afternoon, which means we will have to start the ceremony well before then. Go. Sir John, I shall require you to remain at my side, as possible, and help ensure that everything goes smoothly."

"What of Lanicia, Your Majesty?" Asgarth asked.

Steffan paused. "Put her under your most trusted guards, and send her to my queen's family home. It's not far. I'll have a page direct you. The rest of you lords and ladies will attend me there with our most trusted friends, as selected by Sir John. You, page, run ahead and have the house made ready, with a bedroom for Lady Lanicia to be held."

Steffan looked about him as Asgarth scrambled to assign people to their various tasks. The nobility looked somewhat askance at some of the people Asgarth was pulling out to attend Steffan and Ella, and the newcomers were equally uncomfortable.

At the house, Steffan put the two groups in two different salons, invited them to mingle, and went to another with his mother and wife. The moment the door was shut, Adrianna pulled Steffan into her arms and held him so tightly he could barely breathe.

"Oh, my precious son," she whispered over and over through her tears. A moment later, Ella was held fast in her grasp. Finally, she sniffed. "All Chester would tell me was that you were farmers in Raultberg."

"Yes," said Steffan.

"And where are Barth and Alicia?"

The pain stabbed through Steffan and Ella once more.

"Alicia is in Leiderkeit with our other children," said Steffan.

"Others?"

Ella smiled. "We've had four more since the accident. The twins, Nella and James. They're six. Lorelei, she's three, and baby Steffan. He was born last February."

"And Barth." Adrianna held her breath against the bad news.

Ella glanced at Steffan. "He... He's no longer with us."

"He was killed," said Steffan softly.

"Oh, dear." Overwhelmed, Adrianna sank into a chair.

"It is a great deal to cope with all at once, Mother," said Ella.

"We know the pain you must have felt," Steffan sighed sadly.

"But it's over now," said Adriana, touching his cheek in wonder. "Poor Barth. He's in a better place now, with his grandfather. And I have my son back."

She held him again, then reached out and pulled Ella into the embrace. "And my daughter, and four new grandchildren!"

# CHAPTER TWENTY-FIVE

As the archbishop set the crown on Steffan's head, carrier pigeons were released, and scores of messengers rode out across the land with the news, and still more to the neighboring kingdoms. Moments later, Steffan placed another crown on Ella's head.

"I wish our children could see this," he whispered.

"One can," Ella replied softly.

Together, they smiled through the sorrow.

Bells throughout the city rang and pealed without stop. The celebration, though hastily redone from the preparations for the harvest festival, was sumptuous, and slightly hilarious, especially when Sir John insisted that the new king and queen lead the slip step. Steffan slipped a bit, but it didn't matter, as there were plenty of others slipping, too.

When finally allowed to go to bed, Steffan stayed up for one small luxury, a good long soak in a well-made bathtub with plenty of rinse water and sweet-smelling soap.

"These sheets feel so wonderful," sighed Ella when Steffan finally joined her. "I forgot how much I missed them."

"I know. And no straw digging in, either. I love being completely clean again, and without dragging in all those buckets." He pulled her close to him and kissed her hair. "Soft sheets, soft night shirt, softer wife."

Ella chuckled as his lips found her nose. "Do you wish to continue celebrating?"

"If you're not too tired. It's one thing we shall always have, you know."

"I know." And she gently kissed his lips.


In the darkness, Lieutenant Filfeldt ran and continued running, his terror spurring him onwards when his limbs groaned in protest. Visions of the Murdren boy, of the prince, in his hands, filled his brain, and all the taunts, and that travesty of a hearing before the magistrate, and all the polite digs echoed without stop in an unending nightmare. How could he have known? Lanicia's protection could not save him, and that cheat of a magistrate was probably running just as hard.

Filfeldt ran, hiding in the daylight hours, running in the dark. One night, he burst into the yard of a deserted farmhouse. Out of nowhere, it seemed, a gigantic hulking animal rushed him, snorting and grunting on too-short legs. Horrified, Filfeldt scrambled towards the house. The pig reached the door first and advanced menacingly. Filfeldt backed away slowly. The pig advanced some more. Filfeldt backed himself up against some stone work. Feeling for the rim, Filfeldt hoisted himself on top of the edge and turned, only to step straight down into the well. The pig snorted and went into the house.

Edward Asgarth arrived the next day to collect the livestock. Friederich and Pieter joined him and helped him clean out the stalls, and collect the chickens, talking all the while about the strange turn of events.

"Who'd have thought, right here in our own village," Pieter said for the hundredth time.

"You should see the airs Isolde Dirkman's given herself in the city," chuckled Edward. "And Mrs. Murdren, I mean the queen, was just as nice as could be, which is right kind of her, considering all the trouble the old biddy caused her."

"I wonder if the king is going to come after the Lieutenant," said Friederich.

"I'd hate to be in his shoes," Pieter said.

"Who knows where the man is?" said Edward. "He ran from the square the minute it was announced the ring fit. He can keep on running as far as His Majesty's concerned, too. He don't want to think about what happened any more than he has to. Now, the chickens go to Mrs. Dieterich, and the Birchenwelds, and Daffy goes to the Birchenwelds, too. They're the poorest, and Mrs. Dieterich is too old to keep a cow. His Majesty wants the pig back with him. You know how his son loved it."

"And how he hated it," chuckled Friederich. "What do you think the odds are the creature's going to end up royal bacon?"

"So long even my brother wouldn't bet on it," Edward laughed. "Now, I've got to get going. His Majesty said to tell you and the others that you will be remembered, just as soon as he has a chance, and the mess Lanicia's made of the government's been cleared up."

"He doesn't have to do that," said Friederich. "We weren't all of us kind to him, you know."

"That's as he wants to do." Edward shrugged. "Well, I'm off. The others should be home any day now."

Edward never returned to the village to live. He found himself well situated in the new court. Lyle and Kiffs were both knighted and given small estates. The rest of the village had its taxes waived for ten years, with gradual increases after that time.

Lanicia chose to remain in seclusion, with only her son for company. Steffan really couldn't try her. He had no evidence that she had engineered the accident, and her crimes against the people weren't really crimes, as she had acted well within what her authority allowed. Steffan was content to let her wallow in her own bitterness and ensured that her son could not come to power later on her behalf.

The first week of Steffan's reign was exceedingly busy. Ella remained at his side, taking notes, and sometimes reminding him of details that even he had missed. Late that Sabbath's Eve, Ella received a message, and roused her husband, then went to go get Adrianna, who was also staying in the palace.

"Are you dressed?" Ella called at the dowager's door.

"Yes, but why?" Adrianna opened the door with a puzzled frown.

"The children are here. The coach should be pulling up at the palace gates even as we speak."

Adrianna hurried after Ella. King John's two personal coaches were indeed in the palace courtyard.

The children were sleepy and befuddled. Baby Steffan squawked a little as Ella took him from Gen's arms. His father embraced the others.

"You're really king," said Nella with a bemused smile.

"Want Mama," said Lorelei.

"I'm right here, darling," said Ella, scooping her into her arms.

After all the hugs and kisses, Steffan pulled back and brought Adrianna forward. An old memory stirred in Alicia.

"Grandmother," she said suddenly and flew into Adrianna's arms.

"You remember me?" Adrianna asked. "You were so little, Alicia."

The other children were somewhat shy, but it quickly passed.

King John had brought the children himself, along with the Asgarths in his care. Berta, Giles, and Gen had profited from their time in Leiderkeit but were still nervous about returning home. However, they were not nearly as nervous as Arlette. She had found it awkward facing Berta, Giles, and Gen at first. Spending almost a week in a coach with them had reconciled them all, but there was her father to consider.

Asgarth had been sent on an extended inspection tour of the kingdom, and so was not in the palace when Arlette arrived. When he returned, about a month later, he presented Steffan with a mildly aggravating problem.

"It's well enough that Cyril is foreign minister," Asgarth complained in a semi-private audience with the king. Ella was there, as always, and Alicia, who was in training, and expected to attend as much of her father's business as possible. "He's happy, and he's got what he wanted. But you let Woodman off without a title. Why aren't my principles as important as his?"

"Woodman is still the Chief of the Commoners' Council," Steffan pointed out. "And he does have an estate. Why are you so insistent that you go back to your little farm?"

"Because it's what I know, and what I am. I see the looks Cyril gets from them others. Even Duke Chester gets looked down on, and he's been elevated longer than anyone."

Steffan sighed. "But, John, you don't see my problem. Now that Chester has Raultberg, his old holding of Fin Reache doesn't have a baron to govern it."

"We could find someone else," said Ella. "But there are other considerations, one of them being your oldest daughter."

"I don't understand."

"Well, do you remember that wandering musician who was a friend of mine?" asked Steffan.

Asgarth growled. "Arlette's been getting letters from him."

"So I've been told. They met again while the children were in Leiderkeit. I've been told they're very much in love."

"And what does that have to do with me taking a title?"

There was a knock on the door. Steffan granted permission to enter, and John of Leiderkeit walked merrily in. He had made a point of avoiding John Asgarth until Steffan had paved the way.

"Did he take it?" he asked Steffan and Ella.

"We're still trying to explain the delicacy of the situation," Ella replied.

"You're that musician," Asgarth gasped. "Well, you've turned up a bit finer than I thought. What's your real name?"

"John of Leiderkeit." He bowed, then laughed. "Actually, King John of Leiderkeit. I do confess I lied to you about my status. I sincerely hope I haven't been lying about your daughter's."

"What are you on about?"

Steffan coughed. "My good friend here has a unique way of getting out and meeting his people, not unlike the way that was forced upon me. Under the guise of a wandering musician, he met your daughter, and they've fallen deeply in love. Unfortunately, John's true status prevents him from marrying any woman who is not at least the daughter of some nobleman."

"I've been telling everyone you are a favorite of the king and a well-established gentleman of his court."

"Which would be quite true," said Steffan, "If we could get the man to accept the Barony of Fin Reache."

"Asgarth, you did promise Berencia that you'd make sure your daughters married well," said Ella. "I speak from experience. A king that loves her would be very well."

Asgarth snorted. "You don't leave me much choice. A baron I am, then."

John got down on one knee. "Then, Your Lordship, I most humbly ask that you grant me the hand of your daughter in sacred matrimony."

"If she loves you, you may have it." Asgarth sighed

and looked to heaven for help.

"Then I shall truly live happily ever after," John crowed.

John's excitement caused Ella to catch at her throat. The room waited a moment while she recovered.

"I'm fine," she gasped.

"Sick again?" Asgarth shook his head.

Ella put her arm around Alicia. "Whether he's depressed or celebrating, I always seem to end up sick, then fat and confined."

Steffan flushed and cleared his throat.

They named the baby Felicity because she'd been born into joy. As for living happily ever after, one can say, with some satisfaction, that Steffan and Ella did, more or less. The course of no life runs completely smoothly, and there would be other stories to tell. But they had learned not to depend on outside circumstances to be happy, and so ultimately, they were. As for the others, well, those are other stories. As John and Arlette's began, others continued, some ended, and so life goes on.

# COMING IN SPRING 2018

*And now for something completely different. Here's a sample of my new mystery series, featuring Maddie Wilcox, winemaker and healing woman in Old Los Angeles*

## DEATH OF THE ZANJERO

We knew the value of water in Los Angeles. Back when our great city was still a tiny pueblo, water was scarce and our farms and ranchos were at the mercy of what the heavens produced. Back then we had to pay handsomely to have our fields and vineyards irrigated. Back then the Zanjero, or water overseer, was the most powerful man in the pueblo, which sadly meant he was often the most corrupt, as was Bertram Rivers. I had thought he was my friend.

The dawn was slowly lightening the surrounding hills as we gathered that Monday morning, March 28, in the Year of Our Lord, Eighteen Hundred and Seventy. It had been a fairly dry winter, but not disastrously so. We'd had a good rainy spell the week before, so the Porciuncula River was flowing and there was sufficient water in the Zanja Madre, the main ditch from the river that fed all the smaller zanjas that watered our ranchos and farms.

"Where in tarnation is that son of a b--?" Mr. Worthington snarled, then let loose a stream of tobacco juice.

The expectorant landed near my foot and from the look on my bosom friend Sarah Worthington's face, it appeared that her husband had aimed for me. I suppose a gentle reproof of his language and behavior would have been appropriate. However, it would not have been effective, so I simply stepped aside.

Sarah Worthington had come out with her husband to watch as Caleb Worthington and his men opened the sluice gate to my rancho. She was a tall, sturdy woman, with an elegant bearing and hair the color of freshly tilled earth. Mr. Worthington had been a miner before he and Sarah had come to Los Angeles and bought their lumber business. She was so dear to me, the first woman to befriend me when I'd been brought to this desolate place.

We were both anxious for the gate to be opened. I had been up all night and had yet to see my bed. Indeed, I was wearing my work dress, instead of a decent walking suit. Sarah had some matter troubling her deeply, probably Mr. Worthington. I suspected she wished to unburden herself to me, although I did hope that I could convince her to wait until later that day so I could spend at least a few hours in slumber first.

There were eight of us gathered at the edge of the Zanja Madre. Besides myself and Mr. and Mrs. Worthington, there were five workers. Two of them, Sebastiano and Enrique Ortiz, were from my rancho, the other three were part of the Zanjero's crew. The only person who was missing was the Zanjero, Mr. Rivers. He was needed to verify that the receipt I had gotten the previous Saturday did, indeed, reflect the amount of time I had paid for that Friday and to approve the opening of the gate.

As Deputy Zanjero, Mr. Worthington already knew that I had paid for my allotment, but Mr. Rivers refused to let anyone else open a sluice gate without his presence. Mr. Rivers said it was to protect the good citizens of the pueblo. I thought it a fine sentiment, but at that moment, one that was quite inconvenient.

"Perhaps, Mr. Worthington, you shouldn't wait," Sarah said, after hiding a small yawn behind her hand. "Else Mrs. Wilcox might not get her full allotment."

Mr. Worthington glared at her. He was as big and burly as one might expect of a former miner, with dark blonde hair and small, dark eyes. He was wearing his usual dusty black suit and black tie. He spat out another disgusting stream, this time landing close to Sarah's foot.

"Hombres," he said, with an accent that was truly dismal. "Um, viy-eenay casa Rivers and officina. Diga Señor Rivers, uh, we're waiting."

As it happened, Baldo Vasquez, a short white-haired farmer, and Elias Padrino, a vineyard foreman with dark hair sprinkled with gray, both spoke English even better than Mr. Worthington. They glanced at each other, and at David Montero, a Negro who owned a good-sized tannery in town. Mr. Vasquez and Mr. Montero nodded and turned to do Mr. Worthington's bidding. However, they were saved by the appearance of Will Rivers, Mr. Rivers' youngest son.

He was a lad of thirteen, a tow-head with bright blue eyes. The boy usually wore what his three older brothers cast off, never mind that his father could afford to buy him new clothes. Will was very slight and his pants were generally tied on and his shirts constantly billowing about him as a sail on a merchant ship. One wondered how soon it would be before the wind would catch the garments and blow the lad away with them.

Will was barefoot, as he generally was, and approached at a dead run from the road leading into the city proper.

"Where's your pa?" Mr. Worthington demanded.

"Don't know," Will gasped. "He, eh, never came home last night."

That statement would have elicited a great deal more concern, but the pueblo was a rough place, filled with many temptations for those men who were weak-minded enough not to resist. That a husband and father should stay out the night was, sadly, not that unusual. I wouldn't have thought it of Mr. Rivers, but it didn't surprise me, either.

Mr. Worthington cursed loudly.

"Ma said to tell you to go ahead and open the gates today," Will said, trying to look braver than he was. "Pa will be madder than a wet hen if you miss your scheduled times."

Mr. Worthington glanced over at me, then at Will. Mr. Rivers did prefer that things be done properly. However, there were other rancheros waiting for their water and Mr. Worthington had other duties to tend to, as well. The tolling of the bell from the Clocktower Courthouse softly floated over the Zanja Madre from the center of town. It was six in the morning and time to give me my water.

"Hombres," Mr. Worthington finally yelled and

gestured that they should open the gate.

It was a large panel of wood, painted over and pitched many times to keep the wood sound in the wet. Mr. Vasquez scrambled down the dry part of the brick zanja on my side of the gate and back up to the other side of the bank. Together, he and Mr. Montero and Mr. Padrino tried lifting the panel, but it was stuck solidly. Mr. Worthington took a long pole and began jabbing it around the bottom of the gate. The gate remained stuck. The three crewmen jiggled the panel and Mr. Worthington jabbed and suddenly the gate pulled free, upsetting the men. Water poured quickly into my zanja, rushing and whispering as it went past.

Then through the froth and foam, a dark shape rose up. It was the body of a man, clad in a dark suit of clothes. Sarah screamed but stayed standing. With Mr. Worthington pushing it with his stick, Mr. Moreno and Mr. Padrino reached out and as the water rose, were finally able to pull the body out of the zanja.

The man had been tall and broad-shouldered with dark blonde hair. There was a good solid cut and bruise on the back of his head, just above where his hairline had receded. His suit was torn in spots, presumably from the time in the water, as it otherwise looked to be of good quality. I looked over at Mr. Worthington, whose face had taken on a queer look. My stomach felt just as queer.

"Maddie, stay back," Sarah whispered, holding my arm. "It's too terrible."

I shook her off as Mr. Worthington turned the body over and confirmed that we had found Bertram Rivers.

# CONNECT WITH ANNE LOUISE BANNON

Thank you for sticking it out this long! Please join my newsletter. It's the best way to stay up-to-date on my upcoming projects, blog posts and even games and giveaways.

Sign up here: http://eepurl.com/zH0Ab

Or connect with me on your favorite social media platforms:

Friend me on Facebook: http://facebook.com/RobinGoodfellowEnt

Follow me on Twitter: http://twitter.com/ALBannon

Favorite my Smashwords author page: https://www.smashwords.com/profile/view/MsBriscow

Subscribe to the Robin Goodfellow Newsletter: http://eepurl.com/zH0Ab

Connect on LinkedIn: http://www.linkedin.com/in/annelouisebannon

Follow me on Pinterest: http://pinterest.com/msbriscow

Visit my website: http://annelouisebannon.com

Follow me on Google+: http://google.com/+Annelouisebannonfiction

# OTHER BOOKS BY ANNE LOUISE BANNON

I'm so glad you liked A Ring for a Second Chance! Check out my other novels, available in print or ebook at your favorite retailer:

**Freddie and Kathy Mystery Series:**
Fascinating Rhythm
Bring Into Bondage
The Last Witnesses

**Operation Quickline Series:**
That Old Cloak and Dagger Routine
Stopleak
Deceptive Appearances

**Brenda Finnegan:**
Tyger, Tyger

**Romantic Fiction:**
White House Rhapsody, Book One

And I would be honored if you left a review for this and any of my books on GoodReads or any other retail site. It really helps.

# ABOUT ANNE LOUISE BANNON

Anne Louise Bannon is an author and journalist who wrote her first novel at age 15. Her journalistic work has appeared in Ladies' Home Journal, the Los Angeles Times, Wines and Vines, and in newspapers across the country. She was a TV critic for over 10 years, founded the YourFamilyViewer blog, and created the OddBallGrape.com wine education blog with her husband, Michael Holland. She also writes the romantic fiction serial WhiteHouseRhapsody.com, Book One of which is out now. She is the co-author of Howdunit: Book of Poisons, with Serita Stevens, as well as author of the Freddie and Kathy mystery series, set in the 1920s, and the Operation Quickline series and Tyger, Tyger. She and her husband live in Southern California with an assortment of critters.